Hel

Gitte Tamar

BTW LLC

First Published in 2023 by BTW LLC.

The story, all names, characters, and incidents portrayed in this production are fictitious. No identification with actual persons (living or deceased), places, buildings, and products is intended or should be inferred.

Book Cover by BTW LLC

To those who choose to disregard their pedigree out of
embarrassment over their family tree.

Be careful of what skeletons you try to sweep into the
ancestry closet that you keep.

The blissful ignorance will not protect you from the
karmic debt you reap, it will silently accrue and catch up
with you and, with a vengeance, ruin thee.

Author's Note

Hello to all,

Thank you to everyone, whether your part was big or small.

Thank you to my family and friends; you already know who you are, so I will refrain from listing you by name. I am eternally grateful for your unconditional love and emotional support.

Again, thank you to all my readers for continuing this journey with me. I will forever be in your debt.

Sincerely,

WARNING:
This story includes situations of violence, gore, death,
abuse, implied assault, and swear or curse words.

CONTENTS

Chapter One

THE SMITHS ON BETHLEHEM LANE

NOVEMBER 24, 2011, UTAH

Deep in the mountains of Utah, an off-the-grid town exists among the beauty of the red rock formations. As if the surrounding peaks are not enough to shield the rural community from the outside world, its simplistic design is further veiled between the shadows of two larger cities. Its placement allows the small town of Mountain View to thrive in pious seclusion.

Having no crime, morality is the primary concern of Mountain View, and its appearance follows as a close second. The town elders teach that inner peace and tranquility are to be reflected in the outer presentation of every aspect of life. To implement the practice, each aesthetic, from building to landscaping, is controlled to create a picture-perfect slice of suburbia. Choices require committee vetting and approval to ensure compliance, regardless of the matter's scope.

Despite being visible only from the sky, the rooftops are scrubbed bi-annually, and the gutters are kept in perfect condition, providing pilots flying overhead a view prettier than a painting. In addition, every house and store window receives a daily polishing per the street sweeper's schedule, ensuring a perfect reflection for all passersby. Year-round, the townspeople exchange smiles and waves as they brush away dirt from the sidewalks or shovel snow, depending on the time of year.

In Mountain View, you will not see a single pothole, untidy yard, or molehill; the uniqueness compared to other places does not end there.

Rather than relying on physical barriers like speed bumps to discourage dangerous driving, the inhabitants abide by the rules to avoid the internal guilt of breaking the law.

The small town's residents thrive upon mental subjugation. To reward the population's compliance, the city leadership makes it their mission to dilute all aesthetics, considering unique characteristics aggravating to the mind. A prime example is the careful selection of the building's paint schemes, which are restricted to a limited range of beige muted tones. The elders claim it subdues the wives, making them less temperamental, and deters them from causing headaches for the men when they are away at their respective places of work.

By always putting their residents' best interests first and having an answer to every problem, the population remains beholden.

Whenever an unsuspecting traveler arrives in Mountain View, a grinning local greets them, singing the town's praises, effusing it as the happiest place on earth, much like a salesperson pushing a timeshare property.

One might think they would speak rapidly to cover the excessive list of selling points, but they relay the information at a snail's pace to ensure every syllable is painfully heard. Their smiles expand to the point of baring their teeth as aggressive happiness spills from their mouths in a tinny, brassy tone.

Though their goal is to be inviting to all, the extreme nature of their moral dispositions feels unsettling to outsiders; most find it highly unpleasant.

The subconscious insight is equivalent to visiting a distant aunt's home for the holidays and noticing all her couches covered in a transparent plastic film that smells of saran wrap. Although it is helpful to keep the cushions clean, you feel as if she has already judged you as messy before eating the first bite of food. Without realizing it, a sensation deep in your gut makes you resent the sight of the well-cooked turkey on the table, and you lose your appetite. Then, as you try to relax on the couch after dinner, the stiff plastic texture and shrill squeaks under your seat further fuel your unease.

It is a small lesson in psychology for you and poses quite a conundrum. Every reaction is a product of something so deeply entrenched in our being that we cannot always recognize its origin. The response is purely instinctive.

Lucky for the town, the disconcerting feeling they create in outsiders prevents passersby from desiring to stay any longer than it takes to make a quick bathroom stop or fill their car with gas. Visitors are in and out before realizing why they are uncomfortable or averse to engaging in conversation. Mountain View's population sees nothing off about the behavior of the travelers; they simply chalk it up to them being on a tight-laced schedule.

The residents love their utopia. Because of their naivety, they experience little of the real world and are oblivious to the term *intruder* or the fence's purpose surrounding their community. As a creative bunch, they have established a unique reason for the cyclone barrier's existence. It is not a way of keeping others out, but welcoming them in. The inviting decorative piece, covered in ivy, accents the fresh tops of the pruned forest-green hedges that line each sidewalk.

In the early morning, as the wives take brisk walks while pushing babbling babies in strollers, they admire the picturesque frame circling row after row of stucco homes. The brass numbers on each mailbox and door are the only defining features in the maze of identical structures.

Because of the stark similarities, entering the wrong residence is common. Of course, most would consider barging into a stranger's home a stressful proposition, but there are no such worries in Mountain View.

The residents all dutifully attend church, and their participation makes them trustworthy in the eyes of the Lord. That alone relieves any concern about someone mistaking their home for another. Inadvertently opening the wrong door will always find a warm smile and greeting from a woman who has sacrificed her aspirations to care for her husband's desires and their family's spawn. A playdate will generally emerge from the faux pas, and with a single pointing of a perfectly manicured finger, the unintentional intruder will be kindly guided in the right direction.

From the outside, Mountain View appears so optimistic that one may believe negative thoughts float away into the clouds and tumble back to earth like gentle rain, nourishing the budding flowers in spring.

The residents behind each cookie-cutter home's front door are confident they share the same experiences with their neighbors and live happy, correlated, picture-perfect lives. At least, that is what they are conditioned to believe.

What families show to the public does not reflect their actual situation, and though they may seem alike to their neighbors, the only thing they have in common is the appearance of their home's exterior.

One noticeable difference is the configuration of their offspring. In the absence of a specified number of children assigned by the church, some parents believe that having more babies will increase their admiration from others.

While two children are the average for most households, those wishing to appear abundantly blessed have more. Seeing a well-dressed, enormous family stepping out of their house may make the neighbors take notice, but the family suffers the same problems as the rest of the world. With more mouths to feed, they confront similar difficulties in obtaining enough money to sustain their basic needs. Despite their realities, the community members of Mountain View display their cheerful personas, camouflaging their harsh truths and living lies.

As the sun sets on a chilly November night, there is no need for streetlights in Mountain View. Instead, each window exudes a warm glow onto the black asphalt roads and gray cement sidewalks linking the homes. The paved pathways connect the community's experiences as residents prepare to celebrate Thanksgiving with a holiday meal. Together, they will concurrently sit, devouring their feasts, and, though separated by sheetrock and space, all will give thanks for what they are grateful for.

After settling their children at the dinner table, the wives, in unison, crack open their kitchen windows for ventilation. Smells of fresh turkey and pumpkin pie escape through the wooden sills and circulate through the neighborhood air as if to hail their husbands' arrival.

The moment the men enter, the wives joyfully greet them with pecks on the cheek, hang their coats, and, following them, take their respective places at the table. When everyone is settled, the joyful-toned whispers of the children exude excitement as their supper prayers echo through the walls.

From the exterior, the rows of warmly lit windows, accompanied by inviting smells and muffled chatter, exhibit the church's model—a picture-perfect environment.

That is until you glimpse inside the Smiths' home perched at the end of the cul-de-sac labeled *Bethlehem Lane*. They are one of the more prominent families in the community.

At first glance, their illuminated dining window blends in with the rest, but upon closer inspection, it reveals a truthful depiction of their relationship. As the family of five sits around a big round wooden table, holding one another's hands in prayer, they present themselves as the ideal community model.

The wife, wearing a green dress with red and burgundy velvet accents, patiently listens to her husband's rambling words regarding what he is grateful for and, noticing she has not been included, clenches her jaw. Her muscles ache by the tenth minute of his speech, and she fidgets, drawing her husband's unwelcome glare. In fear of shedding a tear that will expose her genuine sentiment, she refrains from blinking, causing her blueish-colored irises to dry. The depleted moisture removes her eyes' glossy luster and muddies their hue, making her chestnut brown hair seem more fitting.

In a community consisting solely of blue-eyed individuals, the leaders instilled the belief that any color apart from blue is an abomination brought on by Satan himself, dwelling within the bearer's soul.

Maybe the church was onto something. There is a bit of truth to its condemning claim; a pair of brown eyes is tied to a generational chain of horrific acts that now reside within the Smith family's walls, filling the household with lies and deceit.

Mrs. Smith's eyes were not blue at birth; they began as a shade of elmwood brown. Her mother, fearing the child's exile from the community and desperate for a solution, hid the baby while crafting a plan to make her appear more presentable to the public. After countless hours experimenting with natural substances like manuka honey, she stumbled upon a potent concoction to lighten her child's eyes. With enough diligence and hourly treatments, their color turned a muddy shade of blue, and though it could have been better, it made the mark of sin much less noticeable.

When Mrs. Smith was around eight, her mother discovered colored lenses that, combined with the treatment, masked the tainted truth behind their daughter's undesirable eye color entirely. With the local optometrist only offering the option of wire-framed glasses, the community leaders hadn't a clue of the deception. They deemed the overnight hue enhancement a miraculous act of God.

Mrs. Smith finds the holidays the most challenging time of year to conceal her truth. Working for nearly a week over a hot stove preparing for their family's holiday feast dries her eyes. Year after year, the fear of her secret emerging heightens as the kitchen's stove heats and boiling steam wreaks havoc on her contact-encased corneas.

To this day, no one knows the truth. Her parents took the secret to their graves. Not even her husband knows the effort behind her iris's pristinely crisp coloring; she gets up an hour before him each day to ensure that.

Even if it were presented to him, he would refuse to consider it as a possibility, as it would highlight his igno-rance. He takes great pride in his intellectual superiority. His daily actions reflect this belief.

Since there is no head seat at a circular table, he ex-udes his dominance by slamming his hands down onto the tabletop, leaning forward, and loudly declaring his authority as the household's only breadwinner. His words are unnecessary, as his posture speaks volumes regarding his self-importance.

Families usually let their guards down inside the four walls of their homes, but Mr. Smith does not allow it; operating by the book, there are no breaks under his way of life.

Controlling every situation, his dictatorship carries onto his appearance, even synchronizing his shirts to match his wife's daily dress. Everything about his being, from his facial features to his managed way of thinking, exemplifies the community's ideal.

Unlike his wife, his eyes are a natural shade of sky blue that immaculately pairs with the short blond hair gelled to his head. Each strand is perfectly quaffed within a glossy plastic finish.

A wave of steam rises from the freshly baked turkey. As the aromatic scent of gravy wafts in his direction, he fights his growling stomach, and the pair of wire-framed bifocal glasses perched on the bridge of his nose become fogged. Knowing that showing weakness sets a poor example for the children, he refuses to use his hands to adjust or wipe them while continuing to ramble on about the word of the Lord. His sculpted porcupine bristles stay motionless as he fine-tunes their position by wiggling his nose.

As he realizes that his stomach continues to grumble and his vision remains blurry, his underlying annoyance reaches a boiling point.

During his pious diatribe, out of his peripheral vision, he catches his wife's eyes wincing and becomes infuriated by her selfishness. Compelled to force her to listen, he abruptly pauses the prayer and fervently clutches her hand. "I would hate to think that you are passing judgment on a man's direct communication with God, Caroline. Is my declaration of gratitude boring you?" he asks.

The excruciating pain from his grip worsens, causing every muscle in her petite fingers to become numb. Her voice trembles as she tries to speak, but she stops as she feels something putting pressure on her organs; it is a reminder. She tilts her chin to her chest, and as her eyes glance down to avoid unnecessary conflict, she glimpses the tiny baby bump barely showing beneath her dress. A nervous grin sweeps her lips.

She carefully selects her words to address him and quickly sends him a glance in an expression of obedient subservience. "Not at all, Joel; your words are breathtaking," she says.

Her voice trails off to a murmur as her breath runs out and her words become airy. "I apologize if I did anything to cause you or anyone else to feel disrespected on this blessed day of thanks. That was not my intention. The first thing I will do tonight during my evening prayers is to ask God for forgiveness."

Joel scans the chairs equally spaced around the table and releases a grunt.

Their three children patiently sit between the couple, completing the circle. One by one, their palms grasp one another's, each pair of hands slightly varying in size according to age.

Next to Caroline is their eldest daughter, Hannah, seven years old. She is well-taught and obediently keeps her eyes glued to the details of the tablecloth's fall-embroidered leaves. Her head's tilted position displays her dark blond hair but obscures her eyes, which match her father's color. A single French braid, secured by a neat red velvet bow, masks the length of her long untrimmed locks. She is wearing a holiday dress made from the same fabric as her mother's, with burgundy velvet piping accenting the sleeves and waistline.

Madelyn, who has just turned six, sits beside her on an identical shaker-style wooden chair. The girls have the same features, making them look like twins, and both wear matching outfits, further aligning their undeniable similarities. Everything but the height difference, one-year age gap, and slightly turned-up button nose make her a perfect likeness to her older sister.

The last child seated closest to their father is the youngest, a small boy named Jacob, who is five.

Noticing that his son's body is scrunched as he clutches Madelyn's hand for safety, Joel glances over to ensure the small boy's slumped posture has caused no wrinkles in his matching holiday outfit.

Jacob is a carbon copy of his father except for the bow tie secured snuggly around his neck, made from the same velvet used to accent the girl's attire. With his hair as light as a snow-covered hill and his eyes bluer than the bluest ocean, Caroline wanted him to have something that made him look a bit like her, so she added the bowtie, and though subtle, it was enough of a similarity to make her happy.

As Joel finishes his round of glares, he lowers his shoulders to release tension over frustration with his wife. After a lengthy exhalation, he takes another moment to admire his perfect genetics circling the table, and with a sense of renewal, his lips form a rigid smile. "All right, my little blessings. Let us each take a turn to profess our gratitude," he says.

Hannah, restricted from openly expressing herself, takes a deep breath as she prepares to tell her appreciation list. But before she can start her sentence, her mother's grip tightens around her hand, and she immediately stops, knowing it is a warning that she is about to make a mistake.

Ignoring the women's side of the table, Joel shifts his focus to look at his son. "Starting with you, Jacob. Tell us what you are thankful for," he says.

Her father's stern tone reminds Hannah of her place, and her heart races as paranoia sets in over whether he heard her deep breath in preparation to speak. Then, while internally trying to hide, she listens to her brother's voice.

Jacob nervously looks up at his dad towering over him. Worried about his presentation, the child fights a hint of a lisp and murmurs. "I am thankful—"

Joel immediately finds something to correct. "Speak up, son, loud enough for God to hear," he says.

Jacob slightly raises his voice and continues, "I am thankful for Daddy, Mommy, and my sisters," he says.

Joel ensures his son is finished and smirks. Then, with a nod, he turns his gaze to Madelyn. "What about you? What are you thankful for?" he asks.

Madelyn hesitates, still uncertain if it is her turn, and apprehensively glances at her father for affirmation. Noticing him still staring, she knows she dare not ask, and, without hesitation, she begins. "I am thankful for my wonderful family and all our blessings from God," she says.

Her words trigger Joel's grin to broaden into a tooth-baring smile. Satisfied with her response, he gives another stern nod. "Excellent, Madelyn," he says. Continuing to savor the holiday spirit, he directs his attention to his eldest daughter. "Finally, what are you thankful for, sweet Hannah?"

Hannah reacts to her name being called with a large gulp. While looking down at the tablecloth, she stammers, "I... I am thankful for my wonderful life with my loving family, for the food on the table, and for everyone being healthy," she says.

Joel lets his children's words set in, then releases a heavy sigh while making eye contact with his wife. "Well, that was a lovely moment. Now let us eat," he says as he shrugs.

While slicing the turkey, he feels a light tug on his pants belt loop. Without having to look, he already knows who it is. "Yes, Jacob. What is it?"

The small boy looks at his father. "What about Mommy?" he asks.

Unfazed, Joel focuses on continuing to slice and serve turkey. "What about her?" he says.

As Jacob watches a piece of meat hit his dish, he glances at his mother. "What is she thankful for?" he asks.

Joel puts a small piece of meat on his wife's plate and chuckles. "There is a simple answer to that question, Jacob: Why, it is everything I am thankful for," he says.

After returning to his seat, he faces his son to explain. "Someday, God will give a wife to you, and you will be put in charge of speaking on both your behalf. We, as men, are born to bear an enormous responsibility as the head of the household and our wife's mouthpiece, and no one can take that blessing away from us except God. Just remember that."

With a giant grin, he looks at his wife, who firmly grasps her fork. "Isn't that right, dear?"

Caroline stops before taking a bite of food. She holds back her opinion while forcing a smile and gripping her metal utensil.

Her expression softens as she shifts her focus to her son. "That is right, Jacob. A woman is meant to nurture and care for her family, not engage in forming opinions or daily decision-making," she says.

Everyone at the table patiently watches Joel devour his first bite of turkey, and after the lump of food clears his throat, they ravenously start eating.

Chapter Two

SINFUL FEAR

The Smith family's guard lowers as they sit in peaceful silence, eating their holiday meal. Taking advantage of the tranquil state, Joel seizes his opportunity to persist in his control over the dinner conversation. With a passive sneer, he looks down at his son, anxiously shoveling food into his mouth. "You know, Jacob, I have been thinking a lot lately and praying to our dear Lord about you," he says.

Jacob's hunger-filled concentration on his next bite of turkey delays his reaction to his father's statement. He abruptly comprehends that the tiny pause is disrespectful, and his face turns deathly pale, dreading the repercussions.

Joel seethes as he glares at the young boy's fear-filled eyes. "God and I had a serious conversation about your annoying sleep problem," he says while loading his mouth with a forkful of bread stuffing. "Ever since we allowed you to move from your sister's room into your own, you have given us trouble. Your poor mother and I have not had a restful night's sleep for weeks."

Believing he has disappointed everyone at the table makes Jacob feel so ashamed that he refrains from taking another bite and lowers his head. "I—I'm... I'm sorry," he says.

Caroline cannot stand seeing her baby boy disheartened and wants to speak up. But she fights the urge by squirming in her chair. Her husband's ridicule of Jacob and his lack of compassion toward the little boy's nightmares sickens her.

Joel shakes his head, holding his fork in the air, silencing the room. "Just one moment, Jacob. It is my turn to speak. I struggle to wrap my head around how my flesh and blood can be so ungrateful for everything provided. I even considered seeking advice from the community elders, just in case it was an act needing repentance. But, as I took a moment to reflect, I determined that instead of escalating the issue up the chain, we could try working out our differences man-to-man. I would hate for you to face civic punishment for something we can readily fix within the four walls of our home. "

Hearing that the church will not be involved relieves Caroline. She watches with encouragement as Jacob nods timidly.

Joel is content with the signs of compliance from the young boy. "I am happy we agree," he says. Then, taking another bite, he nonchalantly adds, "You know what God told me? When I talked to our Lord above, he said that the only way for you to have a chance in hell to grow into a respectable man is to quit knocking on our bedroom door at night."

Then, using the blunt end of his fork, he sternly taps Jacob's chest. "Fear does not exist in a man. To be consumed by it is a breach of God's will. The only cure is to tackle it alone, in silence."

The thought of sitting alone in the dark and facing the monster plaguing his nightmares terrifies Jacob. His heart pounds while he combats his trembling hands, and it takes every ounce of his willpower to nod his head yes to signify his understanding.

Joel smiles from ear to ear as he takes another bite of turkey. His molars scrape against the fork's metal, creating an uncomfortable shrill as he pulls the meat from the tines. "Good, it looks like we have an agreement. Tonight's bedtime will be a fresh start, and, assuming you keep your word, we can put all of this behind us," he says.

Jacob nods, his head down, and his eyes focus on the plate before him. "Yes, sir," he says.

Upon completing the conversation, Joel continues to enjoy his meal and, overcome by the holiday cheer, hums a merry tune between each bite.

Having been raised on similar routines, everyone in Mountain View, whether they realize it, has a deeply engrained internal clock that is subconsciously followed. So, as the Smiths silently eat away at their food like rummaging mice, the rest of the neighborhood is doing the same, and when the clock strikes seven, everyone's mealtime is complete.

All but one Smith has finished slightly earlier than usual, at a quarter till. The family remains silent, watching Joel finish every morsel on his plate. Then, with a slight scooting movement from him, they all push their chairs out in unison to match the head of the household and rise from the table. The Smith children stand motionless, obediently waiting beside their chairs for parental instructions.

Between homes, the schedules continue to coincide throughout the neighborhood of Bethlehem. As each household finishes its perfect family meal, they carry on with their routine, ending Thanksgiving Day with the wives preparing their children for bed.

Knowing it is time to face his fear, Jacob apprehensively glances across the room at the long hallway that leads to his bedroom. He tries to prepare himself mentally, but it looks darker than he remembers, like a tunnel created by a cave's damp walls.

A foreboding heaviness falls over his feet. Sudden light-headedness washes over him, and his left eardrum rings.

The young child focuses on the floor, hoping to regain stability as his gut warns him of danger. His vision narrows, and he locks eyes on the dreaded bedroom door at the end of the hall.

A faint, raspy voice calls to him. "Come, my boy. It is time to rest. Join us on a magical quest," it says. Even though the ethereal sound should alarm him, he finds it hypnotic, filling him with soothing warmth.

However, as the voice continues, the punctuation fueling each word turns sinister, mimicking a serpent's hiss. "The night is the time your fears take flight as the darkness within is allowed to bite," it says.

Each word lingers in Jacob's ears. His confusion over the shift in tone and his limited vocabulary makes it challenging to compute the rhyme's meaning. Seeking help, he looks to his family, but their complacent demeanor confirms his internal isolation.

As the boy's attention sways, the entity grows louder, reclaiming its hold over his mind and revealing its hatred-filled intentions. "From your soul, my grasp will break, seizing what I thirst for, the light of others, which is mine to take," it says.

Jacob distinguishes its threatening nature and his heart races. He attempts to raise his hands to shield his ears, only to discover that his upper body and arms are paralyzed. As he fights to regain control, his nostrils flare, and the corners of his eyes twitch.

Caroline observes Jacob's muscles stiffening abnormally and wonders if her husband has taken notice. Fortunately, he is oblivious to his son's peculiar behavior, as he is pre-occupied with zealously polishing his coke-bottle glasses with his shirt.

Caroline fears her husband's wrath if he catches sight of Jacob's unauthorized movement and knows she must act fast to protect him. The girls nervously watch as she attempts to block Joel's view by gliding around the table, wedging her body between Jacob and his father. Concerned that their reactions will make her husband suspicious, she chuckles to induce her children to smile. "Well, wasn't that a joyful holiday? Now, it's time to get you three to bed so you can welcome dreams filled with blessings and joy," she says.

Almost as if rehearsed, the sound of her bright tone causes all three children's demeanor to shift to compulsory happiness. The corners of their lips quiver into their broadest smiles just as Joel's glasses reach the bridge of his nose. His spectacle-aided vision is pleasingly met with their grinning faces. After taking a moment to bask in his pride, he nods to acknowledge their obedience. "Off you go," he says.

Despite being relieved by his response, Caroline remains guarded as she calmly places her hand on Jacob's back to comfort him. She then collectedly herds him toward his sisters and, like a mother hen gathering her chicks, ushers them down the long hallway toward their rooms.

The children willingly comply, following her guidance in complete silence.

Caroline stops everyone in front of the girl's bedroom. She opens the door and watches them scurry inside, focusing on her eldest daughter. "Now, Hannah," she says. Hannah pivots to listen. Upon making eye contact with her, Caroline sternly continues, "Remember what we talked about. Since you are getting older, it is time to start learning the role of a household caregiver. That way, you will be prepared to take care of your own family in the future. You may believe it's silly now, but time will creep up on you faster than you think."

She glances at Madelyn, then turns her focus back to Hannah. To ensure they both clearly understand what she is about to say, she speaks slowly and with intent, "From here on, as the oldest, you have the responsibility of ensuring both you and Madelyn get ready for bed."

Hannah's chest confidently rises, and she nods, confirming her understanding of her additional responsibility.

Caroline playfully squinches her eyes while looking at her youngest daughter. "That means, Madelyn, it is your job to listen to your older sister and be obedient. Do you understand?" Concentrating on the instructions given by her mother, Madelyn bites her lip and nods.

The little boy fears that his sisters' responses will end the exchange and expedite his trip to his room, causing him to cling to his mother's leg in anxious anticipation.

Hannah skips to the closet to fetch their pajamas and calls for her younger sister to follow.

A rustling noise catches Jacob's attention, and a warm breath brushes the back of his neck, sending a shiver down his spine. Then a deep, muddled voice with a hint of amusement calls to him from the end of the hallway. "Little boy, it is time for bed. Come and rest your weary head," it says.

Jacob squeezes his eyes shut, listens, and is met with silence. He finally gathers enough courage to open one lid and spots his sisters obliviously getting ready for bed.

Remaining stationed within the doorframe, Caroline quietly monitors their progress. She senses her son's growing anxiety and rubs his back in reassurance. Jacob gives three short tugs on his mother's skirt to get her attention. "Momma, you think I can stay here tonight?" he asks.

Knowing change can be stressful, Caroline giggles and playfully tousles his hair. "Jacob, I will tell you a secret: you don't want to sleep in the same room as girls. They have cooties," she says.

Hannah finishes helping her sister into her matching plaid, red, and green nightgown, then leads her to the bathroom down the hall to brush their teeth. When they return, Caroline greets them with a smile and tucks them into bed.

The sight of the girls saying their prayers overwhelms her with pride. Worried about disrupting their peace, she swiftly turns off the light and nudges Jacob toward the exit. "Sweet dreams," she says.

Both girls yawn, overcome by the sleepiness brought on by their full stomachs. "Goodnight," they say.

As Caroline calmly ushers Jacob out of the room, she shuts the door behind them, and without saying a word, she guides him down the long hallway.

The image of his bedroom door creates internal panic in the little boy. Caroline senses his trembling body underneath her fingers and attempts to calm him. "It will be okay," she says.

Jacob tries to respond, but his dry mouth causes his stammer to worsen.

The two stop in front of his bedroom entrance. Caroline gives him a comforting smile as she reaches for the handle and opens the door. Jacob's eyes widen, and his respiration quickens as he tentatively surveys the inside of his room. Everything appears to be just as he left it. Feeling uneasy about the eerie calmness, he stubbornly plants his feet against the floor.

Convinced that his resistance stems from her husband's lack of sensitivity at the dinner table, Caroline gives him a moment to decompress. "Your father means well. He comes from a place of love," she says. Forcing a grin, she lightly taps his back to nudge him inside the room, then anxiously follows behind him.

On a mission to get him ready for bed, she rushes to his oak dresser, opens the top drawer, and shuffles through the contents. "Let's get you into your comfy pajamas and tuck you in so you can be snug as a bug, just like your sisters."

The floorboards near Jacob's bed release a loud creak, and he takes a step closer to his mother for comfort. Even though she does not acknowledge the noise, his mind still races, and his thoughts further provoke angst.

Everything inside of him tells him to escape, but he does not know where to go; he feels trapped. Unease fills his mind, causing him to remain motionless out of fear.

A second floorboard releases a groan. This time, it is near his feet, causing him to jump. He clears his throat and tries to squeeze out a few words. "But... but what do I do if it comes?" he asks.

Confused by what he is referring to, Caroline pauses momentarily to reflect on his question as she retrieves a pair of red-checkered pajamas from the dresser. Her expression softens as she turns her gaze to her son. "What are you talking about, sweety? When what comes? We both know I am the only one who tucks you in at night," she says.

Her lack of understanding frustrates Jacob, but he knows he must explain. Worried that someone might hear their conversation, he glances from side to side and whispers. "The monster," he says.

Caroline chuckles as she continues getting Jacob ready for bed. She gently taps his nose before pulling his head through the neck of his long John top. "You know, one's mind can be a blessing and a curse. It can play crazy tricks on us sometimes. When I was your age, I used to think something lived in my closet, but as I got older, I realized it was just my mind playing tricks on me," she says.

Jacob remains silent. Taking it as a sign that everything is okay, Caroline escorts him to finish his nighttime routine.

But, as she tucks her son under the covers, she senses his escalating apprehension.

Kneeling beside the little boy, she tries offering him words of comfort. "Remember, faith conquers all," she says.

The young child is so preoccupied with the room's atmosphere that he cannot concentrate on what she is saying. "So... monsters aren't real?" He asks, his voice wavering.

To give him further reassurance, Caroline moves closer and tenderly kisses his forehead. "No, Jacob, they are not real. They only live in your imagination and nowhere else," she says.

As her nose brushes Jacob's skin, he giggles. His laugh makes Caroline smile. "And even if they were, I would let nothing happen to you, so you have nothing to fear," she says.

Despite her efforts to bolster his assurance, Jacob dwells on the discrepancy between her promises and his experience regarding the monster's presence. Still unsettled, he pulls the covers up to his chin. "What about you? If you protect me, who will protect you?" he asks.

The abruptness of his question flusters Caroline, and she pauses. Never being asked anything like this by her children leaves her at a loss for words. "Well..." she says. Then, with a dramatic sigh, she shrugs and attempts to lighten the mood. "I guess that job falls on your father, so there is nothing for you to worry about."

Even though the answer does not bring Jacob comfort, the turkey settling in his belly causes a wave of tiredness to fall over him. "But... but..." he says.

Noticing his eyes beginning to close, Caroline brushes her hand against his cheek. The sight of his nostrils flaring with each tiny snore brings her relief. "Goodnight, my son," she says.

She tiptoes out of the room, leaving him to sleep in peace, and without making a peep, she brushes off their conversation's uncomfortableness and turns off the lights. Then, shutting the door behind her, she quietly wishes Jacob sweet dreams and continues down the hall to tend to the dirty dishes from dinner.

Jacob finds himself in a deep sleep, tormented by what he dreads most. The experience is nothing as his mother had promised.

Rather than sweet dreams, a cold, dark abyss awaits him on the other side of consciousness.

Chapter Three

DON'T SAY HIS NAME

Most people are oblivious to the fact that their brain limits sensory experiences, like pain and temperature, while they sleep. It acts as a barrier to help protect us from our wild imaginations.

Jacob has become exempt from the standard rules of dreaming. Upon falling asleep, he endures what others do not—the experience of being fully cognizant of every moment. It poses no issue if the dream settings remain pleasant in temperature and content. But what happens when the world is filled with terrifying encounters and air so chilling that it could instantly freeze the organs of a living human being?

Most would be horrified by the sensation of bitter cold slowing their beating heart to a state of hibernation, but that is the least of Jacob's worries. Instead, the occurrence is a catalyst, assisting him in uncovering the darkness masked by his naivety: the monstrous entity his mind has been hiding from him.

It has not always been that way. The morbid shift occurred a few weeks back and has remained constant ever since. It coincided with the first evening he slept alone without his sister's company. Even though the thought of changing rooms and growing up seemed scary to Jacob, the constancy of the happy land he went to in his dreams put him at ease.

On the first night of sleeping in his bedroom, before his mother had even left after tucking him into bed, he shut his eyes, ready to be transported to the world he had crafted, *Grüner Hügel*, which, when translated to English, means Green Hill.

Living up to its name, the small town lies tucked away in the countryside of Europe on a hill blanketed with a green blend of ancient pine, cedar, and fir trees. The mix of conifers combined with the snowy scene fills the air on the main street with a smell reminiscent of damp cedar planks. Visitors passing through claim it incites warm, fond memories of decorating their freshly cut trees and homes for Christmas.

Even though the high altitude traps it in a single season—winter—the town makes the most of it by embracing the holiday cheer year-round with wreaths and colorful lights adorning every structure.

Each brick-laden building replicates what one may find in a model Christmas village displayed at a department store during the holidays. The architecture has an old-time feel, with polished cobblestone streets and windows draped in sparkling tinsel.

Caroling bell's chime music on the hour from the spire at the top of the town hall. The residents whistle along with the tune while maintaining perpetual smiles as if under a sunny spell.

Jacob has grown accustomed to its charm, and it resonates as more of a home to the small boy than Mountain

View. Although he does not have blood ties with the residents, he has developed friendships with all the children, allowing him to join in on the holiday traditions.

Since he has never been permitted to partake in sleepovers, his favorite activity within Green Hill's Christmas rituals has become their giant slumber parties.

The dreamy town's population operates similarly to a household amicably split by divorce. The town's parents do not believe in taking exclusive ownership of their offspring. Instead, they share them. That way, the kids do not feel bound to a single-family relationship, and if a child or parent is tragically lost, the blow of grief can be mitigated. Collective parenting fuels the fun practice of rotating sleepovers and provides married pairs time to bond with the village's youth.

All the children favor the tradition. The thrill of the evenings filled with playing games, eating homemade treats, and sharing whimsical stories around candlelight fills them with delight. They especially enjoy reaping the benefits of each couple's passive competition to be their favorite. Every night is a new adventure for the children, as they eagerly wait to see how each house will be more extravagant than the last.

The only rule held strictly by the community is that quiet hours commence precisely when the sun sets. There are no ifs, ands, or buts about it. Since the adolescents are exhausted by sundown, they never challenge the decree or inquire why the rule exists.

It is similar to Jacob's usual routine, making the silent-hour restriction seem normal. One benefit is that it becomes dark later in Green Hill, so his bedtime is slightly later than in Mountain View.

Throughout his repeated visits, he has found it a safe space to share his creativity openly. Within Green Hill, he is free to tell embellished stories, regardless of how outlandish, and without fear of punishment. Allowing him to express himself freely, without criticism, gives him a deep sense of belonging. The more he visits, the more often he wishes not to wake up and face his reality in Mountain View.

Jacob's heart filled with glee as he snuggled under the covers and closed his eyes. The concern over not having his sisters sharing the space was secondary to his excitement, knowing it was the Rigby residence's turn to host the village sleepover.

Several years ago, the Rigby household had fallen victim to tragedy when they lost their only son, Tobias, to "unforeseen circumstances. The loss hit Ada especially hard, as she had always been overprotective of Tobias, rarely allowing him to leave the house. She blamed herself for letting him out of her sight, and his sudden disappearance only confirmed all her fears.

Nothing appeared unusual about the day Mrs. Rigby sent their young son into the forest to fetch firewood. Since it was a chore that many of the village children routinely performed, assigning the task was not given a second thought.

Typically, they would only be gone for half an hour before returning with their arms full of wood. But, after days of searching with no sight of Tobias, they could only assume that he had wandered off in search of an exciting new adventure.

That is how the town handles tragedies—when a sorrowful event happens, the residents create a happier ending or thoroughly brush it under the rug to keep everyone in good spirits.

They believe the Devil is invited into your life if your heart dwells in darkness, so it is imperative to stay positive. They also hold the philosophy that if something does not want to be found, you should not continue searching. It may unearth something you wish to remain buried.

In step with the leadership's communal ideology regarding family, the town council assigned children to visit in scheduled increments until the Rigbys were ready to partake in the holiday tradition again. After receiving positive feedback from the children regarding the couple's readiness, they were finally approved to host their first sleepover since their little boy had vanished.

Aside from being around Tobias's age at the time of his disappearance, Jacob, like the rest of the town residents, knows little about the tragedy's details, or Tobias. He had never met the boy.

Jacob has, however, heard the entertaining tales concerning the annual events hosted at the Rigby's before the disaster and, like the other children, finds them of greater importance. Mrs. Rigby, or Ada, is known for letting the children bake cookies, and, never having been allowed in the kitchen by his mother, Jacob's anticipation of the experience rapidly has become all he can think of.

Jacob could not shut his eyes fast enough to be transported to the warmhearted town where the ambiance felt like Christmas. But this time, things did not go as planned. Despite all the anticipation, the long-awaited gathering is far from what he imagined. What was meant to be a wonderful time became the catalyst for a terrifying transformation of Jacob's trips to Green Hill, as nightmares about the Rigby sleepover consumed him.

An unforeseen shift occurred when he got to his "happy place" on that fateful night. Even though he stood near the town's square in his usual spot, everything was forebodingly different—the air was cold, and the scene was dismal. Each strand of tinsel and bright-colored decoration was murky gray and veiled in a foggy haze.

Still, no matter how alarming the drastic shift in tone is, the only thing on Jacob's mind is finding the sleepover. As a result, he paid little attention to the town's sorry state, attributing it solely to the late-evening hour.

Traversing clouds cross over the bright ambiance of the twinkling stars, casting shadows and blanketing the identities of the tiny creatures scurrying among the surrounding buildings' foundations.

Every bump in the night and mysterious echo makes the little boy tense with apprehension over what may lurk there. His heart races. He tries to ignore it, but the scuffling noises continue to grab his attention. As his eyes dart around, his anxiousness grows. His hands form into tight fists, and he rubs his eyes with them to regain focus. Simultaneously, the clamor surrounding him deescalates.

Jacob releases a sigh of relief until he realizes that the sounds have been cleared to make room for something more significant.

Cackling bellows resonating like a lion's roar fill Jacob's ears, and he winces defensively.

A loud *thud* booms inside the adjacent forest just a short distance away as a tree trunk snaps in half and tumbles to the ground.

Jacob shifts his focus before his imagination can conjure his dark suspicions, locking his eyes on the stars shining through the murky night sky. He cannot look away. His extreme concentration causes him to stop breathing, triggering dizziness, and turning his face blue.

Then, in a sudden moment of clarity, he realizes that his fixation has caused him to forget his most vital human instinct, and he takes a deep, gasping breath.

He is utterly unaware of what is happening at his feet as dark condensation creeps through the main street. The fog engulfs the storefronts like a rising river, drifting to knee-level and consuming every brick and stone that crosses its path.

The small boy suddenly snaps to attention upon hearing twigs cracking in the nearby woods. He turns his head to look, but cannot see through the fog that now meets him at eye level. Jacob frantically scans for any identifiable characteristics of the once-comforting town, and panic sets in as he realizes he can no longer make out the shape of a single surrounding object.

Almost as if listening to his silent appeal, the murkiness disperses like a parting sea, but Jacob finds nothing of the shadowy mist's departure settling. Instead, the observation provokes his belly to drop to his pelvis and fill the void with an unnerving butterfly effect.

The little boy's disquiet over the situation triggers his mind to play through every worst-case scenario regarding how his dream may end. Unfortunately, most of his thoughts involve a monster stalking and devouring him. But even worse than encountering a beast, he fears facing the adults' disappointment over his tardiness and wonders if this is his punishment for missing the town's strict curfew.

Another loud snap resonates from the forest; this time, it is accompanied by the cawing of a crow. The combined haunting noises taunt him, echoing as they clash against the bricks.

Scared of what may come next, Jacob shakes his head to clear his mind. "Negativity invites the Devil in," he says, trying to frighten himself into positive thinking. Then, taking a deep breath, he continues, "The Devil. That—that's right, the Devil."

A gentle breeze brushes his cheek, spurring him to refocus. He knows that if he wishes to preserve his carefree existence in the town, he must craft an excuse to justify his poor punctuality. Calming himself, he looks down and sees his red-checkered long johns and matching slippers. Then, one by one, he wiggles each toe to remind himself he is still in control.

Another burst of wind rolls through the forested terrain, carrying childlike laughter when it reaches him this time. Sensing something ominous approaching, Jacob fights his urge to look. "It's all in your head. Don't look, and that will put the Devil to bed," he says.

Laughter reverberates through the trees, accompanied by a child's whispering words. "Go now, with haste, and do not be late! They are waiting for you to meet your fate."

Upon completion of the statement, the intonation shifts to a frantic helium-deluged shriek. "And do not bother to save me anything sweet. I much prefer things soaked in blood to eat."

Every muscle in Jacob's body freezes, and his voice trembles. "Bl-blood?" he asks. He gulps, then reluctantly listens for an answer. The thought of who is behind the words sends a stream of icy chills down his spine.

But there is no reply from the unsettling voice, leaving him in dead silence.

Jacob takes a deep breath to calm his nerves. Each draw of air is more challenging than the one before it. With every inhalation of frostbitten wind, tiny icicles form in his throat, and the moisture in his lungs congeals. As he exhales, a frosty pathway forms in front of him.

The town's pitch-black windows remind him of the strict curfew. He fears that even with determination, he will not be able to find his way to the Rigby's' home through the wintry darkness.

Branches sharply crack behind him, again shattering the frigid night's silence. But this time, the sound is much closer.

Jacob knows he must move forward, but the mere thought causes his body to freeze in place while he shivers uncontrollably. Sharp, jabbing pains migrate through his stiffened limbs. His body is shutting down from the unrelenting cold. He is running out of time and knows the only option to keep from freezing to death is to get somewhere warm.

The boy squints to enhance his vision while scouring the scene for the Rigby residence.

Although it does not seem possible, everything is darker than before. The only thing breaking through the black abyss is long, flashing strands of Christmas lights connecting both sides of the street, and they, like everything else, appear insipid. A light coat of flocking covers the elongated bulbs, dulling their glow. Rather than providing a constant festive illumination, the wires within the glass walls surge eerily like eyes blinking, one by one.

To combat the hypothermic ache, Jacob tightly wraps his arms around himself, trying to create any form of warmth. His chattering teeth become louder, making it impossible to concentrate, and he clenches his jaw to silence them.

A menacing hiss resonates from the electric current running through the strands of lights. Jacob's gaze shifts toward the unpleasant buzzing, and he notices an odd rhythm in the light's pattern. But, while attempting to focus all his attention on studying the sequence of the dancing flickers, he cannot escape the feeling plaguing the blood beneath his skin. He has never felt cold like this before, and the pain is overwhelming as each vein feels like it is turning to glass.

Whistling breaks through the hum of the bulbs, and Jacob notices something familiar about the melody. Though slightly flat in pitch, the tune resembles a carol traditionally sung by the Green Hill community on Christmas Eve.

In addition, he observes that each downbeat coincides with the blinking of the colored lights draped above.

One by one, each bulb flashes, forming a trail leading to the last house on the street. Its location at the end of a cul-de-sac reminds him of his home in Mountain View, and the similarity convinces him it is the Rigby's. A wave of relief washes over him.

Jacob is elated to join his Green Hill family and for the nightmare to end, yet he stops after taking his first step toward the home. The pressure of his body weight shifting onto his frozen toes feels like tiny needles piercing the skin. Focused on the inviting light in the window, he fights off the discomfort and, little by little, limps closer.

At the end of the cobblestone path, warm candlelight provides a perfect glow in the Rigby house, illuminating the tiny silhouettes of playing children through the kitchen window's leaded glass.

Jacob is unmindful of the whistling melody getting closer because the children's cheerful laughter overshadows the off-key tune. Each animated giggle fills him with optimism.

His face lights up with a smile as he hears the familiar voices of his friends; he has missed nothing.

Anxious about losing more time, he ignores the fiery blur of his windburned vision and the stiffness of his frozen joints. Fighting the ache, he clumsily dashes toward the Rigby residence. "Wait for me! Wait for me!" he says as a joyful warmth penetrates his heart, fingers, and toes.

A loud commotion stirs at the forest's edge, followed by a surge of swirling snow that weaves through the buildings and fills the air near the town square. It clears the way for a pair of heavy leather boots to step from the tree line onto the cobblestone. An eerie jingle accompanies each slow, methodical stomp. As the single rusted bell rattles, a raspy voice hums to imitate the old bell's tune. "Jingle, jingle, jingle," it says.

Jacob is so focused on reaching the destination that he is oblivious to what is happening behind him.

As the entity emerges onto the main street, the colorful lights overhead uncontrollably buzz. Taking a moment of pause, the figure lowers its chin and locks its eyes on the child. Then, with a single jingle of its bell, one by one, the buzz of each bulb escalates in pitch to the point of shattering. The creature sticks out its thick tongue, catching bits of colored glass falling toward the street, and chews each sharp shard with a grin.

The wafting smell of freshly baked cookies creeps beneath the tiny gap under the Rigby's' front door. Overwhelmed by the aroma, Jacob wipes his salivating mouth as he arrives at the front porch's base and almost trips up the three short stone steps to the entrance.

He is oblivious that he is sitting prey.

The entity continues its methodical pursuit, its heavy footsteps echoing off the brick structures as it leisurely approaches the boy. Rather than the typical sound of a shoe sole, every purposeful *thud* forms a different resonance as it grinds glass fragments into the hard cobblestone. Oddly, the closer they get, the more the clamor resembles the clop of cloven hooves.

Jacob is mesmerized, focused on only one thing: eating fresh, hot cookies. Driven by impulsivity, his hand grows a mind of its own and jolts toward the doorknob, but before he can grasp the metal handle, the door flings open.

He gasps, inhaling a large gulp of frosty air, and hyperventilates as he tries to catch his breath. His chilled esophagus causes his throat to spasm, and he chokes on his icy saliva. As he glances up for help, he distinguishes the outline of a woman. Her smile lengthens, stretching her lips thinly from ear to ear, giving the impression that she is overjoyed to see him.

Jacob slows his breath, and even though his vision is blurred from the frigid winds battering, he detects something familiar about her nightgown. The colors perfectly match his pajamas. The woman stares down at him while remaining bizarrely quiet and stationary.

Concerned about wrongly assuming the woman's identity, Jacob wants to ensure it is Mrs. Rigby. He squints to sharpen his vision and scans for any available details that may give a clue.

Upon closer inspection, he sees she is wearing an apron perfectly tied around her waist. It has a pocket of white eyelet lace that sits above her hips next to an embroidered gingerbread man monogrammed with a simple cursive *R*. That is enough proof for Jacob to confirm that it is her, and he is relieved to know that he is precisely where he is supposed to be: in the safety of an adult's care.

The warmth radiating from the open door clears his vision. His eyes wander to assess the woman's details, and her frazzled presence reminds him of how his mother looks during the holidays after spending long hours in front of the oven's heat.

Her appearance is uncharacteristically disheveled compared to other mothers he has encountered in Green Hill. Trails of mascara run down from her eyes and flow over her cheeks. The charcoal streams mix with her peach-toned blush and settle in a pool of smeared strawberry-colored lipstick on her chin. If someone did not know better, they might assume she had been crying for days. The state of her dark red hair strangely contradicts her messy makeup. Her crimson tresses are meticulously combed into a bob with perfectly rolled ends gently caressing her neck.

She glares straight ahead, remaining silent as her grin grows into a gaping smile. The cavernous gap between her lips exposes her discolored teeth stained with hews of pinkish-beige. Although her hands are rigidly positioned by her sides, her fingers spasm, and she attempts to steady them by digging her broken nails into the delicate material of her apron.

He does not think much of her disarray, but he notices a peculiar feeling he gets from the energy she is exuding. Something about how her fingers fidget is unusual; it makes him uneasy.

Wild with excitement, she appears ready to explode with emotion as she falls to her knees, releasing a hysterical cry. "I knew it would keep its word and return you. I just knew... I just knew. No one believed me, but I knew," she says, each word running over into the next.

Her lamentations continue like a broken record. Tears flood her eyes and overflow her lids, sending glimmering streams down her cheeks. Her arms wrap around the small boy, and she breaks into delirious laughter. "Your father didn't believe me, but I knew you would return to us."

Jacob has never seen an adult expressing this much emotion before, and with this being his first time meeting her, he is overwhelmed.

Refusing to let go, her arms squeeze his body tighter like a boa constrictor crushing its prey. Jacob's inability to avoid the overzealous display of affection turns his body rigid, but that changes when the skin of her cheek contacts his. He finds the warmth of her motherly touch reassuring, allowing him to push past his discomfort.

As his lips gain feeling and sensation returns to his tongue, he realizes he has yet to introduce himself, and, worrying about being rude, he stammers, "My—my name is Jacob."

Declining to listen, the woman pushes herself away from him and covers her ears. "That is enough, dear. I know who you are," she says, leaving him at arm's distance. Her finger waves through the air and lands softly on his lips. She cheerfully hums in a minor key while swaying back and forth to the disconcerting tune. At the height of the song's movement, she closes her eyes and mumbles a few words in Latin. "*Mors tua, vita mea.*"

Ignorance is bliss for Jacob, and not understanding a word she is saying, he awkwardly smiles.

At the pinnacle of her gibberish, she takes a deep breath and, unable to contain herself, snatches him into her arms to pull him closer. "Hush now, my baby, don't say a word. You are here now, back in my arms, where you belong," she says.

A haunting moan and faint tinny jingle cut through the winter air.

It strikes a nerve in Mrs. Rigby, and she instantly reacts. With a compulsive twitch, her eyes widen, and her arms tighten around the small boy's torso as if to establish ownership. She glances past him, looking toward the noise, and, with a painful spasm, her lips quiver back into a smile.

Another jingle sounds, but it is slightly closer than before.

As if recognizing what is lurking in the darkness, she gives a slight nervous nod of acknowledgment, then redirects her attention to Jacob. She appears hurried as her excitement builds to a shrill tenor, and her words speed to an auctioneer's pace. "Of course, silly, I know who you are; I am your mother. Your wild imagination is like mine; you are just as cute as I remember. Wait until your father sees you. He will not believe how much you have grown to resemble him. I cannot wait until he sees that adorable little face." Releasing her clutch, she pinches his rosy cheeks and stares intensely into his pupils as if dissecting his soul. Jacob only wants to get inside to play. He stands on his tiptoes, trying to glimpse his friends behind her.

Confident he is distracted, her eyes dart past him to scan the distance. The way she analyzes the darkness is filled with paranoia.

Jacob's attention shifts, wanting to see what she is staring at, and he wiggles to escape her grasp. Panicked, she squeezes his ice-cold cheeks tighter to regain his attention. He winces at the pain and returns to facing her.

Mrs. Rigby lightens her grip and softens her tone to compensate for her crude attempt at keeping him from looking. "I would not do that again if I were you, my sweet child. If you face the icy wind directly, you will only worsen your chilled skin," she says. Then, looking at his chattering teeth, she attempts to redirect him. "You must be freezing to death without a coat. What do you say we get you inside to warm up?" she says.

Springing to her feet, she grabs him by his shoulders. "I have taken care of everything, so don't worry; we—I mean, *you*—are safe."

Jacob returns a shivering nod of agreement. Then, following her nudge, he steps inside to escape the cold. Mrs. Rigby smiles and lunges past him, slamming the door shut. Her heart rate escalates as she peeks through a small crescent-shaped window at the top of the entry, then swiftly locks the door.

The sound of the thick iron latching catches the small boy's attention. He quietly stretches on his tiptoes to observe what she is doing and sees her fastening the last of the door's sizable padlocks. Upon finishing, she releases a sigh of relief and giggles, noticing his curiosity. "These are just to keep the fun in," she says.

Her words spark excitement in Jacob and remind him of the fun time he is about to have with his friends. Wanting nothing more than to join them, he forgets about his troubles as his yearning to play with the other children takes over. He is sure that everyone is in the kitchen baking cookies, and if he is quiet and listens closely, he will hear their laughter.

But disappointingly, he hears nothing, though he stands perfectly still. Aside from the ambiance created by the crackling coals of the nearby fireplace, the room is dead silent. He assumes his ears must still be affected by the cold and closes his eyes to reign in his focus.

Mrs. Rigby pushes past him to cater to the burning wood and, grabbing a fire poker, makes herself busy by stoking the embers. Ignoring her, Jacob concentrates on listening for the others. The fact that he still cannot hear the same noise that led him to the brownstone confuses him. "Where are they? Did they go to bed?" he asks.

Something about the question triggers Mrs. Rigby, and her body freezes. Then, not wanting to answer, she pretends not to hear him.

She gathers her thoughts and, regaining her composure, turns to face him with a smile. "What did you say, my dear?" she asks. Her nostrils flare as she clears her throat. "Mommy is just a bit tired and didn't hear you."

Having a more significant set of issues on his mind, Jacob brushes off the fact that the woman keeps referring to herself as his mother. He is only focused on solving the mystery of the hidden children. The image of their outlines dancing and playing in the window filters through his mind as he happily inquires again. "My friends... I saw them from outside. They were playing in the window. It looked like they were having fun."

Mrs. Rigby knows that answering the child should be like second nature, but she is in no hurry to respond. Unnerved over Jacob's interrogation, her agitation rises. She closes her eyes and listens to the lingering silence and crackling embers, neurotically picking her nails and chewing her fingertips. Then, suddenly, with a spastic wave of her hand, she calls for his attention and spews a reply. "Oh, yes, that is right, sweety. We were baking, but they are all asleep now. I think the heat from the oven made them tired," she says.

Jacob's mouth gapes open as he prepares to ask another question. Her hands wring the lace of her apron, and the creases of her lips twitch. Then, to distract Jacob, she rushes forward and grabs his arm. "Let's go see your father. What do you say about that? I know he is dying to see you," she says.

Jacob has a sick feeling in his gut, and his worry causes him to stutter. "B-but my dad doesn't live here, so I—I want to see my friends," he says.

She places her palm on his back and gently nudges him forward. "Sweety, now don't be silly. I am sure that the cold has just made you a bit confused. Come on now, let us go see your father," she says.

With no other options, the small boy follows her guidance. Halfway across the room to the kitchen, he smells something cooking. The scent is neither sweet nor savory; it oddly combines the two with a tinge of farm-to-table. His eyes widen with excitement. "Are we going to bake cookies?" he asks.

With a chuckle, she lightly pats his shoulder. "Sure, my boy. If that is what you want to do, we can bake as many cookies as you like," she says. Her smile fades, starkly contradicting her chipper tone. They stop in front of the kitchen door, and Mrs. Rigby looks at him with a forced grin. "Of course, we can bake cookies if that would make you happy," she says. The small child impulsively nods with excitement.

Taking a long breath, she reluctantly opens the door, like pulling off a bandage. With a jarring motion, she stops, cracking it just enough not to see inside. "Now... I must warn you, the kitchen is a little messy from earlier, but I am sure you will understand," she says.

Excited to at least take part in some of the activity, Jacob no longer cares if the other children have already gone to bed. "I don't mind," he says. Unable to fight back his anticipation, he jumps up and down, trying to get her to move faster.

Mrs. Rigby manically titters. "Here we are," she says. Her eyes shut tight, and she takes a deep breath as she pushes open the door. The hinges creak, forming a long ear-piercing shrill. Jacob impatiently squirms in anticipation.

Unbeknownst to him, he is unprepared for what lies on the other side.

Chapter Four

IT'S COMING

Aburst of heat billows through the growing entrance, accompanied by the pungent odors of roasting flesh and iron.

Now able to see clearly within the confines of the kitchen, Jacob's eyes widen with fear. Nothing about the room is what he imagined, and the horrific sight causes the small boy to go into shock.

Every detail contradicts the next, putting the room at odds with itself. Where it is clean, everything is misaligned, and where it is crimson-splattered, items sit perfectly organized. Each square foot exposes a vile act highlighting a reign of terror that defaces the walls, counters, and brown-tiled floor.

Jacob is afraid to close his eyes, terrified of what will happen next. His eyes grow dry and sting, turning his vision fuzzy.

Noticing the sound of his pounding heart, Mrs. Rigby offers a nervous smile and lightly rubs the boy's back to comfort him. "Don't be shy. Go ahead. Go on in," she says with a swift, forceful nudge.

Jacob flinches and looks down at his feet, unsure where to take his first step. A red liquid that is as vibrant as freshly spilled paint coats the floor to the bottom edge of the wooden baseboards.

Naive about the substance and unfamiliar smell, Jacob glances at Mrs. Rigby to read her reaction, but nothing about her demeanor varies from before. She behaves as if oblivious to the horror and stares past the mess with a numb, unwavering grin. It is as if everything appears normal to her, and nothing is wrong with the scene.

The extent of her unfazed nature makes the small boy feel like he is overreacting. Raised to be obedient and not wanting to disappoint her, he elongates his stride to avoid the carnage and makes his way inside. Mrs. Rigby's incessant smile causes her lips to quiver as she cautiously watches him enter the room. "There you go," she says.

Not hearing her footsteps behind him concerns Jacob, and as he turns to see if she is coming, he notices something on the backside of the door. An array of tiny bloody handprints covers the wood paneling, some more distinct than others; the varying shades of crimson correlate with how long they have been resting. A few sitting closer to the ground sprout from the coagulated substance pooling beneath the wooden frame, with trailing smudges extending from where the fingernails should be. Every digit has left a spiderlike scarlet trail of gore.

The gruesome sight and the rancid odor cause Jacob's knees to buckle, and his body falters. His eyes migrate from handprint to handprint until landing again on the large pool of burgundy liquid on the floor. A grisly drag mark stretches away from the puddle, painting a path of butchery across the kitchen's cold tile. He reluctantly looks up to see where the trail ends.

Mirroring the turmoil in the little boy's head, chaos secretly brews outside, revealing itself with a pounding knock. Someone is at the front door. Startled, Jacob and Mrs. Rigby hold their breath as they listen to the intruder's aggressive introduction.

Guilt briefly falls over Mrs. Rigby, causing her face to flush. As she had not been expecting company, the late-night visitor perplexes her. Her breath quickens, and her imagination runs wild with scenarios related to the discovery of her debauchery.

Jacob notices a sudden shift in energy as goosebumps consume his arms and legs; he knows something evil is outside.

Another knock cuts through the dead quiet—this time, it is much louder and more violent than before. The blow's forcefulness rattles the home's structure, causing soot to tumble from the chimney's bricks. As it cascades onto the flames, it snuffs them out. The ceased crackling of the embers heightens every noise of the stranger's movement, including the bells' jingling.

Mrs. Rigby recognizes the sound, and her eyes widen with terror. She knows it all too well. Lately, she has found it to be a catalyst for her prolific nightmares.

Jacob senses her anxious energy. With a single shared glance, they can both feel the panic, even without a word spoken.

The jingling tinkles again, this time in a cluster of three notes at a decibel only she and canines can hear. It triggers an innate response inside Mrs. Rigby; her body trembles with terror, and she clutches onto the door frame to stabilize her weak knees. Feeling faint, she tilts her head to ease an onslaught of nausea and spots the bloodstains on the kitchen floor. Each of her breaths becomes quicker, and her heart pounds.

Unnerved over what may come, she recites Fatima's prayer to seek forgiveness for her horrific acts. *"O mi Iesu, dimitte nobis debita nostra, salva nos ab igne inferni, perduc in caelum omnes animas, praesertim eas, quae misericordiae tuae maxime indigent,"* she says.

After she speaks to the heavens, a moment of silence passes, and all appears calm. Assuming the prayer has brought tranquility to the situation, Mrs. Rigby sighs in relief. "God has listened," she says. She glances at the boy, and the lights give a subtle flicker. Mrs. Rigby pays little mind to it while focusing on the child.

Unexpectedly, her shoulders raise to the bottom of her earlobes; she tries to stop them but has no power over their movement. Losing control escalates her anxiety and her heart's pace quickens. Her hands clutch her ribcage; something feels wrong.

An assaulting sulfuric odor drifts into the room. The horrific stench smells of rotten eggs as it rises to their nostrils.

Jacob notices Mrs. Rigby's face tense, and an unusual twitching begins in the outer corner of her eye. She struggles to control her body's movements and can barely muster enough strength to lower herself to her hands and knees on the floor. Then, with a trembling finger, she draws the sign of the cross in the pool of blood surrounding her. *"In nomine Patris, et Filii, et Spiritus Sancti,"* she says.

The words of the Holy Trinity cause her eye's twitching to worsen, and the excruciating pain makes her complexion pale. It is as though something is tearing at the veins in the socket. Unable to handle the agony, she screams and lifts her blood-drenched hand from the cross to paw at her irritated eye. Then, like a piece of driftwood bobbing up from the bottom of the ocean, a small fragment of wood emerges from the center of her pupil.

Taking a deep breath, she secures the tiny object between her fingers, pulls it from her eye, and stares at it in horror. It is a small wooden snowflake. She desperately attempts to bring peace back into the room by repeating her prayer.

Amid her pleas, several locks of her hair mysteriously lift straight up from the top of her head. Jacob cannot divert his attention from the magic trick before his eyes. As he waits for the act's culprit to be revealed, he realizes the perpetrator is not relenting and covers his mouth to hide his fright. Then, in a single sharp movement, the locks of her hair are forcefully yanked backward, cracking her neck, and leaving her no choice but to stare up at the ceiling.

Terrified by the sound of the horrific snap, Jacob jumps back, slipping on a bloody smear. Dumbfounded and afraid, he stares in disbelief as the tube of cartilage forming her throat forcefully expands. She hacks and gasps for air as something significant blocks her airway as it passes through her trachea. Her hands flail at her sides. Then, clenching her fists, she pounds against her sternum to dislodge the object.

A third knock strikes the front door; the heaviness of the impact forces the wood to splinter. In unison, Mrs. Rigby hoists her knuckles and gives one final blow to her chest, dislodging a tiny rusty bell from her throat.

It rolls across the floor and stops in the thick sludge. As it lies in its stagnant position, the top reveals a frayed but neatly tied thin, discolored dark-green ribbon that secures a single dried holly berry.

Mrs. Rigby tumbles to the ground in shock, and her eyes close as she takes deep breaths to replenish her oxygen. Jacob remains fixated on the bloody bell. He has seen its unique kind before. It is similar in shape and size to the one held by jolly old St. Nick while distributing candy canes to the children in the town square on Christmas Eve. He associates the unique object with his happiest memory, but now, as he stares at this gruesome rendition, he questions everything.

Mrs. Rigby does not have to look; the sound is enough to reveal the item's identity and confirm her deepest fear. She pretends it is not there because, from her experience, things only worsen when their presence is acknowledged.

Though they continue to process the chain of events separately, the two are concurrently stopped in their thoughts by an abnormal squeaking from the kitchen window's glass. Jacob looks up and sees the imprint of a hand dissipating from the frosted pane. With a slight delay, Mrs. Rigby follows suit and, upon looking, catches sight of the last finger mark vanishing.

Recognizing it has captured their attention, an eerie deep voice taunts from outside. "Ho... ho... ho."

Although the phrase is familiar to Jacob, its dark, gravelly tone incites panic, and each mocking word sends chills down the child's spine. Seeking someone to protect him, he redirects his attention across the room to Mrs. Rigby.

She knows they have little time and sees the panic emanating from the boy's dilated pupils. They find a sense of grounding in one another's presence, but the shared moment is brief, cut short by brutal screams from outside the window. The acoustics created by the ice formed on the snow-frosted cobblestones amplify each horrid wail.

Even though the sound is shocking, unbeknownst to them, the home's brick walls take the edge off the cry's shrillness, protecting them from the true extent of its brutality. Something about the tone of the voice causes Mrs. Rigby's pupils to constrict. The way the syllables resonate in her ears triggers an emotional breakdown, and she loses control. Trying to fight away her darkened thoughts, she stammers to convince herself that she has made the right decision. "No, no, no. It... it said that if I did as it asked, it would not hurt us," she says.

The blood-curdling screams are so thunderous that the inside and out lights flicker in a strobe-like pattern, matching each shriek's crescendo.

Mrs. Rigby covers her ears to block out the noise and cannot help thinking the worst. Fighting off her negativity, her quivering lips force a grin to reassure the boy that everything is fine.

Even though she is hopeful Jacob is buying it, her smile does not fool him, and he finds no comfort in the effort. Instead, his courage builds, and with a deep breath, he opens his mouth to speak.

She knows they must remain quiet, and his sudden movement makes her frantic. Fighting her emotions, a single tear cascades down her cheek as she lifts a finger to her lips to warn him to be silent.

Another earsplitting blow to the front door feeds the tension in the room and causes more damage to the wooden panels. It shakes the building's structure to its foundation, prompting the electrical wires to buzz and the lights to surge faster.

Though unable to see one another through the strobing flickers, their eyes dart around the room as they hear scurrying in the walls and heavy footsteps on the roof.

The lights return to a slow, consistent pulsation, and after a few moments of silence, they build enough courage to peek out the kitchen window. The lights continue to surge from light to dark. They lean closer to the sill, gazing through the glass while they try to interpret the grim scene between flashes.

Then, without warning, red liquid sprays across the window with the volume of a severed artery, sending them both scurrying backward through the kitchen's coagulated sludge.

The voice dissipates with one final screech, leaving the gruesome splatters displayed in silence.

Mrs. Rigby recognizes that the screaming man is surely dead and loses control of her emotions. Swept up in a powerless lament, she clutches her chest as her hysterical wails break the silence. Matching her energy, Jacob whimpers as he stares at the crimson-coated window. The scene overstimulates him, and he cannot see past the horror of the bloodied glass.

Thinking the worst is over, both remain motionless as they process the brutal turn of events, but then, the sound of something colliding with the leaded glass makes them realize it has only just begun.

Mrs. Rigby does not know how much more she can take but pushes aside her feelings to remain present for the child's sake. Though reluctant, she turns her attention toward the noise. Seeing the bloody mess for a second time causes her pupils to dilate with shock as she watches something join the red paint-like splotches.

A man's mangled palms press against the glass as if pleading for help. Even though she would prefer not to witness the aftermath of human suffering, she feels responsible for the man's fate and, as a punishment to herself, refuses to look the other way, forcing her lids to remain peeled open.

The lights continue to flash, and between each blackened pause, something shifts the body's dead weight, dragging the hands in a slithering motion down the panes and leaving translucent trails through the bodily slurry. The movement creates a loud squeal that penetrates the window's glass and echoes through the kitchen.

Suddenly, Mrs. Rigby notices a glimmer on the victim's left hand and realizes it is a wedding band. Recalling the tone of the man's screams, paired with the golden flecks cast in her eye from the ring's metal, makes her sick to her stomach. She knows her worst fears have come to fruition, as the blatant clues remove any lingering denial regarding the victim's identity.

It is her husband.

As the horror continues, Jacob cannot look away from the image of the man's hands falling from the glass and disappearing into the black abyss.

Witnessing her husband dangled in front of her triggers memories of the loss of Tobias. Mrs. Rigby feels the same anguish she experienced when finding out she would never see her son again.

The idea of losing her only remaining family member causes her mental condition to deteriorate further. She plunges into a state of hysteria, succumbing to her mourning, screaming at the top of her lungs, releasing the sadness over her husband and the pent-up anguish she was forced to suppress for her Tobias.

Between the chaos of the gruesome imagery and Mrs. Rigby's cries of anguish, Jacob is overwhelmed by fear. He closes his eyes, hoping to escape, pleading to return to his bed. "Mommy, please help me! I am afraid and want to wake up," he cries as he stands trembling, waiting to be transported.

Mrs. Rigby hears him calling for her, and her eyes dart toward him. His fear-induced words are the only thing capable of pulling her back to reality. The dire nature of the situation sets in, and, realizing how loud she has been, she worries that her hysterics have drawn unwanted attention. In a reflexive act to silence herself, she thrusts her hand over her mouth and whispers affirmations to calm her mind. "You know this was not how things were supposed to be, but you must remember, you have your child back, and that is all that matters," she says.

Taking a deep breath, she temporarily contains her emotional spiral by spouting confirming words to further soothe herself. "It's okay. This must be a test. It will return Mr. Rigby safe and sound when it is over." Unbeknownst to her, the assertions are ludicrous, but they make her feel much better.

She makes eye contact, wipes her tears, and calmly motions for Jacob to follow her.

The wind outside is tumultuous. Each gust whistles as it sweeps across the cobblestone and brick mortar lines. As it makes its way down the main street, the gusting frost squeezes through the splintered cracks of the Rigby residence's front door and carries the haunting remnants of a jingle.

The unsettling tune creeps into Mrs. Rigby's ear, and its unwelcome lingering causes her heart to race. Her body trembles over the ghastly scenarios regarding the outcome of her future. "It's coming," she says.

Paranoid that her fate will be like her husband's, she stops what she is doing and dashes to check the door's condition. Upon inspection, a slight movement catches her eye through a breach in the wood. The horrific possibilities of what may lie on the other side secure her complete attention.

She tries to convince herself that the darkness is just playing tricks on her as she squints without hesitation to get a better look. Peering through the cracks filled with flickering light, she remains stock-still, intently observing. She blinks to relieve the discomfort of the cold air drying her eyes, and upon opening her lids, she is met with a pitch-black pupil staring back at her. Her fear renders her motionless, unable to break her gaze. The form alters its position, showing more detail as its sagging lip lifts to form a menacing grin that fills the fractured opening. In a state of panic, she gasps sharply and scrambles away from the door.

The creature enjoys the hunt and thrives off inciting terror. Her pronounced shift in demeanor confirms it is successful in its quest. As it stares through the fissure at its prey, its mouth froths with salivation. Changing its tactics, it seeks to manipulate to gain access. "Help... help me," it says. The tone of its voice abounds with familiarity. As each pleading word enters the room, it perfectly mirrors the voice of her dearest loved one.

Immediately, every bit of common sense about what lies in wait behind the entrance leaves Mrs. Rigby's mind, and her eyes water uncontrollably. She knows that voice; it is her husband. Her enthusiasm causes her heart to race. "He's alive," she says.

Overcome with exhilaration; she scampers toward the entrance. She desperately wants to help and struggles to prevent herself from acting impulsively. Concerned that something might hear them, she whispers. "Are... are you okay? Please tell me you are okay," she says. Her guilt fills the silence as she waits for his reply. "I fear I cannot live with myself if it harms you. Nothing bad was supposed to happen. It promised we would be left unscathed, and Tobias would be returned if we gave it what it wanted."

As she waits for his reply, a light scratching sound runs against the backside of the door, like a cat sharpening its claws. Overenthusiastic, and presumptuous of the sounds' meaning, she considers it his response. Deep in her heart, she knows her husband longs for her touch, and the thought tingles through her body. Swarming with emotion, she takes a tiptoeing step closer.

The creature takes time to craft an answer, enjoying every moment of the delay as it feeds off her guilt-ridden energy. Finally, it inhales a long, frost-filled breath, then releases a cavernous groan. Her anxiousness grows as she intensely fixates on each noise from the other side of the door.

The entity shifts its strategy, presenting the man's voice with a sense of panic while pounding on the entrance. With each loud sniffle and plea for help, it attempts to incite Mrs. Rigby's compassion. "Let me in! Please let me in. I am begging you! It's going to kill me!" it screams at the top of its lungs.

Overwhelmed by the pressure, she fights her intuition, ignoring the idiosyncrasies of the wavering vocal inflections, and attempts to quiet her husband's fear by hushing him through the wood. Even though he is not listening, she knows she has much to make up for, and helping him is the only way she feels she can clear her conscience.

While caught up in her thoughts, a quick jingling sound weaves between the splintered cracks and pierces the room's tension.

The noise sends an alarm through her, igniting a chain reaction that tenses every joint and triggers a sharp headache to pulse behind her brows. She takes a deep breath to clear her mind and reconsiders the situation with a fresh outlook.

The jingle sounds again, immediately diluting her momentary optimism. Even though she cannot physically see what is on the other side of the door, she senses the heat of hell's fire radiating through the wood. She closes her eyes and, preparing to speak, stabilizes her shaky voice to confront what is lurking outside. "Is it with you? Right now? Is it out there?" she asks. Her nerves cause her body to tremble. A gust of wind blows against the front of the home, conveniently masking the sound of something larger rustling near the entrance.

While continuing to hide in the kitchen, Jacob hears her voice shift pitch and, feeling her angst, refrains from looking.

Left with little patience, the thing becomes agitated and blurts a response without hesitation. "There is no one here but me!" it says.

The voice's demonic transition confirms to Mrs. Rigby that the thing outside is not her husband, but the beast. Afraid of drawing suspicion regarding her epiphany, she masks her fear as she shifts to survival mode. Her surroundings go silent, and a ringing pitch takes over her ears; her heart feels numb in her chest. No matter how hard she tries to focus, she cannot shake the feeling of shame about her earlier gullibility with the creature.

Knowing she must get away, she carefully takes a slight step backward, focusing on the iris that has resumed its place, peering through the crack in the door. It suddenly shifts positions, and she jumps in fright, bumping the toe of her shoe against the edge of a wobbly floorboard.

Although the board's squeak is barely noticeable, the slight noise abruptly shifts the thing's attention toward her. The creature understands it is losing control of Mrs. Rigby, making the game of torment more challenging. In the years since her son vanished, it has kept track of her, and the information gleaned has helped bolster its capacity to exploit human fear and desperation.

Imitating what it remembers of her reactions, it breathes heavily and exudes a frantic quality, grasping for any emotional tie that may reel her back. "No, I swear it left! Just let me in, please. Please hurry before it comes back," it says.

No matter how easily Mrs. Rigby fell for its lies before, nothing can fool her now. She is only fixated on one thing: returning to the kitchen to be with Jacob.

The room abruptly acclimatizes to the winter temperature outside, causing a layer of frost to dust the walls. She shivers as the icy gusts of air find their way through the door's crevices and brush her skin. The hairs on her arms stand, creating prickly points, and the skin surrounding the follicles uncomfortably tightens.

Instantly, her mind shifts to the room's frigid temperature. As she scans the space for additional breaches in the structure, her attention stops on the fireplace in the room's corner. The flames have been out awhile, leaving nothing to warm the air. Not one bit of glowing life has been spared; even the embers cease to exist in the coal bed.

Jacob is stagnant with fear in the kitchen, quietly listening for what will happen next. As the ice spreads like a plague across the surrounding walls, the numbness returns to his delicate skin, bringing back the tingling pain in his legs. His rapid exhalations leave trails of icy imprints hovering in front of him. Realizing he has no control over his fate, he shakes uncontrollably, his trembling knees matching the tempo of his jittering jaw.

Mrs. Rigby tries to focus on devising a plan of escape but finds it difficult after catching another glimpse of the eye twitching through the door's crack. The sight sends her over the edge, and something snaps, causing her to relinquish her fear and take charge of the situation. She knows they only have moments left and accepts that what she does next will determine their fates.

Mrs. Rigby gives a last look at the pupil staring back at her and, shifting course, runs in a dead sprint toward the kitchen. She gently sweeps Jacob's body into her arms to calm him, whispering comforting words into his ear. "Mommy has something she needs to take care of. I will put you somewhere safe. It would be best to pretend you are asleep. Please promise you will not make a peep." She gives him no time to respond, immediately ushering him toward the back of the kitchen.

Although the absence of steady illumination makes it nearly impossible to see, the light radiating from the oven and the surging bulbs reveals enough of the unwelcome scene. Jacob looks down to see where he is stepping and notices their path coincides with the direction of the gory trail of blackened goop spread like jam across the floor.

Thinking she hears something approaching, Mrs. Rigby skittishly checks behind them. She is paranoid that some-one is watching and pushes harder on Jacob's back, forc-ing him to walk faster. As they near their destination, she firmly grabs his arm. "You understand everything I have instructed you to do?" she asks.

Standing before the glowing oven door, Jacob gulps and, smelling something rank, holds his breath while reluctant-ly nodding. After glimpsing something inside the range from the corner of his eye, he refuses to turn away from her.

Again, Mrs. Rigby senses someone watching them and glances back at the door. Not wanting the child to grasp her paranoia, she pats Jacob's shoulder and playfully laughs to distract him. "Hopefully, the mess in the kitchen is not as bad as you expected," she says. She forces a loud cackle that resonates at such an unnaturally high frequency that the glassware on the counter swivels.

Jacob is at a loss for words.

Before Mrs. Rigby can continue, pounding resonates again from the front entrance, creating more fractures in the wood. It is followed by three distinct rhythmic jingles of a bell. The abrupt noise causes her to jump, and she grips Jacob's shoulder to stabilize herself.

Noticing him squirming underneath her fingertips, she worries he may speak and preemptively covers his mouth. "Don't you dare," she says. Knowing the situation means life or death, her tone harshens.

Jacob whimpers in anguish as she holds him in her grasp. She looks at him sternly while bending down to meet his eye level. "You must hide. That thing senses fear, so no matter what happens, you must be brave, and whatever you do, do not come out until I say it is safe to do so," she says.

Then, leaning closer, she softens her voice while taking on a graver tone. "Swear that you will not come out until I tell you to."

Jacob's gaze appears vacant as he quietly stares at her. His silence makes her eyes protrude from her skull. She wants a solid answer. "Do you promise?" she asks. He timidly nods in response.

"That's better," she says. Even though she would prefer a more convincing reply, she knows it will have to do. They are running out of time.

Mrs. Rigby places her hands on his shoulders and, taking a deep breath, turns him to face the oven while relaying her instructions. "All right, there you go. That is the best place for you to hide, my child."

Jacob does not have to look to know the space she is referencing. Planting his feet, he refuses to budge. Over the years, he has watched his mother put many things into the scorching appliance and seen them come out burned.

Mrs. Rigby takes his lack of movement as a sign of defiance. She tries to hold back her frustration but is livid and loses patience. "I thought we were past this behavior," she says. To motivate him, she slaps him on the back. Her palm striking his ribcage reverberates like a woodpecker pecking on a hollow tree trunk.

The sharp pain makes Jacob gasp, and, not wanting to face further consequences, he sees no option but to listen. With each step, he imagines the unbearable heat scorching his skin. The horrific thought lessens his willingness to take part, but he complies, knowing he cannot escape her clutch. He closes his eyes, again hoping his nightmarish slumber will end.

Mrs. Rigby's hands squeeze tighter around his tiny biceps. Convinced she must force him to comply, she becomes more aggressive as she prepares to shove him inside the oven. Standing beside the appliance's sizable open door, she glances at the wire racks to assess where to put him and is engulfed by a wave of anxiety.

The oven is stuffed to the brim. She had forgotten how full she had left it. Her heart races with panic as she realizes there may not be enough room for the child. Then, in a mad rush, she releases a single hand and frenziedly begins unloading the contents from the center shelf into a pile on the floor.

Jacob remains frozen in place, still convinced that he will soon wake up. Without warning, Mrs. Rigby gives his arm a hefty yank and hoists him inside onto the oven's wire rack, bending his limbs in various ways to make him fit.

As she contorts his body, Jacob's eyes squinch tighter. It is not until hearing the oven door slam shut that he faces the probability of being trapped inside. He attempts to take a deep breath to calm himself, but the putrid stench surrounding him makes it unbearable. Jacob cannot quite place his finger on the odor's identity. He sniffs the air, triggering an intense gag reflex. Reluctantly, his eyes open to solve the smell's mystery.

Flashes of light through the oven door window greet him with intermittent illuminations of a horrific scene. Sadly, the graphic nature of what surrounds him is even more catastrophic than the splashing waves of gore he witnessed outside the kitchen window.

Child-sized limbs stuff the surrounding space. Each appendage's jagged end shows its removal was crudely completed with a wood saw. The rotting extremities fill the wire racks above and below him and appear carefully organized by type. All are trapped in the ghastly confines of the sealed space, engulfing him in the unbearable sulfuric smell of decaying flesh.

The situation makes Jacob not know whom to trust, and he cannot help but correlate the bloody scene with the woman he had thought was trying to save him. Fearful of being next, he opens his mouth to scream for help but finds the oven to be a soundproof vessel. No matter how loud Jacob yells, no one can hear him.

Desperate to escape, he places his hands on the small glass window and, letting out a grunt pushes with all his might, but the door does not budge.

He is met with the grim reality that he may never get away.

Jacob presses his face against the glass to view the kitchen. The window leaves charcoal smudges on his nose, and he realizes that residue from the oven's heavy use is tainting the glass. Using his hand, he wipes the soot away, and something in the kitchen catches his eye. Immediately, his attention shifts to where Mrs. Rigby had unloaded the oven's contents.

In the space lies a mound of children's heads, their eyes fixated on the oven as if searching for their missing parts. The Tetris-like placement creates the appearance of firewood strategically piled up for a bonfire. Decapitation has drained every bit of their blood, causing their lips and eye sockets to turn a purplish blue. A fly buzzes around the pile and lands on one of their helpless pupils, burrowing inside the small tear duct to make a home.

Although he does not want to acknowledge his terror, his heart refuses to comply, beating aggressively against his chest wall as he reluctantly scans the array of faces.

To his utmost shock, he recognizes them all.

He has found his friends.

The emotional turmoil boiling inside causes him to tremble uncontrollably. Hopeful that his eyes are playing tricks on him, he shifts his gaze back and forth from the parts surrounding him to the innocent faces outside, but no matter how hard he tries, he cannot deny the scene. His mouth opens again to scream, but this time, it is for help. "Help! Please help me! I want out!"

One by one, the severed heads' mouths gape open and hum a Christmas carol at a pitch only suitable for a child's ears.

Even though the insulation should make the melody inaudible, Jacob can perfectly hear the haunting tune. In his peripheral vision, he notices the severed limbs beside him pulsating with the song's tempo. Petrified of what may come next, he stops yelling and no longer wants to be freed.

Meanwhile, paying no attention to Jacob's pleas, Mrs. Rigby continues to pace back and forth across the room, babbling about a plan of action to save herself. "Everything will be okay. You only need to do as he asks. He will keep his word, sparing your life, as promised," she says.

Then, mid-murmur, she sees the boy's face peering through the oven's window. Incensed over the possibility that he may ruin everything, she lowers herself to make eye contact and gives him a stern glare. "Shhh! Quiet! I am not risking my life for a little brat!"

All he can hear is a muffled version of her lecture. Having to base the context of what she is saying solely on her crazed facial expressions and wild arm movements, he concludes she is threatening to cook him alive. Not ready to die, he cries while scanning the severed limbs surrounding him. He braces for the worst, anticipating the excruciating pain he will encounter while meeting his friend's fate, but after waiting a few minutes, he notices no blisters or burns marking his body.

He exhales a tentative sigh of relief.

Mrs. Rigby believes she hears something rustling in the other room and, thinking only of her survival, a switch flips off inside her, draining every ounce of empathy from her eyes. She stops pacing while continuing her stern lecturing of Jacob. "You had better stay in there and hide. Because if the Devil finds you, he will devour your insides," she says.

As she takes one last lap around the kitchen, the creature strikes the front door a fifth time. The violent impact causes every one of the vintage appliances to shake. Frightened by the sudden vibration, Jacob curls up into a fetal position and clutches onto the metal rack to stabilize himself. He hides within the body parts and re-adjusts his position to get a better view of the outside world through his oven door portal. Through the soot-smudged glass, he follows Mrs. Rigby's every move.

Treating the knock as a warning, she picks up her haste and gathers an armload of the children's heads from the floor like a game of pickup sticks. With a smile, she places them on the counter, carefully arranging them in a pentagram on its tile surface. After finishing the final touches, she swivels each head so their eyes face the open doorway connecting the kitchen and living room, then bolts to the fridge.

She flings the door open and retrieves several dishes containing a variety of miniature pastries. With great care, she meticulously assembles the macabre confections on holiday plates equally spaced around the counter. Every piece has its unique decorative touch. Tiny fingers with blue-tinged nails stick out from the pressed dough, each surrounded by blood, spelling the word 'Jingles.'

Mrs. Rigby admires their artisanship as she eyeballs them in their decorative formation on the counter. "Beautiful," she says. No matter the circumstances, she takes pride in her creations.

This is what she was made to do: entertain.

Smelling the air, she releases a sigh of accomplishment.

A sixth and final knock sounds on the front door. The impact completely severs the thick wooden panel from the frame this time.

The kitchen's perfection makes Mrs. Rigby complacent about the knock's urgency. She is overwhelmed by her happiness and expresses it with impulsive giggles. Then, realizing her emotions are getting the best of her, she regains her composure, straightens her posture, and adjusts her apron.

As she waits, the last pieces of splintered timber crash to the floor, initiating the next round of chaos.

Chapter Five

JINGLES

A broken man crawls through the front door on his hands and knees, his movements slow and labored. He is followed by an icy wind that masks his raspy breaths and the thud of his heavy boots striking the floorboards as he inches forward. As he descends into the living room, his body leaves a trail of wet, muddy snow and intestinal matter.

Blind to what is occurring on the other side of the kitchen wall, Mrs. Rigby maintains her brave face, and the only hint of her angst is a slight quiver of her lips. She keeps her eyes locked on the open door across the room as she listens for anything recognizable.

A mangled hand plunges through the center of the doorframe as if part of a demented puppet show. Having not heard a single sound preceding its entry, the movement startles her, and her heart races as she scans the details of each digit. She gasps upon seeing that a wedding ring identical to her husband's resides on its finger. Believing he is already gone, the possibility that it is the ghost of her deceased partner drains the color from her face. She gets caught up in her thoughts, questioning her earlier choice to abandon the person outside. "Is that you?" she asks.

The arm advances into the room, exposing its forearm, while each finger twitches with a spasmodic motion. Then, suddenly, an accompanying voice speaks. "You abandoned me," it says.

The accusation provokes guilt over her earlier decisions. Her eyes dart around the room as she scrambles for an apology. "You must understand—I didn't know what to do. You were not acting like yourself," she says.

Abruptly, the arm's wrist goes limp, causing the hand to flop downward as if in sadness. "You deserted me. I would never have done that to you," it says.

Trying to make up for what has happened, Mrs. Rigby stammers to find the right words. "You are here now. That is all that matters. So, let us just put it behind us," she says.

Rather than consoling her, wicked laughter echoes from the other room. The abrasive tone causes Mrs. Rigby to flinch, and, shunning away, she notices something on the floor: the bell she coughed up earlier. She stands in silence as tears descend her cheeks. "Why are you doing this to me? I have done everything you have asked," she says.

With a loud grunt, the corpse to which the mangled limb belongs rises to its feet and staggers through the doorframe. Its knees buckle, and as the body lands hard on the tile, it bumps into the tin bell, causing it to roll in her direction. Mrs. Rigby avoids looking at the object as it inches toward her.

Despite the body being mutilated and appearing dead, it still convulses. The sight of the battered figure causes her face to flush. She surveys the remaining identifiable features, and there is no longer any uncertainty; it is her husband.

Her lip quivers at the thought of wanting to take his pain away, but she contains her emotion, fearing the creature smelling her weakness. Then, taking a long sniffle to stop her tears, she clenches her jaw, ready to confront the thing tormenting her. She glances beyond Mr. Rigby toward the entrance, where the limb still dangles in the middle of the door frame.

Its fingers wiggle playfully as the lone extremity moves further inside, revealing a serrated end where the shoulder should be. Mrs. Rigby shrieks, realizing that the beast's long, lanky arm extends from the severed appendage as if wearing the man's flesh like a sock puppet.

With no warning, the arm retracts, leaving the kitchen in silence.

As the creature lingers outside the door, it takes pleasure in its ingenuity while stripping the limb remnants from its own, revealing a decayed, leathery hand.

The glove of human flesh dangles from the creature's fingertips, blackened claws still entwined with the putrid tissue. Each jagged nail is curled up to form tiny hooks that pierce through the finger's tendons. No longer needing to control the body part's movement, the creature does not bother taking the time to unhook its talons. Instead, in a jerking motion, it flings the flesh from its hand, tearing it away and leaving only a few scraps of meat on its nails.

Trapped and terrified, Mrs. Rigby's confident posture wanes. She clenches the muscles in her abdomen to regain her calm.

Jacob, restricted to the view through his small window, cannot see above her trembling legs or what is occurring on the other side of the kitchen's center island. With his limited line of sight, he is forced to fixate on the strange movements of her lower limbs and the watery substance trickling from her knees onto the floor. Before he can process what the liquid may be, the sight of a small circular object slowly moving toward her gets his attention. He squints for a better view and gasps in horror upon recognizing the object as the bell. Remembering he was told not to make a sound, he remains silent as it finishes its roll and stops at her feet.

Mrs. Rigby watches the remnants of her husband's hand instantaneously snatched from sight. Left with no visual sign of the creature's next move, she silently listens, and her imagination helplessly goes down a dark spiral, knowing the beast guards the only exit.

After a brief silence, an abnormal growl echoes into the kitchen, followed by loud crunching resembling the sound of pliers crushing bones. She recoils in horror as she envisions the creature feasting on the severed limb. The beast snarls again, followed by the slurping sounds of sucking each of its fingers clean. Her hands anxiously wring the fabric edges of her apron.

Mrs. Rigby continues her surveillance of the doorway and catches a slight stirring at the bottom of the wooden frame. Refraining from sudden movements, her gaze fixates on the fetid toes protruding from the worn ends of thick black leather boots as they extend into the room.

As the rancid digits touch the tile, a large, bony kneecap protruding from underneath a pair of stained velvet burgundy trousers also appears. Her eyes slog their way up the limb, and oddly, she is not afraid as she stands motionless, staring in awe.

Although she has heard its voice many times before, she has never glimpsed its physical appearance. Unbeknownst to her, it has been a complete mystery to all since anyone who has laid eyes on it has vanished without a trace.

The opportunity has a certain enchanting quality that makes her feel special. For the first time in her life, she believes she is the chosen one.

Taking its sweet time, it bridges its spine backward to prolong its entrance and, with face-up flattened palms, extends its boney arms beneath the archway. Each joint, from its elbows to its fingertips, is hyper-extended, giving the appendages a very unnatural appearance.

A single bell rests on top of one of its skeletal palms. Mrs. Rigby's eyes fixate on the metal's shine through the flickering strobes of light. She finds something about its luster mesmerizing.

With an abrupt flick of its wrist, the creature tosses the circular object into the air and catches it between its long, spindly fingers.

She notices that this bell differs from the rest; its sound is more vibrant.

The creature carefully pinches the object between its thumb and forefinger and, holding it in front of itself, stands in the doorway like a statue. Then, with sinister intent, it quietly watches Mrs. Rigby with its beady black irises. As it waits for her next move, it tilts its head to study her reactions.

Even though the tiny bell is across the room, she can see her reflection on its shiny surface, causing her eyes to widen with wonder. The exterior reflects her desires for what she has imagined her life should be, and she finds a glimmer of hope for her happiness in the snowflake carvings forged into the metal.

It is as if it was made solely for her as a gift, and something about its hypnotic presence takes her sadness away.

The creature continues to move slowly and deliberately into the room. As the rest of its torso enters, it reveals a worn leather belt slung around its waist. The long piece of stained leather has been modified to carry a variety of special tools, each secured with hooks made from children's canine teeth and locks of woven hair.

Attached to the right side is a collection of chains with iron shackles and custom-made scissors with burlap-covered handles. Everything about the abnormally long design of the shears' blades is unique, each crafted from repurposed twelve-inch filet knives. The sharpened tips are rusted from years of hard use, and their oxidized shade masks the bloodstains on their surface.

A square satchel made from pieces of human skin dangles off a tooth on the opposite hip. Each patch comprising the object varies in size and color; all are sutured together with a fishing line. Packed inside the peculiar pouch are unique bells. Hanging from the adjacent hook is a whip made of birch sticks braided together. Since the branches are still green, they are pliable, making them better for whipping and allowing them to form a bullwhip-style coil.

Mrs. Rigby's eyes continue to follow the bell, still captivated by its intricacies. She is surprised to discover that it holds her happiest moments with her young son before he was taken away, and the more she stares at the item, the more memories she has sadly forgotten return. As her concentration deepens, each recollection becomes more vivid.

Amused by her self-serving curiosity, the creature craves a better view. The backs of its kneecaps snap to an inverted position, creating a bend that allows it to step through the doorway and complete its descent into the kitchen despite its massive height.

No matter what is happening around her, Mrs. Rigby refuses to be interrupted. She is captivated by the emotional gratification that the object brings and utterly unaware of the dire consequences she will bear for her choice to relinquish reality.

When the day of reckoning arrives, her eyes will turn milky white, and she will fall blind because of her unwillingness to face her self-created existence.

Jacob is restricted to forming judgments based on the information he can collect from his limited view through the tiny window. The muffled sounds are useless, leaving him to rely solely on body cues for understanding. He is relieved to see Mrs. Rigby's trembling subside and, believing it must be a good sign, releases a small sigh of relief.

The creature is energized by its ability to manipulate the woman, reveling in the feeling of power it gets from understanding her predictable behavior. To it, the world is nothing more than an enticing experiment using humankind like lab rats.

The beast keeps its gaze angled toward the floor, savoring the moment of fully unveiling its identity. Its towering stature quickly becomes apparent as its spine straightens, the vertebrae emitting loud cracks as they slide into place. The creature's appearance is no longer a mystery.

Its shirt, which is long and draped, is created from the same burgundy velvet material as the pants. Curly tufts of children's hair, varying in color, line the cuffs and collar, mimicking pillowy clouds. The shirt's loose neckline allows ample room for its neck, which is slightly askew from its head.

Not a single feature on its face fits together proportionally, but each has a similar characteristic: the fleshy coverings are raw and chaffed. Burn scars mar its skin with signs of hell's flames and provide a dark history of how it attained its blackened heart.

Only slight indents, each sealed with the same thin skin that protects an eardrum, sit where his nose and ears would be. Unlike other creatures, every facial indentation is a permeable intake for its senses, allowing it an extraordinary cognizance of its surroundings.

Just under the nose-like concavity, in place of a philtrum, thick, hardened skin protrudes, and below that are a pair of thin, dark, tarry lips. The jutting formation lifts the upper lip from its bone, making the creature unable to close its mouth fully, displaying its blanched gum line. Discolored, needlelike teeth break the mouth's pallid skin in jagged rows.

Two large sanpaku eyes, positioned midway up its skull, fill the upper half of its face. Crusty mounds line the top and bottom edges of the concave orbs where the eyelids used to be. Loathing sleep, it tore them away long ago, and scabs are all that remain. Each pitch-black pupil has a dash of red dead in the center. The odd structure resembles a fertilized egg cooked sunny-side-up. No matter the lighting, the pupils do not dilate, appearing soulless and devoid of empathy.

It wears the scalps of others sewn to its head and jawline to replicate the beard and hairline it cannot grow because of its deep scarring. The color and texture are of no matter to it, leaving it with a patchwork quilt of shades from white to black. To provide extra security to hold the scalps in place, a moth-bitten, floppy pointed hat, made with fabric matching the rest of the outfit, sits snugly on top of its head. A ball of matted curly child's hair, tied to the pointed tip, dangles over the deep indentation underneath one of the creature's high cheekbones. It has securely stitched the cap through the brim into its skin's scar tissue, making it permanent.

Though she had previously looked forward to seeing the creature's face, Mrs. Rigby was not interested in the revelation. Instead, she remains fixated on the memories displayed on the bell's surface. Her smile stretches from ear to ear while consumed by the reminiscence of sledding with her son. "Such a good boy," she says.

The words spark the creature's attention, and it watches her reaction with a twisted grin as it playfully shakes the object between its spindly fingers, testing her response. Fearful that her joy may vanish, her eyes wildly track the bell like a cat after a ball of yarn.

In one swift movement, it extends its hand, holding the bell toward Mr. Rigby's maimed body, desperately clinging to life. The ends of its thin lips drift further up its cheeks, touching the bottoms of each eye, as its slithering tongue salivates to prepare for presenting a conundrum.

"What will you choose, oh faithful wife, your desire for happiness or his life?" it asks. The anticipation of her response thrills the creature and provokes a cackle that quakes the room. "Hmm? What will it be, the bell or he?" Then, abruptly pausing, it stares at her, waiting for an answer.

Mrs. Rigby acts as if nothing else exists; she has yet to take her eyes off the bell tightly clutched between its fingertips. Quickly giving one last attempt to grab her attention, it points its boney digit in her direction and continues. "Now, you must remember, only you can decide what fills you with glee deep inside."

Her lips drool, and her eyes glaze over as she stares intensely at the reflection cast by the metal. While basking in the silence of her obsession, the thing creeps closer to her husband's body.

It extends one of its legs and taps the man's ribcage with the tip of its foot. With no answer, it uses its grubby boot to give the body a solid kick. The force causes Mr. Rigby to roll onto his back, and the creature rejoices in extracting the anguish from the excruciating expression in his eyes.

Once finished, it shifts its attention back to Mrs. Rigby and patiently waits for her answer while maintaining its devilish smile. "Well? Which is it, wife? Your happiness or his life?" it asks.

Subconsciously, Mrs. Rigby has decided, causing her vision to blur and delirium to take hold of her mind.

The smell of her selfishness causes a bead of saliva to drip from the creature's mouth. It tumbles from its lips, and the acidic droplet lands on Mr. Rigby's neck. Like a parasite feasting off a host, the venomous substance consumes his skin and eats away at his flesh. Even though the pain is excruciating, his immense blood loss has taken away his motor functions, trapping him in torment. The fluid gurgling in his lungs provides the only expression of his agony.

As the creature awaits her reply, it delightfully watches the whites of her eyes engulf her irises, and without a word spoken, it can gather the answer it seeks.

It rapidly becomes tired of her boring ways and, losing its enthusiasm for the game, flicks the bell from its fingers, causing the small sphere to fly across the room. Upon hitting the ground, it creates an unmistakable jangling sound as it rolls across the floor.

Mrs. Rigby is left in complete darkness as it leaves her peripherals. The presence of the bell is not merely a portal to her memories with her son; it has become the only beacon for her vision, and she is blind without it. Consumed by thoughts of being imprisoned alone in an endless abyss, she turns her animalistic. Trapped in her hysteria, froth spews from her mouth as she scrambles to her knees and sightlessly searches through the puddles of blood in search of the bell.

A sinking feeling overcomes Jacob as he witnesses her erratic behavior. He shimmies himself further back onto the shelf to hide, watching with horror as her apron becomes soaked in the blood of his friends.

Paying no attention to her rummaging, the creature smells something in the air, and its head snaps toward the scent of blood gurgling from Mr. Rigby's mouth. "Well, isn't that a shame? Oh, what a wicked game. She cares more about her memories before your small boy was slain than rekindling the love of your smoldering flame. Leading up to the day when her cold-heartedness came, she believed herself an excellent mother, but for his fate, she was solely to blame. I watched from a tree where I hid away as her son ran to escape from becoming her prey, but alas, he was too small to keep her at bay, and she left him dead in the snow where he once loved to play. He was too weak to escape his horrible fate, and now, it is time for hell to welcome dear Mrs. Rigby through its fiery gate," it says, each word rolling freely off its tongue.

With its eyes locked on Mr. Rigby, its spindly fingers retrieve the long-bladed scissors from its belt, and then, grabbing a fist full of his hair, it steadies his skull. Needing him alive, it carefully thrusts the man's head into the tiled floor, cracking it just enough to suit its purpose. Then, the creature carefully digs a single blade of its scissors underneath the skin at his hairline and scalps him. Grabbing his naked cranium with his hooked claws, it twists off the upper portion of his skull, exposing his brain.

Swiftly returning the scissors to their hook, it reaches into the satchel to grab a bell. Holding it to its ear, it listens for the ring and snickers. "No emptier than a heart without a beat, I will soon provide you a quite special treat," it says while unhinging the upper half of the metal and opening it like a locket.

Mirroring a game of operation, it uses its long nails to perform a surgical procedure and, with great precision, plucks out the man's amygdala. Then, like choosing a prime piece of meat, it ponders its selection, and with a quick flick of its bony wrist; it filets off a slice of the asset holding the emotions surrounding Mr. Rigby's reminiscences, the hippocampus. The severance releases an aroma of fear as it escapes the bloody matter, causing a bead of saliva to drip from the creature's bottom lip. It masks its hunger with a devious grin while carefully tucking the two pieces of brain matter into the bell for safekeeping.

"Joy to the world," it sings while admiring its new treasure. It catches a slight twitch in Mr. Rigby's comatose gaze.

Without breaking its stare, the creature hurriedly places the bell back in its pouch and ties it shut. It sniffs the air and finds the scent of the man's vulnerable state alluring. The sweet stench overcomes him with urgency.

Mr. Rigby lies silent in his last moments, yet his exposed brain still pulsates, causing the creature to lose control. Focused on tasting his warm blood before the man perishes, it snarls as its stomach grumbles. "Ho, ho, ho, what a feast this shall be for my dear friends and me," it says.

Then, it untucks its shirt and lifts the stained velvet while looking down at its belly. A face crudely carved into its thick blue skin looks back.

The creature lowers itself to the floor, causing the sculpted figure's enormous mouth to open. The flickering light bounces off its long serpent tongue as it coils around Mr. Rigby's leg like a frog catching a fly, pulling him closer. Its belly gapes open like an anaconda's jaws, then chomp after chomp devours him whole. In his brain-dead state, Mr. Rigby has no hope of survival and succumbs to slowly being eaten alive.

Muffled hissing noises sound from the creature's wrists. It pushes back its sleeves, exposing two small faces protruding from mounds of scar tissue. Two more peer out from below its pant cuffs, one on each of its twisted ankles. The carved formations resemble smaller versions of the one on its stomach.

Blood drips from their lips as they hiss in unison and bare rows of chattering, stained teeth. "Hungry..." they say.

With Mr. Rigby's body already partially devoured by its carnivorous stomach, the creature chuckles. "Hush, my greedy little ones. Don't you see? There is plenty to go around for both you and me," it says. Every word it articulates causes it to spit.

The tiny beings extend their tongues and frenziedly lick each droplet of the creature's spittle that falls within their reach. Their heckling turns angry, and their expressions scornful. "Where? Yes! Where? Take us there so we can have our share," they say.

Each snarling face turns upside down, creating morbidly dramatic frowns. "If you are lying, you had best prepare to face the consequences of our cynical glare."

Annoyed by their complaints, the creature hisses to silence them. "Your reward depends on your patience, my friends," it says.

A sizzling effervescence echoes through the kitchen, and immediately Jingles projects a devilish laugh and shifts its attention to its belly. While digesting the corpse's flesh and bones, its acidic stomach fluid froths like a boiling volcano.

The beast's internal organs shift to make room for the last of the meal, causing a tickling sensation to plague its gut and jitters to run down its spine. The prickly feeling makes the creature release a raspy snigger.

Upon consuming its last bite, the abdominal face seals over with scars, concealing its presence until it is beckoned for its next feast.

The creature spots some forgotten remains of Mr. Rigby on the floor—the portion of his skull removed in its quest for brain matter. In a swooping motion, it scoops up the chunk and, tightly clutching it in its fingers, drops to the ground and takes a seat on its tailbone.

Still hungry and waiting for their turn to indulge, the mouths on its wrists gnash their teeth at the flesh and bone hanging from the beast's spindly fingers.

While keeping the chunk out of their reach, the creature uses the slippery floor to spin itself to face the opposite direction. Then, spotting Mrs. Rigby, it chucks the last bite into its mouth and antagonistically chews slow and loud, inciting the tiny enclave of parasitic faces to jeer in unison.

Reveling in the energy captured from its recent victim, it tunes out the faces' humbug attitudes by belting a Christmas carol. "Here Comes Santa Claus," it sings. Each munch of bone creates an unsettling echo in the kitchen that startles Mrs. Rigby and causes her body to stiffen.

Oblivious to her surroundings, she moves forward on all fours, searching for the missing bell, steadily getting nearer to the creature without realizing it. "Come out, come out, wherever you are," she says. She listens for a response and, hearing nothing, frantically picks up her pace.

Entertained, the creature watches her quest as it chomps on the last bit of bone. Then, with a full mouth, it speaks, projecting bits of hair and tiny bone fragments in her direction. Her palm lands on top of the slimy particles, but on a mission, she casually flicks them off.

The creature chuckles at her naivety and, not wasting any time, pulls up each pant leg and sleeve to expose its companions. "See, you should be thankful I made you wait. That one is more alive than the last, leaving its flesh in a far fresher state," it says to them. Knowing what is imminent, they drool, ravenously fixating on her clouded eyes.

Jacob remains quietly hidden in the back of the oven, shielded behind the pieces of children. His mind replays the last glimpse he had gotten of Mrs. Rigby, looking crazed and crawling like an animal on the floor.

As the creature leisurely stretches its limbs to stand, Jacob briefly glimpses the movement and assumes it is Mrs. Rigby. Desperate to find out if she is back to normal, he scoots forward on the shelf and squints to get a better view. But, as he takes in the details of what is standing near the center island, he soon realizes it is not her and panics. The monster's presence fills him with terror, yet he is strangely drawn to it, unable to look away.

Unaware of the small observer, the beast continues watching over its prey. The tiny parasites smile and fall silent as they get a glimpse of their meal. As they prepare to feed, beads of pus salivate from their mouths.

Then, with a wiggle of each leg, the creature gracefully arches each foot to stand on its toes and, slinking toward Mrs. Rigby, tiptoes through the pools of blood.

Jacob fixates on the monster's backside as it approaches the kitchen door. Under the assumption that it must be leaving, he relaxes. His immediate assumptions regarding the creature strangely fill him with guilt. Having been taught never to judge a book by its cover, he tries to find something positive about the beast, and his attention shifts to looking at the hat on its head. Even though it is different facially, something about the creature's outfit reminds him of Santa Claus. The similarity causes his favorite song of Christmas to pop into his head—" Jingle Bells."

As the figure leaves his limited view, thoughts of the holidays put a smile on his face. Simultaneously, as the child naively basks in optimism within the safety of the kitchen appliance, Mrs. Rigby feels something on the floor in front of her. Overcome with joy, she seizes the item, desperate to return to her son.

The creature wiggles its toes beneath her grasp, momentarily breaking her concentration.

But Mrs. Rigby's pause is short-lived before her infatuation reignites, and she resumes her fervent search. "My son. Where is my son?" she asks.

The creature remains quiet while studying her movements.

There is only one thing she desires. It is the immediate return to cherished memories with her son. Overwhelmed with desperation to see the visions, she manically claws at her eyes until bloody tears run down her cheeks.

The beast watches and smiles from ear to ear as it takes joy in her festering dismay.

A waft of air carries her emotional anguish through its porous skin, absorbing into its rancid organs like a sponge. Its posture straightens. Then, with a whirl of its wrist, it clenches its hand into a fist and blows a frigid breath between its bony knuckles. The frosted exhale forms tiny snowflakes upon exiting the fists' other side. They gracefully swirl before tumbling to the floor. It whispers a raspy melody while swaying its hand to a silent beat. "Jingles, Jingles, Jingles. Jingles is my name. I will give you this gift today for the soul I wish to slay," it says.

Focused solely on her desires, Mrs. Rigby curls forward into a ball and rocks back and forth as her teardrops turn to a wail. "Woe is me," she cries.

After watching her tantrum, Jingles slowly opens its fingers at a pace reminiscent of a sprouting rosebud. The very bell Mrs. Rigby has been tirelessly searching for rests on the palm of its hand. It positions the tiny object between its fingers and gradually crouches on the floor to get her attention.

Each parasite adorning its body exudes a massive smile while trying to contain its excitement.

The creature extends the bell toward Mrs. Rigby and gives it a shake. With one last sniffle, she removes her hands from her face. The idea of the object being just before her nose brings excitement. However, wary that its sudden appearance comes with a catch, she shifts her attention to see who is holding it and is greeted by the rosy cheeks of her long-lost son.

Everything inside her wants to touch his flushed skin, but she stops, anxious it is too good to be true. As she fights her urge, she fixates on the prior experiences the bell provided. The memories had typically played like movies. She cannot remember one instance of being fully immersed in the memory. Overridden with caution, she knows she must make a move, so testing the waters, she whispers. "Tobias... is that you?"

The small boy remains frozen in the same position, patiently presenting the bell in the palm of his hand. Finally, after several moments of silence, he gives her a mischievous grin and nods.

Her maternal instincts kick in. She knows it is her son; nothing can convince her otherwise. Overwhelmed with joy, she ignores her desire to ask questions and scans him to ensure he is okay. She finds the room's stillness unsettling and can no longer contain herself as her anxiety grows. "I knew you would come back. You were always such a good little boy," she says rapidly.

His recognizable outfit further affirms his identity, causing her eyes to widen with excitement. It is the same outfit he wore the day he went missing: a down-filled navy blue snowsuit and brown boots.

Still, in disbelief over the miracle, she fumbles for something in her apron pocket. Her fingertips dig into the bottom of the fabric, and the feeling of a piece of crumpled paper makes her smile. It is a sepia-colored photograph that depicts Tobias standing outside in the snow. Grabbing its worn corner, she pulls out the image and extends it in front of her, her fingers trembling. Even though the print is water-damaged from long bouts of crying, it still provides clarity that the small boy is a match.

Her lips quiver into a smile. "Perfect. You are just as perfect as I remember," she says. Yet, even with this confirmation, she still finds herself in utter disbelief, and, leaving her eyes locked on the child, she carefully places the picture back in her apron pocket.

He extends his hand closer, offering her the bell. His grin is eerily unwavering, and something about its statuesque positioning triggers an odd feeling in her gut. A rush of emotions overtakes her, and, thinking the worst, she fears she is hallucinating.

She shakes her head to rid her mind of illusions, then scans the room from left to right. Everything looks different; every inch of the floor is covered in snow.

Taking a moment to compose herself, she closes her eyes and, upon opening them, is met by rays of light shining through the trees. She is near the forest's edge, and the kitchen no longer surrounds her.

A child's laughter carries through in a burst of a stiff wind. The sound is jarring. Its tone reminds her of Tobias, and she glances around to see if he is nearby.

He makes eye contact with her as he stands the same distance away as before, his skin red from the cold, extending his hand and offering the bell. As they continue staring at each other, his grin turns to a coy smirk. Setting aside her concern, she gives a soft smile in return.

His hand fidgets to draw her attention to the shiny object. "Mommy, I found this for you," he says. Allured by the light reflecting from the metal, her gaze breaks from him to look. Tobias wiggles his hand again to entice her to take it. "Don't you want to be together?" he says.

Worried that he does not comprehend how much she has missed him, she widens her smile to mask her concern while reassuring him, "Of course I do. What would make you think that?"

The child jostles the bell again and shrugs. "You didn't try hard to find me," he says.

His words devastate her, and she becomes defensive. "Who told you that?" she asks. He squirms as he refrains from answering.

Her face turns red. "Tobias, answer me," she says.

The child's smile vanishes, replaced by an abrupt stream of tears. "Don't you like my gift?" he says.

Realizing her harsh tone may have frightened him, Mrs. Rigby sighs and refocuses on the item in his hand. "Yes, of course," she says. Then, with a smile, she takes a step forward and stops. "Now, once I take this beautiful gift from you, what do you say we talk about where you found it?"

With a single loud sniff, Tobias stops crying and grins. He knows he has her right where he wants her. His eyes intently watch her hands as they reach for the bell, and the nearer her fingers get to the metal, the wider his stare becomes.

She has many questions and knows she must take part to receive the answers, so she grabs the bell from him. In that instant, he disappears.

A child's laughter resonates from the woods. " Tobias? We are finished playing games," she says. After a roll of her eyes to show her annoyance, she charges toward the forest.

Mrs. Rigby screams in anguish as a searing pain engulfs her head. Amid her torment, her confusion escalates as her words slur and her vision fades.

Tobias peers out from behind a nearby tree and mockingly chants, "It's going to get you. It's going to get you. It's going to get you."

Mrs. Rigby barely has time to identify his fuzzy outline in the distance before her knees give way. She falls to the ground, but instead of landing on a bed of snow, the unforgiving tile of the kitchen floor greets her.

As she slips in and out of consciousness, she tries to move but cannot. Her gaze remains fixed, forcing her to stare at the monster hovering over her.

After removing the two small pieces of her brain, it places them inside a metal bell. "I would have given you a bit more time to play, but I can no longer keep my friends' hunger at bay," it says. The parasitic limb dwellers hiss.

While hushing them, it seals the bell's lid shut. The creature lifts the object to its face and absorbs the scent, but something smells different. "What is this, I see? Are you concealing something from me?" it asks as a string of saliva drips from its lips. Wanting to move the memories forward in time, it shakes the bell's contents, then watches her moments with Jacob. "Tsk, tsk, tsk, Ada, what do we have here? It appears you have hidden a child very near."

Placing the stuffed bell back in the satchel hanging from its waist, it grins as it contorts its body around Mrs. Rigby to allow the parasites to feed. They snarl like crocodiles as they pick away at her flesh and bone. As they ravenously eat, blood soaks the creature's velvet attire.

Intrigued by the child's whereabouts, it becomes impatient that they are taking so long. "Jacob... Jacob?" it whispers.

Still huddling in the oven, the small boy hears something, and rather than the usual muffled words, the sound of his name is clear as day. Tightening his arms around his knees, he tries to curl up into a smaller ball to hide.

Having retained the child's scent from Mrs. Rigby's memories, Jingles lifts its head, sniffs through the room's aromas, and smells his lingering fear. As another trickle of acidic saliva drips from its mouth, it looks down at the tiny faces still feasting away. Unbothered by its distraction, they continue to eat voraciously.

Not wanting to disrupt them from their banquet, the creature tightens its hold around Mrs. Rigby's marred body and, remaining seated, scoots backward toward the oven. "Dear child, come out from where you hide; it is your only chance to survive. Cross my heart and hope to die; I will try my best not to eat you alive," it says.

Jacob uses his hands to cover his ears and block out the noise. The closer the monster gets, the colder the air inside the oven becomes, causing the boy's skin to adhere to the metal rack.

Continuing to slide across the ground, the creature drags Mrs. Rigby's body, leaving an extensive trail of gore behind. Jacob tightens his eyelids and shakes, refusing to look at how near the creature is.

Jingles stops shy of the oven door and stares at Mrs. Rigby's dead weight on its lap. Tired of dealing with her and wanting to eliminate the extra baggage, it hunches forward and unhinges its jaw to aid in her immediate consumption. It stuffs the entirety of her skull into its mouth and, crunching through her bone, swallows her bite by bite.

The snapping sounds resonate through the oven door. Jacob winces. He reacts without thinking by opening his eyes to see what is causing the noise and comes face-to-face with the demonic beast.

Mrs. Rigby's blood drips from its face, covering its chest. Already having swallowed her head, the beast uses its teeth to sever each vertebra in her neck. Then, feeling the eyes of the child watching, it turns its focus away from the woman. With a smile, it continues chewing her flesh while making direct eye contact with the little boy.

Jacob screams. The beast leaves its mouth gaped open as it blissfully inhales his fear.

Panicked, Jacob tries to scoot further back into the oven. He frantically wiggles his body to free himself from the oven rack, tearing bits of frozen skin from his legs.

After pushing off the mutilated corpse, the creature crawls closer to the child's hiding place. "Are you naughty or nice? Do not make me ask twice," it asks tauntingly.

The demonic faces chime in. "Naughty, nice, naughty, nice," they say.

Caught up by the temptation of the hunt and overcome with excitement, the creature's tongue extends and licks the oven's glass door. Unsatisfied with the taste, it wants to get closer and presses its face against the window to see inside, leaving a fiendish smiley face smudge. "Ho Hum, which will it be? Is he a good little boy? Or a bad one like me?" it asks.

With little patience remaining, it notices something in the glass's reflection. The bell Mrs. Rigby had coughed up earlier is lying on the floor near the kitchen's butcher block. Jingles licks its teeth, stretches out its arm, grabs it, and gives it a few quick shakes. With each flick of its bony wrist it says jingle at a tempo reminiscent of the child's favorite Christmas song.

Jacob attempts to ignore the creature's tactics, but watching it is captivating. Fighting through his legs' pain, he whimpers along with the melody, curling up tighter in a ball to keep his bare skin from contacting the rack.

The creature presses its head against the glass to analyze the child's response, smudging its facial imprint. Then, happy to get a reaction, it sings, "Jingle bells, jingle bells, jingle all the way!" Cackling, it conducts the song with flicks of its wrist.

Jacob cannot close his frozen lids, leaving his eyes peeled open in terror. As the creature hums, the temperature drops, causing the child's heartbeats to slow and every organ in his body to shut down. He gasps for air, and his mouth fills with ice from the condensation of his breath. Jacob's pupils shift from the right to the left, following the music, and his mind falls into a hypnotized state.

Jingles, obsessed with feeding off the child's adrenaline, listens closely for his heartbeat, and the sound of it slowing makes it seethe with anger. It is not enough to satisfy his insatiable hunger for fear. Frustrated that the thrill of the hunt is nearing its end, it attempts to reignite the boy by tapping the bell against the oven window's glass to get his attention. Jacob's fingertip gives a single tap back in reply.

Having a revived audience causes the creature's grin to stretch until the outer tips of its blood-stained lips reach the corners of its eyes.

"Hello, Jacob. My name is Jingles. Yes, Jingles is my name. I am here to reveal a wonderful game. You are quite special, and to my dismay, unlike the others, your bell is empty on this momentous day. But do not fear. It will soon ring with terror in your brain. From this day forward, I claim your dreams as my private domain. You, my dear boy... shall be my most prized claim," it says.

Jingles speaks into the carved sides of the metal bell. Its raspy words produce a haunting whistle as the accompanying puffs of air pass through the object's gaps. "Cherish this always and hold it tight; you will fear for your life if left out of sight. You must follow this rule. I will not tell you twice, or you will be a child considered naughty, not nice."

As the sentence leaves its lips, the instructions translate differently into Jacob's subconscious, resonating like his favorite song's melody. His mind tucks every detail away, and the longer he stares at the metal, the deeper he falls into a trance-like slumber.

When he wakes, he is left with the memory of Jingles and the blood-splattered bell, now hidden beneath his pillow. It is enough to jog his remind him of what he has been tasked to do.

Jingles' entrance results in a terrible shift in his life. His dreams of innocence are now filled with nightmarish realities; he can see his breath, experience the cold against his cheeks, and feel the pain of his frostbitten skin peeling from his bones.

Jacob is afraid but cannot share his experience with those around him. According to the church's teachings, any ungodly occurrence in a dream shows the Devil's influence and requires intensive reprogramming. He understands that if the bell is discovered, it will be taken away, and fearing Jingle's wrath more than the church's doctrine, he conceals the bell, repeatedly swallowing it to keep it close.

Little did he know, his compliance invited the beast into his dreamland and tethered him to the creature—Jingles.

Like a tick, it will feast upon Jacob, draining his sleep and extracting every bit of happiness from his waking hours.

Chapter Six

THE UNRAVELING

THANKSGIVING NIGHT, THE SMITH HOUSEHOLD

No one could have predicted what would result from Jacob's turkey-laden coma.

Shortly after his tired eyes transport him into the misery of his dreams, a point of no return is reached, and the fate of every family member is cast in stone.

As everything in the house continues its regular holiday evening schedule, little idiosyncrasies, chalked up as clumsy mistakes, cause the routine to go awry.

The matriarch is the first affected by the unlucky streak.

Caroline returns to the dining room, clears the table of dirty dishes, and takes them to the porcelain sink to clean. She coddles each special holiday platter, even making extra trips to avoid overloading her arms. But, upon entering the kitchen with the last dish in hand, her foot slips, and she fumbles, almost dropping the plate.

Every household in Mountain View is granted one intricately designed heirloom set of porcelain tableware for use during the holidays. The priceless collections are handed down from one generation to the next.

They are irreplaceable.

Upon regaining her balance, she scans the floor for the cause of the slip and, seeing nothing, shakes her head, laughs it off, and chalks it up to clumsiness triggered by her distraction. She delicately puts the last dish in the sink and then follows church protocol, quickly expressing a prayer of gratitude for not breaking the china.

With an irritated sigh, she analyzes the extent of the mess awaiting her attention. "So many mouths to feed," she says.

As part of the guidelines for the Thanksgiving dinner, using electric dishwashers is prohibited.

The time-consuming holiday chore is a church teaching to humble women. They believe that by stripping them of the frivolities used in tidying the house, the women will better understand the sacrifices made by their ancestral matriarchs and grow an appreciation for their blessings.

Already drained from her day's toil, Caroline does not wish to clean dirty plates by hand, and the longer she looks at the extent of the soiled dishware, the more her reluctance builds. Her eyes remain fixed on the enormous pile of soiled dishes, and she is not excited about the laborious process of scrubbing each one.

Finally, pushing past her frustration, she closes her eyes to do the mandatory commencement prayer. O Lord, grant thy blessings upon the female church ancestors that have come before me. Through their wombs of light, I have been gifted with the strength to persevere and the insight to become the best mother I can be. In this, I pray. Amen," she says.

A burning feeling travels through her throat as each word leaves her lips. She clenches her jaw to battle the discomfort and attributes it to acid reflux.

With a sigh and an eye roll, she reaches for the faucet's handle and turns it, but the spout remains dry. Not a drop comes out. Her eyes widen with confusion. Overcome with concern, she turns the handle on and off, hoping to make it work.

Meanwhile, the gleam from the fluorescent lighting overhead casts a reflection off the dishwasher's chrome facing. Tired and at her wit's end, she wants things to be easy. The appliance's shine captures her attention, and its alluring pull causes her to weigh her options. As she gives into her impulsivity, she envisions ways to hide the sinful act from her husband.

Caroline reaches into the sink to retrieve a plate and is met by a stream of boiling water shooting from the spigot. Startled, she jerks her hands away in shock. Taking the incident as a sign, she fights her disappointment, adjusts the temperature, and begrudgingly cleans the stack of plates.

In each neighboring home, the women's hands crack and bleed from continuous scrubbing while their husbands fulfill their only task: bringing illumination to the holiday season. Milling outside, each man patiently waits beside their house's exterior to flip on the pre-strung Christmas lights.

Joel wants to ensure everything is perfect before the countdown begins, so he takes one last circle around his home's perimeter to confirm that each strand is in order. A sudden icy wind blows through the streets as he frantically analyzes every bulb.

Averse to the chill and wanting to get back inside to sit by their warm fireplaces, the men nonchalantly check their wristwatches. Then, glancing at the neighbors beside them, they silently agree to start early and, in unison, make their way to their respective light switches.

Joel remains focused on inspecting each bulb, oblivious to the group's decision. To his dismay, he spots one with a slight crack and worries that the faulty bulb may ruin the rest of the strand. As he ponders how to fix it, a wave of fear washes over him upon noticing the other men kneeling near their light switches out of the corner of his eye. Torn on what to do, he takes a chance on the bulb's functionality and, trusting in faith alone, changes his trajectory and dashes to his switch.

Upon his arrival, they look at one another, then in perfect unison, countdown three, two, and flip on their holiday displays. As the electricity surges through each strand, it fills the streets with a buzzing hum.

The men stand in unison, brushing the grass off their knees with pride as they admire each other's glimmering lights and exchange proud nods of respect.

Even though he knows he should remain attentive to the tradition, Joel cannot stop thinking about the problem lightbulb and the harm its failure would cause to his reputation.

After delivering his last compliments, he shifts his gaze to the dud on the roof's edge. As his eyes strain to get a better look, the defective object greets him with faint, mocking blinks.

The flicker causes sweat to accumulate at his hairline. His heart pounds as he imagines the worst possible outcome and wonders if anyone else has noticed. As he prepares for the faulty light to cause the entire strand to burn out, he quietly concocts excuses for his failure to the community.

Following a last flicker, the bulb resumes a consistent glow. The sight stops Joel's spiraling thoughts, and he releases a deep sigh of relief.

In the meantime, he has become complacent about what the other men are doing, especially his neighbor Wallace, who watches his every move. The man's stare is blatant.

Many would be grateful for living next door to someone concerned about their well-being, but Wallace always has ulterior motives. He is the tattletale of the community.

Joel senses someone watching him and, from his peripherals, catches sight of Wallace, looking smug and wearing his usual off-kilter Santa hat. Seeing his stare sets Joel on edge.

Not wanting to anger the elders by appearing unneighborly, Joel plasters on a smile and proceeds with a typical greeting. "Hi-De-Ho, there, Wallace!" he says. Then, with a swooping wave, his hand completes a full circle, ending with a motion toward Wallace's elaborate light display. "I don't know how you manage it, but you outdo yourself year after year."

His neighbor remains silent. Joel cannot read his reaction, causing him to fidget. As he waits for a response, he wraps his arms tightly around himself to control his body, shivering from the cold. "Well, I would bet a slice of my wife's apple pie that this might be our coldest year yet," Joel says. Still, without a reply, he shrugs and releases a deep sigh of frustration.

The other men in the community gather for the closing prayer. Joel takes notice and quickly tries to wrap up the one-sided conversation. "I hope you and the family have a blessed night," he says.

Still acting suspicious, Wallace takes his time to straighten his forest-green dress shirt and a brown leather belt that holds up his navy pants. Then, after a moment of silence, he eases his stare. "That's nice of you, Joel. I sure hope you and the family have a super one, too," he says with an exceedingly chipper tone.

They continue to smile at one another across the yard with passive animosity. Unfortunately, neither man is willing to show weakness by looking away first, leaving them uncomfortably glaring in a wide-grinned stare-off.

All the other men bow their heads to pray, and Joel and Wallace follow along, ending their competitive streak in the name of the Lord. The flock mumbles a few words to thank the heavens for the beauty of the twinkling bulbs that display cheer in the community.

As the last word, "Amen," is spoken, a gust of wind barrels through the street, carrying a flurry of snowflakes that dust the rooftops with a blanket of white.

Shivering, the men lift their heads and, looking at one another, give cheerful nods, then quickly scurry back inside to warm their cold limbs. Upon entering their homes, they hang their coats and, taking a moment, listen for water running in the kitchen sink.

The silence confirms they are on schedule for the big event: Black Friday shopping. On Thanksgiving night, the tradition of Black Friday sales rules each household. It is the only time of the year when it is appropriate for couples to have a bit more freedom.

After Thanksgiving dinner, the children are put to bed, and Christmas music is played quietly in the background. Each tune is meant to create a holiday mood as husbands and wives gather around their home computers to shop for gifts Santa Claus will give on Christmas Day.

Solely reserved for the occasion, the church grants each household a single computer. Most families have them stationed in their living rooms beside their vintage RCA television with an adjustable antenna.

Since financial hardships are common, especially during the holidays, the church believes that setting shopping guidelines prevents spousal arguments and makes the Christmas season more enjoyable.

Religious officials promote the event as an act of unity that strengthens family foundations. The annual occasion also provides wives with a temporary feeling of equality by giving each woman the power to share opinions with her husband regarding what gifts to buy. By permitting the onetime-per-year opportunity, the church feels each woman is less likely to question her lack of independence.

Despite how the men present the activity, boundaries remain, with husbands controlling the mouse and clicking to purchase and wives suggesting additions to their online shopping carts. The women's job is to disclose the gift ideas she has secretly compiled over the prior months.

The Smith household does not shy away from the norm. Like all the others, they keep the big electronic box on a small table in the far corner of the family room.

Seeing the layer of dust sitting on the flattened top of the computer causes a wave of pressure to blanket Joel's chest. He wrings his hands and cracks his knuckles to prepare for the marathon. Even though the event seems like a chore this year, he works to remain positive, forcing a grin.

Unfortunately, nothing about the task is enjoyable for him. For someone battling anxiety, the distance to the table appears catastrophic.

It is unlike the prior holidays, where he was soaring with excitement. On the contrary, the mere sight of the device triggers resentment and an aching sensation in his gut. As he attempts to divert his irritation, he recollects his earlier encounter and sarcastically mutters, "I'm sure Wallace is already sitting at his computer, buying everything his family needs," he says.

Caroline thinks she hears something while finishing in the kitchen and, worried about not appearing to be a supportive wife, shouts to make sure he is not calling her. "Everything okay, dear?" she asks.

"Yes, everything is fine, dear," he says and rolls his eyes.

Caroline shrugs and returns to drying dishes.

Joel feels the room stretch around him, and he loses control of his nerves. His cheeks flush with anxious energy as he reluctantly walks to the chair and sits in front of the computer. Exhausted, he struggles to sit up straight, but eventually, his tiredness wins out, and he settles into a stooped posture.

As he reaches to turn on the monitor, the sight of his reflection in the screen's glass causes him to pause. He finds his appearance unsettling. Rather than seeing his typically confident and youthful expression, he appears stressed out, with heavy bags under his eyes. Although his outward signs of concern make it nearly impossible to conceal his inner turmoil, he knows he must hide his weakness from his wife.

Taking a deep breath, he forces a look of happiness on his face to mask his stress. "This is a time to be thankful, Joel. Jesus, it's Black Friday. You should smile just thinking about the money you will save and the looks on your children's faces when they open their gifts on Christmas morning. Pull yourself together; it's only one day in the year. You are the head of this house, and no one can take that from you. Man up. They are relying on you." He says.

As he continues his pep talk, Caroline puts away the last of the dishes, folds the drying cloth to highlight its floral pattern, and hangs it from the oven's handle with a smile. Feeling a sense of accomplishment, she releases a sigh and puts on a cheerful face, ready to start the portion of the night she enjoys.

She is determined to make everything perfect.

Joel focuses solely on his internal battle and does not hear her enter the room.

Straight away, Caroline spots her husband's odd posture, hunched over the keyboard. Worried he may be in a bad mood, she takes it upon herself to cheer him up. She quietly glides toward the desktop space in the living room corner and gently grasps his shoulders to give him a massage.

He jumps. The touch of his wife's fingertips fills him with anger. Annoyed by her lack of boundaries, he swats her hands away. "Not now, Caroline!" He says.

Caroline is shocked by his hostile reaction and nervously picks at her fingernails, fearful she is in trouble. Refraining from aggravating him further, she stands still, looking over his shoulder at the computer monitor. She notices he has yet to turn it on. The sight of his face blankly reflecting at her from the black glass escalates her nerves. At once, she scrambles to smooth things over. "Is this about dinner? Did I upset you? If I did, I promise..."

Joel lifts his hand to silence her, then places it across his forehead and rubs his temples. "I don't know. Did you?" he asks.

She remains quiet to avoid further irritating him, even momentarily suspending her breathing. Met by her silence, he fixates on the room's tension through the reflection cast off the screen.

Suddenly a wave of honesty comes over him as he notices Caroline's ribcage not moving. He can no longer contain his angst and compulsively blurts, "There will not be a Christmas this year."

His mood swings constantly plague their relationship, so his behavior does not shock Caroline. Thinking it is just another of his dramatic episodes, she inhales deeply, relaxing her posture. "You know we should not talk like that, dear. Things are never as bad as they seem. I am sure whatever has happened is something silly that can easily be fixed," she says.

Her words' overly optimistic tone strikes a nerve in Joel and worsens his headache. Finally, the gnawing pain causes him to snap. Swiveling his upper body to face her, he glares at the naivety in her doe eyes, and his hand lowers from his forehead, revealing his beet-red complexion. "Goddamn it! Stop making light of this, Caroline. This is serious," he says.

Never having heard him use the Lord's name in vain, Caroline takes a small step back, her heels digging into the floor to secure her stance. Knowing she must try again, she softens her voice to comfort him. "Please, give me a chance to understand. Whatever it is, I want to help relieve the burden on your shoulders," she says.

His silence further wreaks havoc on her nerves.

Embarrassed by his temper, Joel stares at the floor, dwelling on his wife's disappointment. He is reluctant to face her, feeling ashamed of his behavior and the secret he is keeping. Finally, he concludes that there is no other option but to tell her the truth. "Well, I guess I might as well tell you because we are going to be the laughingstock of the community soon enough," he says.

Caroline is confused. Ignoring her perplexed body language, he continues. "Realistically, we probably won't be allowed to partake in our community gatherings after this comes out. We may even get excommunicated, and if the church casts us aside, we will be forced to rely on each other." The thought of their roles becoming less defined makes his eyes widen, and he shakes his head. "Our relationship dynamics might have to change."

Overwhelmed, he clutches his face as he wallows in self-pity. "I feel like a failure; I have let you and the children down."

Regardless of how vague he is about the issue's details, his voice's dismay immediately turns Caroline's face a shade of white. Although she can usually see the brighter side of things, she can tell by his inflection that this is something different. Things are serious.

It is usually unacceptable for her to question her husband, but her curiosity overpowers her, and she timidly speaks up. "What—what did you do?" she asks.

Joel is frustrated to be in a state of vulnerability. "It is not what *I* did. It is what my employer did to me. They conducted a mass layoff at work and dismissed me on the spot," he says. The memory of the incident causes his jaw to tense with anger. "They treated me like I was disposable, like a piece of trash."

Caroline's eyes widen in shock. She cannot fathom anyone doing such a terrible thing to another person, especially one with a family and during the holidays. "I cannot believe that they did that to you. They—they laid you off on Thanksgiving?" she asks.

Joel overreacts to the question and, taking it incorrectly, behaves like it is an assault on his dignity. He grits his teeth as he fights back another outburst. "No," he says. "It wasn't on Thanksgiving. The company let me go a little over a week ago."

The news causes Caroline's eyelids to flutter; she is flabbergasted. She cannot believe she overlooked the clues, as she remembers those mornings when she kissed him goodbye and wished him a good day as he left the house. No matter how hard she tries, she cannot wrap her head around the idea that he has lied to her.

She wants answers.

"I watched you walk out that door every morning, and you said nothing. I don't understand. Where have you been going if you did not go to work?" She asks.

Joel's anxiety heightens, causing him to run his fingers aggressively through his gelled hair strands. "Yeah, I get that this doesn't look great. I did not want our neighbors to think I was some loser who could not care for his family, so I maintained my daily schedule. The only difference was that, rather than reporting to a job, I just drove around," he says.

Caroline is sickened by the revelation.

Feeling misunderstood, Joel throws his hands into the air in frustration. "I did not want the church to recite some pity prayer for us," he says.

Joel cannot believe he is being forced to confide in his wife regarding money matters, and he lets out a sarcastic laugh. "I mean, at this point... I don't know which is more demeaning—the community's awareness of the situation or this conversation with you."

Trying to remain supportive, Caroline gracefully lifts her skirt's front hem and kneels on the floor next to her husband's chair. She submissively scans his eyes. "I know you are upset and how much you enjoyed your job at the genetics company. I am sure other jobs are available where you can do the same research. Or maybe they will realize they've made a mistake and hire you back," she says.

The sound of her forced positivity fuels Joel's anger to the point of nausea. "What don't you understand, woman?" he says. Overwhelmed by frustration, he jumps up and paces. Then, to avoid disturbing the children, he lowers his voice to a whisper and ridicules her. "Yeah, because the area is flooded with companies specializing in ancestry testing. Caroline, use your head. There are only a couple of those types of companies in the country. Most people don't care where they come from anymore. They only care about the here and now."

Not wanting to aggravate him further, she ignores his pacing and focuses on the chair. Without stopping to look at her, he rambles on. "I thought the company was doing well," he says. His pacing speed intensifies as he reflects on the extensive overtime he has given the corporation. "Did you know we just received millions of dollars in funding to launch a new beta program for at-home DNA testing? Accessible to everyone? Who do you think was behind that idea?"

Realizing the intensity of his rant, he takes a moment to collect himself. "Me! He chuckles in a passive-aggressive manner. "As an early bonus, they gifted the employees involved with the new product early access. It was supposed to be a small token of thanks before its public release. I had been saving the results to read together as a family at Christmas. I thought it would be exciting, but now, I don't give a shit! "

The idea of how the holiday has been ruined makes him angry. He releases a loud sigh of frustration, then continues, "I still can't believe that all they gave me was some stupid paper related to the test results and my termination notice."

Overloaded with the information, Caroline struggles to process everything as she stands in silence. Stuck in a Pollyanna-ish delusion, she is convinced there must be a way to fix it. "I am certain something can be done," she says.

Joel grunts angrily, frustrated by her inability to comprehend the situation. "What part of this aren't you listening to?" he says.

Worried his outburst will wake the children, Caroline quickly pulls herself onto the chair, hoping her shift in position will redirect him. The office chair's wheels creek as she sits, catching Joel's attention.

Under the assumption that he was the only one in his household allowed at the computer, he is confused by why she has taken a seat and erratically jumps to conclusions. "Get away from the computer. I already told you we do not have the money right now to buy gifts," he says.

Rather than being obedient, she ignores him, turns on the monitor, and boots up the system. Her assuredness takes him aback, and he lashes out. "You are not helping the situation," he says.

Caroline smiles as she releases her finger from the computer's power button. The purr of the processing fan is like music to her ears, bolstering her confidence. "Stop it, Joel," she says. It feels good to assert herself.

With newfound conviction, she launches the web browser and quickly types into the search bar. Even though her bullishness takes him aback, the clicking keys entice him, and, wanting to see what she is doing, he slowly approaches to get a look at the screen.

Caroline remains fixated on her mission, paying no attention to him. Throughout their eight-year marriage, she has learned that her husband's response to conflict is to shut down. She has discovered that the most effective method to snap him out of his slump is by steering him towards a subject he is enthusiastic about. In this scenario, it is his genetic research.

With a few frantic clicks, she pulls up his former employer's website. "You said you were in the beta program, right? Aren't you even a little curious about your results?" She asks. She knows the one thing that always makes her husband happy is his love for discussing ancestral history.

Her question throws him off, and he stammers to gather his words. "Well, yes, but why would I want to look at anything from a company that abandoned me after years of loyal service?" he says.

His stubbornness irritates her, and she rolls her eyes. Finally, after sorting through the website's tabs, she stumbles upon the members-only section. Now on a mission, she snaps her fingers at Joel to get his attention. "It says you need an ID number. Do you still have the piece of paper they gave you?" She asks.

Not thinking she would get this far, her computer proficiency throws him off. His eyes squint with skepticism over what else she may be hiding. Finally, with reluctance, he entertains her interest. "I hid the letter under the keyboard," he says.

Caroline lifts it, and her eyes widen upon seeing the sealed envelope underneath. She grabs the item and quickly tears it open. After carefully scanning the contents, she pinpoints the login information and slowly types in the credentials, ensuring the information is correct. Then, with one last click of the mouse, she successfully logs into the portal.

Having never seen the website team's final design of the members-only area, Joel's curiosity overrides his mood. Intrigued by the layout, he takes another step forward to get a closer look. Caroline's eyes strain as they scan the page's information. A small envelope-shaped image catches her attention. At the center of the icon, signifying a notification is a bold number one. Sitting beside it is a tab labeled *Results*.

Shrugging off her curiosity, she moves the mouse to click the *Results* tab. The sight of the small envelope catches Joel's attention, and he places his hand on hers to stop her. "Hold on. Wait a minute," he says.

She gets impatient, needing to understand what could be more fascinating than reading his DNA profile. "What?" she asks.

Guiding her hand, he moves the mouse toward the alert. "The messaging section—it's that small envelope. We made the area a place where those who share DNA can connect with relatives. To put it simply, it is a platform for cyber-family reunions. What's odd is that there appears to be a notification. As far as I knew, that feature was not supposed to be available until next year, when the company goes public," he says.

Caroline allows him to take the lead. "Huh," she says. A smirk forms on her lips; the idea of them playing detective together thrills her. "I feel like a young Nancy Drew," she says. As she slowly tracks the mouse's trajectory with her eyes, the mystery triggers a spike in her adrenaline. "Do you think they planned to release it early because of the layoffs?"

Unsure what to think, Joel's hand stops moving the mouse and hovers the cursor over the icon while he ponders. "I mean, considering my termination completely blindsided me, I guess there could be other things they were hiding. Nothing would surprise me," he says.

Impulsively, he presses his finger on Caroline's to open the message. A small spinning wheel encompassing a map appears on the pixelated screen. Their eyes grow wide as they wait for the page to process.

As the messaging portal opens, the subject line and sender's username display across the top. Not recognizing the name, Joel quickly glances past it and reads the preview of the message. "Hello, dear relative. I hope this finds you well. A sizable inheritance belongs to you, waiting to be claimed," he says. As he reaches the end, he realizes it is cut off. The only way to reveal the rest is by fully opening the link. Already thinking the whole thing is odd, he pauses. "This must be a scam, Caroline. Maybe we should sleep on it tonight and investigate again tomorrow. The link may contain a virus. No one gives out free money."

She jumps in, adding her opinion. "The gentleman living a few houses down from ours gave us money when we came up short at the grocery store the other day," she says.

He does not appreciate being challenged; his face turns red. "That's different. He is from our community," he says. With a dismissive shake of his head and a clearing of his throat, he attempts to regain his authority as the head of the household. "We should have enough money to make another month of mortgage payments. That will give me time to find a job, so we do not have to resort to accepting help from a stranger. We are better than that."

Caroline's frustration with his prideful behavior leads her to act boldly. She swats his hand away. "That's not enough for Christmas, Joel. The kids need gifts, and you may be entitled to an inheritance. What if you could buy everything for Christmas and never worry about working another day in your life? Wouldn't that be amazing," she says. He is at a loss for words. Not having a rebuttal, he bides his time by muttering to himself.

His lack of motivation to see her side causes her to dig her heels in further. She has yet to dismiss the message's validity." So, you're telling me someone hacked into your company's website?" she asks.

Between his wife's interjections, the flood of confusing details, and the discoveries about his company, Joel is at his wit's end. Not knowing if he can sacrifice any more of his ego, he becomes flustered. "I—I don't know what to think," he says.

Before he can gather his thoughts, Caroline snaps back. Manically smiling, she points to the screen and says, "Doesn't the church teach us to keep faith in dire times, Joel? Well, this could be our sign. A direct gift from Heaven," she says. Her patience is wearing thin, and she suddenly gives in to her impulses and clicks on the notification to uncover the rest of the message.

Joel struggles to respond as he tries to adapt to his wife's new opinionated nature and logical reasoning. Caroline does not care if he is ready to hear it and reads the correspondence aloud. "Hello, Smiths," she says. Then, pausing, she quickly grabs his hand with excitement. "That's us!" she says.

Unlike his wife, Joel does not find the revelation exhilarating. He finds it exhausting.

He quickly scans the document to review the details while searching for red flags. "Where in God's name is *Mittlerhaus*?" he asks.

Caroline is lagging several sentences behind him and, to catch up, hastily looks for the name in the message. "I guess that's where your ancestors are originally from," she says.

Joel cannot wrap his head around the information. Since he has never heard his elders mention the place, he insists it is inaccurate. "No, that is not right. I am pretty sure the church originated in Switzerland, like my heritage," he says. Convinced that the company is playing a trick on him, he moves the cursor to click on the results of his DNA report. "This is some sick joke."

They watch the cursor spin like a wheel as they patiently wait for it to project the information on the screen. Then, suddenly, a pie chart highlighting Joel's lineage appears in front of them.

Caroline attempts to fight back a snicker. Joel is quiet. "Huh," he says. As he processes the new information, he scratches his head. "It looks like 80 percent of my lineage is from *Mittlerhaus*...."

While Joel is distracted by his epiphany, Caroline snatches the cursor and navigates back to the message icon to read the rest of the letter. "Glad that's settled. Now let's see what your generous relatives have to say," she says.

Despite Joel's world being turned upside down, he still wants answers. His eyes light up as he sees the greeting reappear on the screen. The allure of sudden riches begins to take hold, and he inches closer to the monitor to get a better look.

Caroline points to the center of the screen, barely able to hold in her excitement. "Joel, this could be our way out of this mess," she says. Her smile lengthens. "It says your lineage is part of the town's founding families, and you have a substantial inheritance waiting for you, including a home and a large tract of land. Maybe this has to do with God's timing. This could be why you were fired! What if this has all been divinely orchestrated?" she says.

Joel mumbles as he rereads the message to himself. "It can't be. Something about it feels too good to be true," he says.

Tired of his negativity, Caroline won't stand for another word. She takes a deep breath, faces him, and gently grasps his hand. "What if this is God's way of sending us a miracle? Let's write back to them and let them know we are coming. There is no harm in trying." She says.

Quickly, Joel thinks about his choices and nervously polishes his glasses. "I suppose it may be worth a shot. If nothing else, it will buy us time while we sort things out."

Caroline takes the lead and begins planning. "We can use part of our savings to buy tickets and leave on the next flight out. If anyone asks, we will tell them we are going on a mission trip to preach the word to the people living in the land of your ancestors," she says.

The idea sparks Joel's attention. "You may be on to something, Caroline. It could be a gamble, but if this email is true, our payout would far surpass the risk. Worst-case scenario, we get to experience a few days in Europe."

His demeanor shifts as he thinks of all the money they will soon gain, and, grasping onto his faith-filled life raft, he ramps up his enthusiasm. "You go grab the passports and wake the kids. I will book the flights and write back to let them know we are on our way."

Excited that they agree on something, Caroline jumps from her seat. "Great. You take care of the details, and I will round up the children and pack our suitcases," she says, scurrying out of the room.

Joel sits on the office chair and smiles upon noticing his reflection on the monitor. "Everything is going to be okay," he says.

Before typing a response, he closes his eyes and says a prayer. "Thank you, Lord, for this immense blessing. I promise not to ruin the opportunity you have graciously laid before me." He pauses and listens intently in his moment of faith for a reply.

Something is stirring around him.

As he continues to wait, he does not consider that his blindness could mask the validation he seeks or, worse yet, conceal a sign meant to make him rethink his decision.

In desperation, people will often turn to the universe for answers. Most are too proud to admit that they will only listen if the guidance supports their defined agenda.

Joel is no exception. As he waits for his prayer to be confirmed, he is blind to what is occurring directly in front of him.

The computer screen glitches from dark to bright, and appearing between each malfunctioning flash is the faint outline of a malevolent grin.

Chapter Seven

DON'T WAKE ME UP

There is a skip in Caroline's step. She is ready to tackle her assignment and prove her worth to her husband.

Without warning, Caroline storms into the bedroom where her daughters are sound asleep, flips on the lights, and garishly shouts to wake them. "Rise and shine, my beautiful angels! Santa has an early surprise for you this year!" she says.

The abrupt sound stirs Hannah and Madelyn, prompting them to open their eyes. As the youngest gains her bearings, something about her mother's words sparks her attention, and she springs up from her covers. She spastically scans the room with an unrestrained eagerness. "Santa?" she asks.

Caroline rushes toward the girls to maintain the room's excited energy. "Yes! Can you believe it? Of all the families on this street, he visited our house early this year. Isn't it wonderful? I would say that it is a Christmas miracle!"

Hannah looks enthusiastically at her mother standing between their twin beds. "What did he get us? Tell us. Please tell us!" She says.

Madelyn chimes in, saying, "Yes, what did he get us? We have to know."

Scanning her daughter's joyful expressions, Caroline smiles from ear to ear, swinging her hands to call them to lean in closer. "Something huge," she says. Then, with a jump, she wiggles her fingers to build anticipation for her grand reveal. "He gifted us a vacation!" Her eyes enlarge, and her mouth gapes open to encourage their looks of surprise.

Rarely allowed to leave the town, they are in disbelief. The children glance at one another and pinch themselves to ensure they are not dreaming. The youngest child cannot hold back her curiosity and wants to guess where they are going. Quickly, she blurts out the first thing that comes to mind. "Is it to go get ice cream?" she asks. Her smile fills the lower half of her face as she waits for a response.

Caroline anxiously twists her hands together while pondering. "Not quite! It is somewhere even better!" she says. Then, wanting to make the trip sound fun to her children, she nervously extends her arms from her sides and skips around the room, making buzzing noises with her lips. "We get to go on an airplane," she says while pretending to fly.

Their eyes bulge in disbelief. They scramble out of their beds to join her, making a conga line of planes that circle the room. She can tell from their expressions that they are fully engaged. Caroline directs her gaze to the closet, encouraging them to continue gliding around the space as she fetches their two suitcases.

After booking the last details of the trip, Joel shouts from the living room to get his wife's attention. While unzipping the bags, Caroline hears his holler echoing down the hall and stops to listen. "Hey Caroline, they have a flight leaving at five in the morning!" he says, and without waiting for a response, he pushes the button to book it. "Booked! We are all set!"

Immediately, Caroline thinks about all she must do to prepare for the journey and takes a deep breath to center herself. She shouts back, "Perfect, dear! We will be ready." Then, with a smile, she quickly drags the girls' empty bags into the center of the room and looks at Hannah. "All right, I'm giving you a critical task. I am putting you in charge of ensuring both bags are packed for the trip."

Never having packed before, the eldest daughter glances at the open suitcases on the floor with uncertainty. Caroline notices her daughter's hesitancy. "You think you can handle that?" she asks. Not wanting to disappoint her mother, she nods.

Caroline is pleased by her compliance and releases a sigh of relief. "Okay, good," she says. Then, consumed by the tight time constraints, she sprints toward the door. As she crosses the threshold, she feels she has forgotten a crucial detail and stops to shout over her shoulder. "Hannah, pack enough for a month."

The girls are thrilled about the adventure ahead. Even though the eldest daughter does not know where to start, she rushes to their dresser and begins throwing various pieces of clothing into their bags.

Caroline can hear their scurrying feet and, figuring they have it handled, doesn't bother looking back. Instead, she continues her mission, heading to her son's room.

In the mere seconds between her encounter with the girls and descending the corridor, Jacob's dream status worsens. He is fast asleep and trapped in a nightmare; this time, it feels all too real, as if his waking and imaginary worlds have collided.

As he tosses and turns underneath his covers, his eyes anxiously flutter in and out of REM sleep. Rather than dreaming of the town of Christmas as he had done before, the nightmare has come to him, trapping him in his bed.

With a drawn-out creak, his bedroom closet languidly opens—his heartbeat races. Droplets of sweat trickle from his forehead, entering between his lids and stinging his eyes. A thick mist smelling of sulfur enters the room through the open door, covering the floor with a low-hanging fog and chilling the room's air to the temperature of a meat freezer.

Suddenly, the covers around Jacob's body tighten. They squeeze his ribcage like an anaconda, controlling his oxygen and shallowing his breaths. On the verge of a gasp for air, he hears a jingle bell ringing, and the chilling sound triggers him to fall silent.

A pair of heavy footsteps follow the familiar noise. Each floorboard groans as the intruder's weight shifts from one foot to the other.

Jacob's immobility makes it impossible to see what is occurring past his footboard. Closing his eyes tighter, he uses the surrounding noises to put the pieces together and notices the jingle is disjointed from the direction of the approaching steps. Immediately, a sharp ache fills his gut.

Breaking the silence, a low, raspy voice whispers from across the room. "I know where it's hiding," it says.

Jacob startles in response to the intonation, and his eyes pop open. His gaze fixates on the ceiling as fear causes his world to melt around him. "Jingles," he says in a whisper. A grin appears on the beast's face. In unison, Jacob's gut gurgles. The sloshing of stomach fluids causes the metal bell to release a chime only Jingles can hear as it passes through his system.

Jingles takes notice of the muffled melody and laughs with glee. Taking a moment, it feeds off his terrified silence, then exuberantly responds. "Yes, it is I, your friend Jingles, dear boy. Are you taking good care of my magical toy? " It asks.

The child feels like a sitting duck, helplessly waiting for the monster to pluck him from his bed. Worried about becoming its next victim, he fights to free himself, but each squirming attempt at escape causes the comforter to tighten its grip. Glimpsing out of his peripheral vision, he can see the dark silhouette of the creature lurking in the shadows. As it approaches, its presence is even more ghastly than before; the velvet-textured coat is now covered in blood, and its cuffs, lined with human hair, drip with human gore.

A sliver of light escapes from the hallway underneath the door. Slowly, Jingles raises two fingers into the soft illumination and snaps three times to commend him. "Bravo, my boy, for hiding in your dreams and depriving me of your innocent screams. You think you can elude me with the utmost ease, but I believe you need to remember whom you are meant to please. I am sad to say your luck will turn with the enthralling news you are about to learn," it says. Then, stepping closer, it snarls, revealing its pointy teeth as it spews spittle-laden words. "Now, it is time to teach a lesson and let misery churn."

Jacob, terrified and unable to escape Jingle's torment, silently cries.

Jingles slides its putrefied foot a step closer. "Devouring your family will be quite grand. Hmm, let us see. Shall I start with a foot, a head, or a hand?" It says.

As it snarls again, the door leading to the hallway abruptly flings open, releasing Jacob's paralysis and allowing him to turn his head. The small boy sees that the creature has vanished, and his mother stands in the doorway.

Assuming he is upset because of a nightmare, Caroline rushes toward him and places her hand on his chest to comfort him. Jacob is in a state of confusion and is startled by her touch. He is stuck between his dream state and reality, and, not able to tell the two apart, he goes into a frenzy, thrashing and shouting as he attempts to conceal himself beneath his sheets.

She frantically peels back the covers and scoops his sweat-drenched body into her arms to calm him. "Jacob, hush now, it's okay. It was just a bad dream," she says.

Jacob looks at her blankly. His pupils constrict as his brain accepts the relief from her caring touch. Her presence grounds him and causes his heavy breathing to slow. Caroline smiles softly, exuding her love while playfully tapping his nose. "See, I told you, I will always protect you. You are safe now," she says.

He continues to take slow, deep, calming breaths. The ache in his gut persists, and unable to bear the acute, stabbing sensations, he cries and paws at his belly. "My tummy hurts," he says. Caroline wants to remove his pain and gently rubs his stomach, hoping to reduce his discomfort.

Realizing they are off to a challenging start and short on time, Caroline attempts to shift the mood by inciting Jacob's excitement about the fun adventure. She bounces on the bed to rock him and rubs his stomach faster. "I have some exciting news: Santa came early this year," she says.

The news instills fear in Jacob and differs significantly from what he had hoped to hear. Consumed with thoughts of Jingles's blood-stained velvet suit, his tiny body trembles, and his face turns pale. "B-but it's not Christmas," he says.

Thinking he is stammering out of excitement, she ramps up her holiday spirit. Her cheeks puff out with air as she pretends to be Santa. "Ho, Ho, Ho," she says.

Jacob's terror outweighs his pain, flooding his body with adrenaline and kicking his mind into fight-or-flight mode. The small child's arms and legs flail wildly as he panics to escape. Caroline's grip tightens around him. "Stop it," she says. Still feeling him squirming, her squeeze intensifies. "I said stop it."

Her firm hold causes Jacob to quit his fight. Unfortunately, he no longer has the strength, as each struggling effort causes the ache in his intestines to return, even worse than before.

Masking her irritation with a smile, Caroline tries again. "Jacob, now listen to me. Santa was nice enough to bless us with a wonderful trip for our family, so you must show gratitude," she says. Still consumed with the pain, he whimpers and forces a nod.

"We don't have much time and must pack in a hurry," she says. She springs off the bed and swivels to face him. "Think of it as a fun adventure."

Jacob does not mirror her enthusiasm. Instead, he hunches over and grasps his abdomen. Having often dealt with his stomach issues, Caroline assumes his stress has caused another episode. "Let's take you to the bathroom and see if that helps," she says.

Jacob wants to feel better, and he allows her to help him off the bed. The gurgling movement of the object in his gut makes him wince. His mother is oblivious and hears nothing, even though, with each step, the noise becomes louder in Jacob's ears.

Caroline quickly shuffles him to the restroom across the hall. "I know you are Mommy's big boy. I will leave you to take care of your business while I pack your bag," she says.

Overwhelmed by the thought of being left alone, Jacob panics. He hesitantly stands in the bathroom doorway, and she nudges him inside. "I will be back to check on you," she says, motioning for him to walk toward the toilet. Fighting his pain, he clenches his stomach and follows her instructions. She takes a moment to ensure he is where he needs to be, and, satisfied, she shuts the door, leaving the small boy by himself.

Jacob stares at the toilet bowl in front of him. Having swallowed the small metal object many times before, he has become accustomed to stomachaches, but this feels different. The blockage has caused the wall of his intestines to swell, pushing them to their limit, and the pain is unbearable. A growl rolls through his abdomen, and, trying to keep it inside, he grasps his belly to make it stop.

The bathroom light fixture flickers, reflecting off the white porcelain bowl, creating a luring shine. It provokes the child, and like many times before, he fears losing the object that keeps him safe. Unable to hold it much longer, he fights with all his might to clench his cheeks, but he feels himself having an accident and panics. Not wanting to get in trouble, he frantically edges closer to the toilet seat and reluctantly pulls down his pajamas to sit. As the blockage passes, his upper body slumps forward with relief. He is exhausted.

Hearing his loud sigh, Caroline rushes back through the door with a fresh set of clothes for him. Noticing his relaxed posture and the color of his complexion returning to normal, she claps in delight. "Looks like someone feels better," she says. Still a little lightheaded, Jacob nods.

"I am so happy your stomach has stopped hurting. We have a long travel day ahead of us, so the last thing we need is for you to feel yucky," she says. Then, with a nervous giggle, she hoists him off the toilet and cleans him up.

While regaining his strength, he hears a tinkling sound behind him. He anxiously presses on his stomach and, not feeling a bulge, scrambles to turn around. "Wait," he says. But it is too late. Caroline has already flushed the toilet. Jacob frantically scans the churning water for the bell.

As the contents swirl, he catches a shiny silver glimmer making its way toward the septic system. "No!" he screams. Overcome by desperation, he lunges forward and reaches inside the bowl to grab it.

Caroline restrains his hands just before they dip in the contaminated water. Then, knowing there is insufficient time to address the issue, she brushes off the bizarre incident and continues helping him prepare for the trip.

The young boy is consumed by panic and uncontrollably hyperventilates. Ignoring his odd behavior, she assumes he is stressed over the chaos surrounding the last-minute travel and finishes dressing him. She sternly grabs ahold of his shoulders. "I know planes can be scary, but we cannot let our fears get the best of us," she says.

She ushers him back to his bedroom, and he fights her grip every step of the way. Finally, realizing he cannot escape, he nervously tries to explain. "B-but the monster," he says.

Caroline firmly forces him through the door, sits him on his bed, reaches for a pair of his lace-up boots, and puts them on his feet. "Please, Jacob—I'm begging you to stop with the monster stuff. It would be better for all of us on this trip if you calmed your imagination," she says. Her rough handling of his feet reveals her annoyance.

Feeling ashamed of his behavior and upset by her reaction, he straightens his posture to appear obedient. This is the first time he has seen his mother become angry, and her rising emotions only intensified his already unbearable anxiety.

Caroline drives her point home with a firm look. "We are all a little nervous right now, and in times like these, we must be brave and assist one another. Sometimes the need for support can be different for people," she says. As she finishes lacing up his last boot, she rises and continues. "For example, if you would like to help me, you need to try your best not to tell silly stories that put extra stress on me." Taking a moment of pause, she looks him in the eyes to ensure he follows along. "Do you understand?"

Jacob is still terrified. He glances at the floor and, not wanting to upset her further, gives a muffled response. "Yes, Mommy," he says.

She smiles at him and reaches for his mustard-yellow roller suitcase packed with clothes. "Perfect. Now, put a smile on that face and look excited. You do not want to disappoint your father," she says as she rolls the bag in his direction. Doing what she asks, he nervously smiles and grabs the handle.

The two girls enter his room. Madelyn is dressed in a colorful rainbow-striped cotton dress, black tights, and Mary Janes on her feet. Hannah stands tall, proud of accomplishing what she was asked to do. She wears a pair of heavy gray leggings, a pink sweater, and sneakers. "I think we got everything," she says.

Caroline looks at their matching braids and her eyes well with tears. "Just perfect," she says. She taps the free space beside Jacob on the bed for them to sit, and, with purple suitcases in tow, they take a seat.

Seeing everyone ready to go suddenly makes Caroline realize she still needs to pack for herself. She notices the children's eyes locked on something behind her and turns to see what they are looking at.

Joel is standing in the doorway, still wearing his Thanksgiving Day outfit, and holding two suitcases—one for her and one for him. "I figured you were busy with the kids, so I packed for both of us," he says.

Caroline stares at him in astonishment over his uncharacteristic act of kindness. Her eyes drift over his choice of attire. Following her gaze, he peers down at his outfit and chuckles. "Since we only have one set of dress clothes, I thought it best to remain wearing our holiday outfits to make a good impression. I hope that is okay with you," he says.

Having always held the responsibility as caretaker to the family, she is thrilled to have someone assist with the duty, so even though the crinoline of her dress is slightly itchy, she does not challenge him. Instead, she gives him a smirk and follows his lead. "That is a perfect idea, Joel," she says.

Her response brings him a sense of relief. "I left a note on our door for the neighbors to let them know we are out of town on a mission," he says.

Caroline smiles in disbelief over his sudden helpful behavior. "Guess that means we have a flight to catch," she says. "I have a good feeling about this."

Sharing a moment, they look deeply into each other's eyes, sparking something between them. The sensation causes Joel to blush, and he glances down to check his watch.

"Well, we should probably get going," he says. "*Mittler-haus*, here we come!"

Chapter Eight

WELCOME HOME

There are many questions you may ask yourself right now.

To begin with, one may wonder why a family that is so sheltered even has use for a passport, and the answer is simple: it involves their faith. Every Mountain View community member must complete at least one service trip in their lifetime, usually in young adulthood, to fulfill Christ's teachings. To accommodate the obligation of answering God's call on short notice, the elders walk parents through filing paperwork for the government-issued ID for their child at the time of baptism. Annually, the church requires residents to prove that every household member has a current passport. Even though only a lucky few are chosen for international travel, all are ready to answer the vocation at the drop of a hat.

Joel and Caroline would have welcomed the opportunity, but it was never offered to them. Since they were married relatively young, they were omitted from the possibility of international service. The church believes that wedded couples need more time to build their home and family together, and a shorter trip within the States is considered more conducive to that.

This trip feels like a redo to them, which may be why they are both so mindlessly enthusiastic. Deep in their hearts, they yearn for the adventure they were denied. The prospect is thrilling, with a sprinkle of taboo; it makes them feel alive.

As they gallivant to the airport, they expect to feel sad watching their hometown get smaller in the rearview mirror, but that is not the case. Instead, it brings them a sense of contentment they have never felt before.

Every inch the car wheels travel, an ounce of their repressed personalities is restored. Caroline is the first to be affected. Her once-starched posture transforms into slouching in her seat and uncrossing her ankles. As Joel drives, he freely itches his nose and refrains from acknowledging every car he passes; he does not wave at a single one.

Noticing their parents' stiffness fade, the kids' smirk at one another. The brief exchange of happiness allows little Jacob to escape the terror that still eats away at his gut.

The siblings play a game of I Spy with My Little Eye in the backseat. Taking turns, they scan license plates on passing cars and minor details of the scenery to contribute to the guessing game. For the first time, the children go unreprimanded for acting their age and expressing their excitement.

It is as if, by leaving the boundaries of the small town, a veil of constraint has been lifted off the Smith family's vehicle. There is something about the chaos that feels more natural than their usual daily routine, and even better, no one is judging them. Of course, that is not to say they will not struggle to break the restrictive patterns instilled since birth, but their lengthy car ride acts as the perfect catalyst for the change.

Beginning with their on-time arrival at the airport, things seem to fall into place for the Smiths, and all goes as planned. As they pass through the chaos of security checkpoints, the disruptions remain trivial, such as coordinating bathroom breaks for their children and locating their departure gate. Once onboard, they all find the long flight a perfect time to catch up on much-needed sleep.

According to the map provided by the ancestry website, Frankfurt is the closest airport to Mittlerhaus. Joel considers it divine intervention that a nonstop flight from Salt Lake City to Frankfurt was recently added. He views the flight as the backbone of their journey, believing its perfect alignment assures that they have nothing else to worry about and that all other aspects of the trip will work out in their favor.

The ease of it makes him naively optimistic. He feels that no matter how much of the journey he has left unplanned, it will be remedied with divine assistance.

From an early age, Joel was taught to hold faith in the highest regard and trust in relatives' unwavering hospitality. Although unclear about what to expect upon the plane's arrival, he has complete confidence in his long-lost family's good intentions. He is convinced he does not need to talk directly with them about their plans to visit.

So before leaving the house, he did what any relative would do; he sent their itinerary through the ancestry website portal. If they were like him, he did not need to explain any specifics; they would be waiting at the airport upon their arrival to pick his family up.

As the plane nears its final descent, the airstream encounters turbulence, and the violent movement jars the entire family awake. Terrified, the children's eyes widen. Caroline immediately leans over to check their seatbelts to ensure they are secured.

Each clutches onto the armrests of their seats while turning to peer through the windows. Having yet to grasp the substantial time difference, they expect to see the sunny blue sky greeting them, but it is pitch-black outside, and the frigid temperature produces a murky mist and low clouds. Everything is not as expected in Europe's glorious promised land; it is gloomy.

Regardless, they are eager to deplane. Exiting their flight, they shuffle through the long line at the immigration checkpoint to retrieve stamps on their passports, then collect their bags.

With their suitcases in tow, they head toward the arrival pickup point. Every section of the airport they walk through seems indistinguishable from the others. The aesthetics are unappealing, with white walls and dirt-stained tile floors. It looks like an unkempt hospital.

Troves of people filtering through the same checkpoints swarm through ropes strung to create controlled pathways for the mass exodus. All lanes end in the same location, a large cold room lined with row after row of waiting individuals. Each holds a handwritten sign with the names of the people they are there to pick up.

As the Smith family funnels along with the crowd, they are swept further into the chaos. Joel was overwhelmed by the massive group of strangers. Dazed by jet lag and the unfamiliar surroundings, he struggles to gain his bearings.

Then, playing the role of the protector, he springs into action and herds his family together, diminishing the gap between them. "Don't want anyone to get lost," he says, chuckling nervously. Overstimulated by the movement and noise, the children willingly huddle closer together.

While maintaining command of their formation, he scans the distance, trying to read the signs. Caroline stands on her tiptoes and glances over the crowd's heads to see what Joel is looking at. She wants to help. "Is there someone we should watch for?" she asks.

Joel brushes off her question. "I have it handled," he says.

Her lack of sleep causes her to lose patience. She is not sold on his conviction. As she analyzes him further, she notices his persistent expression of confusion while he scans the crowd. Once again, she asks her question in a more straightforward manner. "You have transportation scheduled for us, right?" she asks.

He raises his eyebrows, pretending to spot what he is looking for. Then, with an enthusiastic smile, he waves. "Oh, look, there they are," he says. Springing forward, he holds up a hand, signaling her to stay put. "Wait here. I will be right back," he says.

Before she can respond, he is already vanished, and she can no longer see him in the sea of travelers. Taking a deep breath, she focuses on her children, who appear overwhelmed by the chaos. She swiftly guides them to a nearby concrete pillar to get out of the way as they await his return.

Joel sifts through the dense crowd, making his way to each paper sign. "Come on... they must be here somewhere. They are family, and family has each other's backs," he says. As he nears the end of the line, he has yet to find their name. "What if they misspelled it?" Convinced he must have missed it the first time, he takes another lap, focusing on each person's facial features. "If we are related, I should be able to recognize them, right?"

Despite the cold temperatures outside, the densely packed room of travelers exudes warmth. Caroline pans the scene optimistically as she watches the families reconnect. Seeing everyone exchanging hugs makes her feel nostalgic. She puts her arms around her children. "Isn't that just wonderful? I cannot wait," she says while scanning the wide assortment of people.

Standing right before them, a family uses a translator to greet distant relatives arriving from their flight; everyone in the group is overjoyed to see one another. Caroline sighs. "Can you believe that will soon be us? It is just so beautiful," she says.

As Jacob fixates on the children within the group, he daydreams of the kids he will get to play with. Suddenly, an abrupt ringing penetrates his ears, ending his happy thoughts. After seizing his attention, the high-pitched noise is substituted by the gentle tinkling of a bell. Recognizing the haunting melody, he hyperventilates while his eyes frantically scan the room to see where the sound is coming from, and he soon finds what he seeks.

An unidentifiable presence sits on the floor in the room's farthest corner, ringing a tinny bell. A dingy, discolored Santa hat rests beside it, and as people pass by, they flick coins into the fur brim's opening. The individual's spine is slumped, and the grungy hood of its cloak conceals all facial features. Something about the back's curvature appears familiar to the small boy, sparking panic in his gut.

He frantically tugs on his mother's skirt to get her attention. "Mommy, Mommy," he says. Ignoring him, Caroline shifts from observing the reconnecting families to wondering when her husband will return. The young boy's sense of urgency reminds her of how long Joel has been missing, and she moves her attention to scanning the crowd.

Jacob tugs on her skirt again. The interruption irritates her. Before responding, she pauses to calm herself. "Yes, my darling, what is it?" she asks.

His heart races as he continues to stare at the suspicious being. "It's... it's..." he says. Anxiety causes his throat to tighten, making it hard for him to form a sentence.

She becomes impatient with his stammering. Then, quickly peering across the room, she spots what is holding his attention. "Where are your manners?" she asks.

Her sharp response confuses him.

Sternly, she grabs his shoulder and turns him to look at her. "You know better than that. Do not stare at the homeless man. It is not acceptable behavior, Jacob," she says.

The stirring jingle sounds again, this time louder. It is all Jacob can hear.

Oblivious, Caroline turns her attention to her daughters to lighten the mood while playfully patting their backs. "Come on, girls. Help me look for your father," she says. Searching the crowd is like a game of I Spy to the girls, and they are excited to take part. Caroline stands on her tiptoes, continuing to scan the sea of heads for her husband.

Even though Jacob wants to please his mother, his curiosity gets the best of him, and he continues to observe the mysterious figure from the corner of his eye. Caroline is too focused on engaging the young girls to notice.

A traveler wheeling a suitcase passes by the cloaked individual and flips a gold-colored coin into the Santa hat. The nonchalant interaction eases Jacob's nerves, and just as he relaxes, something brushes against his shoulder. Startled, he turns to look.

It is a small boy dressed in a puffy winter jacket. The woman accompanying the child grabs his shoulder, stopping him after noticing he has run into someone. She turns him around to face her and lowers herself to lecture him. "I taught you better than that," she says.

Jacob's stomach drops. He tries to convince himself that it is only a coincidence that the little boy wears the same-colored coat as the one in his dream.

"Now, apologize to the sweet boy you bumped into," she says. Underneath the oversized snow jacket, the small boy anxiously fidgets, his boots tapping against the hard tile, worsening Jacob's anxiety. Not receiving an answer, the woman becomes irritable and gives him a scolding glare. "Where are your manners, son?" she says. Then, strengthening her grip on his shoulders, she turns him to face Jacob, allowing him a clear view of the boy's features for the first time. She peers out from beneath the hood of her cloak, watching eagerly for his reaction.

Horror grips Jacob as he stares at the twisted features of the child's face.

The small boy's complexion is deathly white, as if all life has been sucked from his skin. Deep claw marks mar his cheeks, mangling him to the point of being unrecognizable. His lower jaw, ripped from its sockets, dangles from a single piece of cartilage.

Lost for words, Jacob quivers with fear as he watches the boy try to speak. A puddle of pink drool runs from the edge of the child's detached jaw and pools on his collar.

As Jacob's gaze slowly shifts upward, he sees something equally horrific: the boy has no eyes. They have been sloppily carved from their sockets, leaving jagged pieces of flesh that have scabbed around a pair of rust-covered jingle bells.

The woman's hands grip tighter around the boy's shoulders. Then, smiling, she whispers in his ear, "I did not hear you say you were sorry." In response to her crushing fingers' pressure, his neck kinks unnaturally, and his shoulders lift, releasing the unnerving sound of snapping bone.

Consumed with fear, Jacob's eyes hesitantly drift to look at the woman. Even though he is confident of her identity, the eyes staring from beneath the hood bear no resemblance to anything he has ever seen before. Her overly large pupils, surrounded by a sea of white, have no shine or capacity to dilate. Their humanity is missing. "Mrs.... Mrs. Rigby?" Jacob asks.

Hearing her name prompts her to remove her head covering, exposing a short A-line bob with perfectly rolled ends. The color of her dark red hair matches her strawberry-colored lipstick. Her grin takes on a demonic quality as her lips peel further back, displaying jagged yellow pieces of filed bone jutting from her tar-black gums.

Jacob cannot look away. The longer she stares into his gaze, the more she uncovers his darkest fears.

Her thin tongue wiggles to the roof of her mouth as she speaks. "We are so glad to have you home, aren't we, Tobias?" she says.

Jacob is hit with an overwhelming sense of panic, causing him to struggle for breath. "Home? I'm not—I—I..." he says. Convinced he may be in a nightmare, he tightly closes his eyes, hoping to break the sleep cycle. "Wake up," he whispers.

His pathetic attempt at escape makes her chuckle. "You are awake, my child," she says. Her words prompt the chaos of the airport to go mute; the only sound that remains is the methodical jingle of a bell. Mrs. Rigby continues to smile as she glances toward the noise echoing from the hunched figure across the room.

Her stare incites movement, motivating the motionless person to rise from the ground and lean against the wall to stand.

Mrs. Rigby's tongue flutters in her mouth while slowly chanting, "Jingles, Jingles, Jingles." Tobias continues to drool while clapping along to the rhythm of her voice. She glances back at Jacob. "Today is the day you have come to stay. The beast will give a lump of coal or, if lucky, a bell to house your soul. If it is the bell, it will trap your fears, entombing them in its metal for the rest of your years," she says.

As the figure straightens its posture, its limbs extend, revealing its lanky stature. Jacob watches in horror as the beast shifts its position to a hunting stance, locking its stare on its prey.

His eyes follow the thing's line of sight, and he realizes it ends with his father. Suddenly, he finds his voice and screams at the top of his lungs while wildly gesturing. "Daddy, watch out!" Over the hustle and bustle, Joel hears the shriek and, not knowing what's going on, skittishly jumps; he looks from left to right as he tries to identify the noise's origin.

Simultaneously, Caroline's attention shifts toward Jacob's pointing finger; she notices it is directed at her husband. "Good. You found him," she says. She squints to sharpen her vision as she looks across the room and attempts to comprehend what he is doing.

Joel is on his third lap around the waiting area; he slows down his pace to read each paper sign, thinking the words will miraculously change since his last two rounds.

Caroline's fury grows as she realizes he has been aimlessly wandering to pass the time, evidenced by his confused expression. As she continues to watch, the uselessness of every effort only intensifies her anger and confirms his dishonesty. "Just as I expected. Your father did not plan a ride for us," she says. Her foot neurotically taps, and her fists clench.

Her irritability and absence of fear confuse Jacob. Stunned by her nonexistent reaction to the beast, he wants to know why she isn't crippled with fear and quickly looks toward his father.

The creature is gone. Losing track of the entity triggers Jacob to panic; it could be anywhere. He rubs his eyes to ensure he sees clearly, then swiftly scans the room from floor to ceiling. As Jacob checks the place previously occupied by Mrs. Rigby and Tobias, he realizes they have vanished too.

His heartbeat escalates, and his palms sweat. As his mind spirals, something grabs him, stopping his thoughts. He jumps. Terrified, Jacob refrains from looking as he reaches to feel what is holding on. He is relieved to find it's his mother.

Caroline scoots Jacob closer to his sisters. She is on a mission to confront her husband and begins herding them in his direction. "Come on, kids, keep a firm grip on your belongings; we are going to find your father. Then, pushing on their backs, she guides them through the diminishing crowd. As they snake around the last lingering families, she signals the children to link hands, and they eagerly comply, clutching tightly to one another.

Caroline locks her sight on Joel.

While glancing over at the only remaining handwritten sign, he notices his family approaching. He looks around; there is nowhere to hide. Trying to mask his defeat, he scratches his head and, pretending to be surprised to see them, lifts his hand to wave. "Hey there, I was just..." he says, stammering to craft an excuse.

Not wanting to hear his flimsy excuse, Caroline clears her throat to stop him. "Knock it off. I know you don't have a ride planned, Joel," she says.

She tries to cool down her frustration by looking away and notices a sign featuring a yellow car. Beneath it, an arrow points to the door below. Even though the words are foreign, she recognizes the image and takes matters into her own hands. She motions with her head to draw Joel's attention toward her discovery. "Let's just put this all behind us and grab a taxi. I don't know about you, but I would like to take a hot shower and change out of these clothes," she says.

Her reaction was much calmer than he had expected. Wanting to preserve the peace, he remains silent and nods. Joel's lips tighten to form a nervous smile as he submissively bows his head, signaling them to go first. "After you," he says. He pushes his slipping glasses up the bridge of his nose and follows close behind them.

Upon exiting the building, they scan the brick exterior. The usually bustling international airport appears barren as the remaining two families load up in vehicles and drive away. It quickly becomes apparent that the Smiths were on the last flight for the night.

Caroline looks from arrow to arrow leading to the pick-up area designated for public transportation and notices that only one cab remains. "Well, guess it's better than nothing," she says.

Inside the bright yellow car with chipped black stripes, a middle-aged man with graying scruffy facial hair sits behind the wheel. His seat is fully reclined, and it appears he has fallen asleep to pass the time.

Without warning, the building's automatic doors close, followed by the security guards pulling down metal gates over the windows and securing the locks. The sound of the steel hitting the ground loudly echoes between the building's overhang and sidewalks, startling the family.

The vibration rattles the cab, jarring the driver awake mid-snore. Flustered, he fumbles for the keys sticking out from the ignition and starts the engine. Noticing the headlights flip on and the engine revving, Caroline drops her children's hands and frantically runs to catch him. "You can't go! We need a ride!" she says.

Unable to hear her over the vehicle's hum, he focuses straight ahead, slowly putting pressure on the gas pedal. Caroline, now in a dead sprint, struggles to catch her breath. Desperation kicks in as she reaches the vehicle, and she throws herself onto the car's hood, pounding on the windshield to get the driver's attention.

The thrashing woman terrifies the cab driver as he tries to gather his bearings. Paranoid that he has hit something, his arms stiffen, and he slams on the brakes. The smell of burning rubber saturates the air as the tires let out a loud shriek against the wet pavement.

Tired of dealing with the situation, four months pregnant, and wheezing for air, Caroline rolls off the hood and seizes the passenger side door handle. The sound of the car door opening catches the man off-guard. Quickly, his head snaps to look, and he encounters a heavily breathing woman with a crazed look in her eye. Convinced she is a crazed psychopath, he flails his hands to shoo her away. *"Aussteigen! Aussteigen! Aussteigen!"* he says as perspiration drips from his brow.

Caroline signals him to pause, holding up her hand as she tries to catch her breath. Despite the language barrier, she senses his distress and tries to reassure him by smiling nervously. "I'm so sorry to bother you," she says. Concerned about losing their opportunity, she motions for her family to come quickly.

Joel has never seen this side of his wife before, and her aggressive behavior dumbfounds him. Regardless of his concern, he motions for the kids to grab their luggage, and they sprint to the cab, dragging their roller bags behind them.

Standing at the open door, Caroline notices something interesting about the cab's aroma. It stinks of cheese. While waiting for her family, she scans the cab's interior for the source of the smell, starting with the man in the front seat. The driver's unkempt appearance and body odor suggest he needs to prioritize showering. He is dressed in dingy brown woolen pants, a food-stained scoop-neck white tank top displaying the coils of his graying chest hair, and a charcoal-gray wool button-down sweater. The car is equally disheveled. The once cream-colored seats are now beige to black, with day-old crumbs in the creases and dark yellow stains on the carpeted floor mats.

She attempts to hide her disdain while considering how barging in may have seemed rude. Uncertain how long they may be stuck in the car together, she knows she must try to communicate and slow her speech to bridge the language barrier. "It is okay. Me... come... in.... peace," she says. "I nice," she says while pointing to her heart. Then, to add insult to injury, she pretends she is driving an imaginary car and, while making tractor sounds, continues, "We need... ride."

The driver rubs his head as he tries to decipher the conversation. Though confused by most of her charade, there is one thing he understands: she wants him to drive. He releases a loud sigh and, with a shrug, pushes the button to open the trunk. "*In Ordnung,*" he says. Then, tilting his head, he motions to the back. "*Sie können Ihre Tasche in den Kofferraum legen.*"

The trunk unlatching makes Caroline smile; she knows she has gotten through to him. Appreciative, she nods to pay homage and places her palms together to make prayer hands. "Thank you, thank you, thank you," she says.

Joel and the kids get there just in time. Noticing the open trunk relieves him, and he ushers for the children to hand him their luggage. He loads everything into the back with haste, closes the lid, and pulls on it once to ensure it is securely shut.

Little did the driver know, the eccentric woman had an entire entourage. Before he can process what is happening, Caroline slides across the back seat and signals for her children to follow. Then, one by one, they funnel in after her.

Realizing there is not enough room in the four-door sedan, she pats her lap. "You can sit on Mommy's lap, Jacob. Come on. We can all squeeze in," she says. Excited to get more attention than the others, Jacob seizes the opportunity and hoists himself onto her legs. She carefully adjusts herself, giving her stomach adequate space.

Meanwhile, Hannah helps Madelyn buckle into the seat beside them before sitting and latching her own.

Joel peeks into the back and, realizing no room left for him, makes his way to the front passenger door. Nervously opening it, he lets himself inside and takes a seat. The driver glares at him with a deadpan expression.

Trying to make the best of it, Joel attempts to lighten the mood. If he has learned one thing, a happy greeting can turn any situation around because a smile is contagious. "Well, hi there, friend. My name is Joel. Thank you so much for—" he says.

Before he can finish, the driver becomes impatient and hushes him. Wanting to be done with the obligation, he hastily asks where they want to go. *"Wohin musst du gehen?"* he asks.

The jet lag, mixed with his naivety, has made Joel briefly forget that there could be a language barrier. He is convinced that the man is using a garbled form of English. "What was that you said?" he asks.

Annoyed, the man's glare deepens, and having little patience left, he asks again, in simpler terms. *"Die Adresse?"* he asks.

Able to match the latter part of the sentence to English., Joel fills in the blanks. Then, laughing off the temporary misunderstanding, he promptly clarifies. "Address?" he asks.

The driver nods emphatically in response. *"Ja, Adresse,"* he says.

Joel cannot avoid being awkward. "Oh, yes, of course. You need the address. Silly me," he says. Fumbling through his coat pocket, he pulls out a piece of paper and chuckles. "How would you know where to take us without it?" Swiftly, he flattens the creases and points to the address. Then, using his best German accent, he reads it aloud. "There it is... *Mittlerhaus.* That is the place we are headed to."

The man perks up; it's a name he does not hear daily. *"Ach?"* he asks. Believing it to be a joke, he laughs and snatches the paper from his hand. *"Warum willst du da hin,"* he says as he looks closer.

Instantly, Joel feels the man is mocking him because he is a foreigner. Although he is generally a good sport, given the circumstances, he is not okay with being the butt of someone's joke. Angry and wanting to set things straight, his jaw clenches, and he clears his throat to give the man a piece of his mind. "That place you are making fun of is where I am from," he says, and his chest puffs.

The driver finds his voice annoying and ignores him. Continuing with his rant, Joel proudly points to himself. "You heard me. We are just as much German as you," he says as he pivots in his seat to get his wife to rally with him. Exhausted, she does not want to feed the conversation and looks away.

Even without scanning over the paper, the driver knows exactly where they are going; he only asks to ensure he hears them correctly. "*Die dummen Amerikaner,*" he says, shaking his head. Chuckling again, he hands Joel the paper and proceeds to drive toward their destination. "*Ich werde dich dorthin bringen.*"

Joel cannot contain his enthusiasm and turns to his wife to share the moment. "You hear that, dear?" he asks as an excitement-filled jitter rushes up his spine. "Did you see how he understood by directions? "It's official," he says. "We are considered locals."

Caroline feels her exhaustion bringing on a headache. She wants him to turn back around but listens to his jabbering with a smile instead. "That is great, Joel," she says. The children grin at one another and watch out the car's windows as the airport fades in the distance.

Joel confidently shoves the paper into his coat pocket and feels something cold brush against his fingertips. His eyes light up. "Oh, boy, I almost forgot!" he says. Joel removes his fisted hand and holds it out in front of him. He inhales a deep breath and continues, "All right, kids, close your eyes, including you, Caroline. I picked up a surprise for everyone back at the airport."

The thought of getting a gift makes the children squeal with anticipation. Aside from Christmas, it is not normal. Squirming in their seats, they can barely contain their excitement. In unison, everyone, including Caroline, tightly shuts their eyes.

Proud of being able to keep the secret for so long, Joel snickers as he checks to ensure no one is peeking. "All right, now hold out your hands," he says. Caroline and the kids extend their flattened palms, and Joel leans over the seat, dropping a small gift on each pair of hands. In anticipation of their reactions, he shouts exuberantly. "Now, open them!"

As everyone's eyes open to look, they are greeted by a tiny jingle bell. The sight of every surprised expression brings joy to Joel. "So, what do you think?" he asks.

Jacob is caught off-guard and is conflicted about how to react.

The girls, swirling in anticipation, begin shaking their gifts to play music. But the bells disappointingly produce no noise. Feeling discouraged, the youngest daughter's gaze falls to the floor. "Daddy, I think mine is broken," she says.

To comfort his daughter, he playfully laughs. He has another secret to disclose. "No need to be sad, my sweet little girl. That is how they were made. I think it must be a German thing," he says. Then, with a smile, he taps the side of his temple. "The jingle is whatever you want it to be. All you have to do is use your imagination." Hearing a parent, especially his father, encouraging one of them to be creative renders Jacob speechless.

He holds the bell in front of him and tries to enjoy the momentous occasion, but unfortunately, his experience differs significantly from that of his sisters. No matter how hard Jacob tries, he cannot look away from the metallic shine of the bell. From the corner of his eye, he spots his sisters rolling their gifts in their hands and laughing with glee. Jacob shakes his gift, trying to find the happiness they are experiencing, but instead, he is met with a trigger: each shake resonates with a child's scream. He is horrified as he examines the bell and realizes it is the same one lost in the toilet before their journey.

As the children play, Caroline holds her gift close to her face to better observe its intricacy. "I can tell these are handmade. The amount of detail put into the carving is incredible," she says. Fascinated, she carefully analyzes each precise nick of the metal. "Where in the world did you find them?"

Joel is bursting with pride about how well-received they are and can no longer stay silent. "This might sound a little out there, but I saw this hooded guy selling them for cash. Well, based on the stature, I assume it was a man. It was hard to make out the face. I am guessing he was mute because he did not speak. After sensing God's calling, I approached him and noticed a small for-sale sign next to the bells. I thought to myself, what better way to be charitable and have trinkets to remember our trip by," he shares. Rummaging into his pocket, he pulls out another bell. "I even got one for myself."

Caroline is stunned. Her husband's rare show of thoughtfulness brings a joyful gleam to her eye. "Wow. That is just wonderful. Not only did you give money to someone in need, but we also gained a cherished memory," she says. Then, she turns to the children. "Isn't that wonderful, kids?"

The girls smile from ear to ear, thrilled with their souvenirs. Still trapped in terror, Jacob wants to express his concerns but stops, remembering his earlier conversation with his mother. He knows he must uphold his promise and does not want to cause her stress, so he nods with a nervous gulp.

Her husband's kindness makes Caroline forget the chaotic ordeal at the airport. Taking in the moment, she touches the bell to her bosom. "Such a wonderful gift. I know we will cherish these for the rest of our lives," she says.

As the loving exchange occurs, the driver glimpses the bell in the rearview mirror and gives them a strange look.

Overwhelmed with happiness, Joel beams as he tucks the bell back in his pocket and faces forward in his seat. Taking her husband's lead, Caroline carefully puts hers in her pocket and, looking at the children, motions for them to do the same. " Now, put them somewhere safe. You don't want to risk losing them," she cautions.

Both Hannah and Madelyn look at her. Then, in unison, they put their bells away for safekeeping. "We won't," they say.

Wanting to face his fear, Jacob squeezes his bell between his trembling fingers. As he moves the object toward his pocket, he sees something on its surface. He holds it near his eye to get a closer look and realizes his initials have been carved into the metal. Terrified, the little boy frantically shoves it into his pocket. "Yes, Mother, I will keep it safe," he says.

Caroline notices the girl's eyelids drooping as fatigue sets in. She peers through the window, admiring the silhouette of the passing scenery; grinning at its beauty, she whispers, "Change is good."

The distance to Mittlerhaus is greater than anyone had expected. After nearly an hour of driving on the main highway, they finally turn onto a side road leading up a winding hill densely covered by enormous trees. The soothing vibrations of the wheels against the bumpy terrain put the Smith family to sleep.

Well, not everyone. Jacob only pretends to be asleep because, in the small boy's gut, he knows that something is off, and the further up the hill they get, the more he feels thrust into his nightmares.

Chapter Nine

GUESS THIS IS OUR STOP

The road twists and turns, becoming narrower and more treacherous the higher the altitude. With every passing mile, the forest grows darker, making their drive seem like a descent into the abyss.

Jacob's heart rate escalates, and he tries to distract himself by nervously counting every tree that passes by his window.

The driver struggles to see through the darkness and snow flurries, relying only on his dim headlights to illuminate the road ahead. He hunches over the steering wheel to get a clearer view.

The front tires hit a small patch of black ice, abruptly throwing the car off-kilter, and it skids. Caught off guard, the driver tightly grips the steering wheel and frantically attempts to regain control, swerving the vehicle back and forth. The jarring movement tosses everyone around in the car, forcing the rest of the Smith family to wake up.

Fearing that his car cannot handle the severe conditions, the driver panics and slams the brakes. Everyone braces themselves as the car slides to a halt.

The glow of the headlights illuminates an enormous, dilapidated wooden sign bearing the words *Willkommen in Mittlerhaus.*

Refusing to risk going further, the cab driver puts the car in park and points out the windshield toward the inclement weather and sign. "*So weit kann ich gehen,*" he says.

Joel quickly cleans his glasses on his shirt, then puts them back on to see where the man is pointing. Everything is dark. He needs clarity. "Are we here?" he asks.

Without saying another word, the man hits the button, unlocking the car. Caroline takes the cue and reaches for the handle. "This must be the place. The names on the sign," she says.

Joel does not find the sign to be convincing. He peers outside to scan their surroundings; nothing looks as he envisioned. With his only example of German culture coming from pictures of Oktoberfest in textbooks, he expected the town to be a little livelier. "Huh. I suppose you must be right. I just thought it would be different," he says; disappointment lingers in his voice.

The driver is irritable and wants to get back down the hill before the weather worsens. After the long day, he is eager to go home. Losing his patience, he snaps, pointing to the door. "*Gut, raus hier,*" he says.

Joel senses anger in his voice and reaches for the handle to leave but pauses, stopping before opening the door. "But why is it so dark?" he asks.

Caroline is solely focused on wrangling the children and does not have time to entertain his question. "I don't know, Joel. Maybe it's because everyone is sleeping. It's not even early morning yet. Usually, people turn the lights off when they go to bed," she says. The girls are fussy and fight with her directions as they struggle to wake up.

Her words make sense to him, and he shrugs. "I suppose you are right," he says.

Trying to be patient, Caroline encourages him to move. All she can think about is getting somewhere to take a hot shower and change out of her itchy holiday dress. His continuing stagnation sparks her irritation, and she raises her pitch to a threatening tone. "Hurry and pay the man so we can get going," she says.

That is Joel's cue; he cannot procrastinate any longer. Reaching for his wallet, he turns to the driver. "How much do I owe you?" he asks.

The man's attention locks on Joel's fingers, sifting through the stack of cash. Without giving much thought, he highballs a number. "*Einhundert,*" he says.

Joel pretends to understand him and impulsively pulls a cluster of euros out of his wallet. Without looking, he hands the money to the man with a smile. "That should cover it," he says.

The driver's eyes widen as he receives more bills than he expected. He quickly counts the money and tries to hide his happiness with a nonchalant nod. Joel takes one last look at him. "All right, I guess we should go now," he says. He lingers a little longer. "You know, we appreciate all you have done. So, thank you for playing a pivotal role in reuniting us with our long-lost family," he says.

Caroline can tell he is trying to stall, and she snaps her fingers at him to move. "Come on, Joel, we need to grab our luggage from the back," she says.

After taking a deep breath, Joel grits his teeth and opens the door, bracing himself for the frigid air. Caroline follows closely behind, lecturing her children while she exits. "It may be slick, so be careful, and no running!" she says.

The children respond with a nod, then slide to the seat's edge, following close behind her. She helps them from the car, and after ensuring each has a solid footing on the slippery road, she turns to check on her husband. He is just grabbing the last bag from the trunk, then slams the lid shut. The noise breaks the wooded serenity as it rumbles through the trees.

The engine revs, and noticing the car's brake lights fade to black, Caroline grabs the children and pulls them to the side of the road. Huddled together, they shiver as they watch the man speed down the hill and leave them in the dark.

A strong breeze rustles through the surrounding trees, causing woodland creatures to relay warnings to take shelter. Jacob, already on edge, jumps at each sound as his eyes spastically dart around, searching for the source of the noises.

Caroline tries to make the freezing temperature more bearable by rubbing her children's shoulders to create friction to warm them. "What do you say we open those bags and get out your coats?" she says.

Hannah crosses her arms to shield her body from the chilling wind; her teeth chatter as she opens her mouth to speak. "But—but how will we see?" she says.

Joel seizes his opportunity to chime in. "I have an idea," he says. Then, unthinkingly fumbling in the front pocket of his luggage, he pulls out a dated cell phone. The screen flashes, notifying him that the battery is almost dead. "We can use this as a makeshift flashlight," he says.

Caroline's stare goes blank, and she is lost for words. Everyone knows cell phones are prohibited in their congregation. The elders believe their use gets you one step closer to hell.

"When did you get that?" she asks. Feeling he is taking too long to answer, she snatches it from his hand and, glancing at the screen, notices the words *Low Battery*. Using the screen's light, she moves quickly to assist everyone in finding their jackets.

Caroline's curiosity reaches a boiling point, and she blurts out the question that has been consuming her. "How long have you had this?"

Nervously shuffling his feet, Joel's response comes out like word vomit. "Since I started at the company. They gave it to me to use on-site. Our building was so big; it just made sense," he says.

Despite answering her question, she is skeptical. No matter how hard she tries, she cannot help but wonder if he is hiding other secrets, but she puts her insecurities aside, recognizing that it is not the right time or place to bring them up.

Caroline spots her husband's jacket, snatches it from the bag, and tosses it to him. He quickly puts it on while frantically apologizing. "Please don't be mad. You must understand—I thought I was protecting you by not saying anything. You know how the community views cell phones," he says.

While ignoring him, she helps the children finish zipping their coats, then puts on her own. Even though she disagrees with his behavior, she does not want to add stress to the situation, so she spins her negativity into something positive. "Well, now that we know you have one, can't we use it to call the relatives and let them know we are here? I am sure they would want to greet us and show us where to go." Not knowing how to use a cell phone to make a call, Caroline hands it back to Joel.

Her suggestion leaves him speechless; he had not thought of the phone being helpful in this situation other than its use as a makeshift flashlight. Not wasting any time, he grabs it from her and starts frantically tapping the screen, but nothing works. "Crap!" he says.

Caroline instantly covers the children's ears. Her husband has never cursed in front of the kids before, and she gives him a furious look. "Language, Joel," she says.

Embarrassed by her scolding, he quickly changes the subject by turning the phone toward her to see. "Go figure—there is no service," he says. Unable to read the small display from a distance, she squints to get a better look, but he pulls it out of her sight before she can see anything. His frustration grows as he scrolls and taps on the screen. "I should have known those pieces of trash would cut me off from their plan. I think they enjoy kicking me while I'm down...." He catches himself before saying another curse word and stomps his feet to let off steam.

The kids silently watch their angry father's tirade as they huddle together to keep warm. Finally, weary of his shenanigans, Caroline reaches for the hands of her two youngest children. Hannah grabs Madelyn's free hand, forming a human train. "Choo, choo," she says.

Frustrated with knowing she cannot rely on her husband, Caroline forces on a cheerful expression and responds. "All aboard!" Then, summoning the last of her energy, she tries to motivate them to walk. "Who's ready for an adventure?" She asks.

The children look at each other, unsure of how to react. As Caroline anxiously waits for their response, she squeezes their hands. She glances at her husband for a split second to see if he is paying attention to the conversation, but he is not. Instead, he stands only a few feet away, wholly engrossed in his phone. The dim light illuminates his face and reflects off his glasses as his finger scrolls over the screen.

She can tell by the mirrored image on his lenses that his actions have nothing to do with helping his family. Instead, he appears to be deleting things. Caroline does not have time for his shady behavior; she has her children to worry about. Shifting her focus, she looks at Jacob and responds to the group, saying, "I know, I sure am."

Jacob looks at their luggage sitting in the snow. "Should we grab our suitcases?" he asks.

Pleased that someone was finally communicating and irritated that it was not her husband, Caroline answers sarcastically. "That is a brilliant question, sweety. You know what? Your father is a big, powerful guy. He can get them for us."

The kids look past the town's sign, nervously fixating on the forest's darkness. Caroline swings her arms back and forth to get the children to loosen up. "It's okay. I promise it won't be scary. Remember, I will be right here beside you every step of the way," she says. Her words bring comfort and temporarily ease their worry.

As they prepare to set out on their journey, Caroline notices something in the direction they are heading. Her posture becomes rigid as her ears detect a buzzing sound reminiscent of a hive of bees. A sudden realization hits her. The hum she hears bears the same characteristics as the one produced by their vintage Christmas lights back home. Its echo from a distance, beyond the sign, causes her optimism to grow. "You hear that? It sounds like home," she says as she fixates on the direction of the buzz. "All right, let's march, my little soldiers."

Confident about where they are going, she hurries forward with the children in tow. The sound guides them through the forest as they wind their way among the trees, heading toward the village.

Caroline is resolute in her decision and does not bother turning around to see if her husband is following. His extended work hours have accustomed her to not having him around, which is preferable.

She is confident in her ability to manage the children alone, irrespective of his decision to join them, and, for the first time, is not concerned about making him happy. Upon further reflection, she could not recall a single instance where he had been content and realized the man's impossible to please.

Joel remains fixated on his cell phone as they move out of sight, completely oblivious to their departure. His only focus is on the small screen.

He feels a sense of satisfaction as the noise dwindles around him, bringing him the tranquility he believes he deserves. While the peaceful environment allows him to concentrate better, the woodland creatures' fading sounds suggest something more ominous.

There is a thing hidden from view lurking deep in the forest, and it has gotten a whiff of the family and driver's flesh as they parted ways just moments ago. Joel is unaware that the longer he stands stationary, looking at his phone, the more likely he will become its prey.

There is a reason for the growing silence; as it approaches, it purposely annihilates each noise-producing creature that does not flee, mercilessly grinding them into the frosted soil with each heavy step. Looking at the tiny, mutilated bodies beneath its feet, it lifts a finger to its teeth. "Shhh... now, remember, little ones, we must not disturb what is set in stone as the Smith family settles in their new home," it whispers.

It captures a slight movement next to its boot. A tiny door mouse lies crushed and dying. Perplexed by its survival, the creature briefly pauses its pursuit to analyze it. As the helpless rodent watches, the beast grins deviously and bends to one knee. Then, with a flick of its discolored nail, it decapitates it.

A gust of frigid wind carries Joel's scent through the air. Upon catching a whiff, the creature's tongue snakes from its mouth and licks its teeth.

Joel uses his alone time to reflect on the last few days; he is in disbelief over his evolution and how much he differs from before. In the past, he never would have allowed his wife an opinion or tried to bond with the children; that was Caroline's job. He considers himself progressive.

In addition, Joel ruminates on his past mistakes and concludes that Caroline is the sole cause of his sinful transgressions. He finds the revelation that he is not to blame freeing. Not only has he determined the origin of his weakness but also, in keeping with the church's teachings, all men's sins are forgiven, releasing him from any culpability.

As it observes Joel pondering his newfound epiphanies, his deliberation intrigues the creature. Silently crouched on the forest floor, it watches. It cannot help but wonder what is going through the man's mind as it waits expectantly for him to speak.

Joel determines he wants to remain in control of his situation's outcome. He recognizes that since Caroline has learned of the cell phone, she will be on her toes, and he cannot risk her getting ahold of the device again and finding out his dirty little secret. To start fresh, he needs to clear the device's history. The sight of the battery draining makes him frantic, and he worries he may not have enough time to scour through the miscellaneous folders to erase his past.

As his finger scrolls through the camera roll, he sees a thumbnail featuring a wonderful memory from the company's recent holiday party; the sight of it makes him reminisce about the double life he had once led.

Before allowing himself to push delete, he checks the battery and takes one last trip down memory lane. "For old times' sake," he says. While browsing through photos of coworkers, his eyes light up as he stumbles across one featuring a friend who is especially dear to his heart. The picture depicts a blond-haired woman wearing a cute Santa Christmas sweater sitting on his lap, each holding a glass of champagne.

"Oh, Barb." The woman's full name is Barbara Miller; he strokes the screen to touch her one last time. "I will miss you most of all."

When the photo was taken the weekend before the layoff, he viewed the woman as meeting every need Caroline could not fill; Barb was everything to him. He had believed her to be the complete package: intelligent, compassionate, free-spirited, and genuinely interested in his hobbies. While admiring the photo, he finds he is not ready to let her go and pulls up the text messages they shared, including the most recent one, where he had updated her on his flight to Germany.

His wife's suspicions were correct; there were other lies. For one, his employer had not purchased the phone. He did. Joel bought it to keep in contact with Barb outside of work hours. He had no phone plan attached, so that nothing could be traced. He knew the data log would not be stored if he messaged her from an app that ran on Wi-Fi.

Infuriated by his lack of time to reminisce—solely because he could not sneak away from his family at the airport to find a power source and charge his battery—he hesitates. Joel holds the image closer to his eyes, and while he struggles to delete the last photo he has of them together, a soft breeze blows past him.

The dense fog parts just enough to reveal a bright yellow full moon. At the same time, the dimly lit phone screen cynically flashes 1 percent battery life. To him, the contradiction of the dying phone and vibrant moon is a direct message from Heaven. Looking up, he grunts to unleash his anger. "I'm trying to do the right thing here, and still, you mock me!" he says.

Like the flip of a switch, the once-repenting man's demeanor shifts, and he furiously glares at the sky as if it is to blame for his current situation. His conviction of having lost all power over his freedom intensifies his frustration. "You think this is funny, God? Huh? Is this my punishment? I must choose between the two of them?" he asks. Quickly, he takes another look at the photo and laughs. "You love to see me miserable, don't you? I'm nothing more to you than a little science experiment."

He is tired of playing the *good guy* role and waves his phone to taunt anyone listening. "You know what? Fuck you. Plenty of people make situations like this work; even plural marriage is becoming more acceptable. This is the same thing. Barb told me this is an open relationship. So, yes, there are many ways I can make this thing work so I can have them both, and if Caroline does not like it, she can kiss my ass," he says.

The long rant leaves him out of breath, and, holding up a finger; he hunches over to take a moment to refuel. "Woo, that felt good!"

Joel's hateful words are like a sweet melody to Jingles's ears, making its mouth water. The spectating faces on its body hiss, "Kill the hypocrite. Kill the hypocrite. Kill the hypocrite."

The creature pulls on its sleeves to hush them. A string of drool drips from its lips as it imagines Joel's flavor. "Oh, boy, look at him go, ranting and raving and stomping through the snow. The man is providing us with quite a show while spewing about things he does not know," it says.

The entities sneer while disguised by the velvet clothing. "Yes. Yes. Look at him go," they say.

Still recovering from his tirade, Joel remains hunched over, huffing and puffing.

Convinced that he is taking his final bow, the creature claps its bony hands together, each *thwack* sounding like the sharp crack of a whip. It startles Joel, and he springs to his feet, thinking it is thunder.

After contemplating, he deduces that the noise is in response to his outburst, and he falls to his knees to beg for forgiveness. "Please don't smite me for my moment of weakness. I'm—I'm ready to repent. Please, I take everything back, I said. I swear, I did not mean it," he says. He throws his hands above his head, offering his soul to the Lord. "I promise to be a changed man from this moment on."

The beast quietly crawls closer to get a better view of the theatrics. Seeking further amusement, it claps again. The spectating faces hoot with laughter.

Joel scurries to escape, concerned that a punishing lightning bolt will be sent to strike him. "I'm sorry!" he says, his desperation worsening. Having nothing to lose, he holds his cell phone toward the sky and makes another gesture, trying to prove himself as a repenting man. "Look! See? I will do whatever you want. Heck, I will delete it now, right in front of you. Then you can be a firsthand witness to the eradication of my sinful ways." He bows his head respectfully while dramatically moving his finger toward the phone's screen. "Here I go." He says.

Upon touching the cold glass front, he immediately realizes something isn't right. There is no deleting click. The only thing visible on the flat black screen is fingertip smudges. The battery has died.

As Joel checks the phone, his eyes widen. "Oh no, no, no..." he says. In a state of distress, he frantically shakes the device. "You can't do this to me." His finger spasms on the power button as he tries to reboot it repeatedly, but nothing works. The screen remains black. He panics as he realizes he has taken too long to reminisce.

As Jingles continues to watch Joel's spiral, his fear soaks into its skin, causing it to tingle.

With a deep inhalation, Joel tries to calm himself but is taken aback when it carries a foul sulfuric stench into his nose and mouth. The smell is stifling, and he cannot ignore the air's horrific odor as he tries to fight back his gag reflex.

The pungent sting from the fumes causes his nostrils to burn. He can no longer control his exasperation, and he cynically chuckles. "Jesus Christ, just when I thought I had already hit rock bottom... It gets worse? Is there a broken sewage line around here? It smells like shit," he says. The inconvenient odor pushes him to his breaking point. Frustrated, he scans his surroundings to identify its origin.

Still, in the early morning hours, the sun remains hidden behind a mountain range of mismatched peaks. A dense haze makes it appear as though time has traveled backward. Everything is much darker than Joel recalled, and he adjusts his glasses to ensure it is not just his poor vision impairing the view.

As the clouds shift through the sky, the moonlight bouncing off the backs of their billowy surfaces creates a glow. A lone ray of light pierces through the clouds and lands flawlessly on the mound of suitcases belonging to the Smith family. The reflection cast by the beam hitting the bags' metal accents sends a tiny glimmer through the grove of trees and catches Joel's attention.

Until now, he has been entranced by the phone and has not given a single thought to his family's whereabouts. Their twinkling luggage triggers concerns over his earlier rant. "What if they witnessed my unholy outburst?" he asks. He tries to remain positive by spewing affirmations. "No, there's no way she heard me. It is too quiet."

Staying low to the ground, the beast creeps closer, only pausing behind the occasional tree to mask its premature discovery.

In unison with the creature's unhurried approach, the wind generates snow flurries that grow stronger with each chilling gust. The sudden blasts of wind produce a high-pitched whistle that drives Joel to the brink of insanity. Questioning the suitcases' apparent desertion, he calls to see if his family is nearby. "Caroline!" he shouts. As he waits for a response, his mind plays tricks on him. "What if they are hiding?" He grabs fistfuls of his hair, giving him a frenzied appearance as he turns in circles, mumbling to himself. "No, they wouldn't do that to me."

Joel's irritation reaches its peak. He extends his hands to block the wind's fury and, quickening his pace, shouts louder. "Jacob, Madelyn, Hannah?" He listens for a response and, hearing nothing, fears his abandonment. Little did he know that the thick grove of trees acted like a soundproof room, muffling each of his cries.

Unwilling to wait any longer, the creature slogs itself across the ground. Wiggling its torso like a snake, it creeps toward the town's sign while remaining hidden from the moonlight. The closer it gets, the more its excitement builds. It digs its nails into the frozen soil, propelling itself faster. The bony end of its spindly middle finger gets stuck. With a sudden and vigorous tug, the bone dislodges with a resounding pop. The crack mimics the snap of a branch as it echoes through the trees, stopping Joel dead in his tracks.

He wonders if it is Caroline.

As he gains his bearings, he pinpoints that the sound is near the sign, not the luggage. The unexpected proximity triggers his heart to race. He places his cold, trembling hand on his chest to calm his nerves and slow his breathing. "There is nothing to fear. It's only nature. Probably just a branch snapping from a wind gust or the weight of ice." He says. He releases an enormous exhalation, and as the breath leaves his lips, it forms a small cloud that hovers around his face and fogs his glasses.

During his one-person pep talk, the beast finishes its descent. Upon reaching its hiding spot behind the dilapidated boards, it rises to its feet. Shifting its weight to its toes, it quietly hunts for a place to observe Joel and stumbles upon a massive wormhole. The sharp splinters stab into its leathery skin as it presses its cheek against the wood to peek at the man's unraveling.

Angry that they cannot partake in the fun, the companions complain. "We want to see the hypocrite lose his wits," they say. The creature hushes them to be quiet, the sound merging with the deafening wind. Not listening to their master's command, the faces continue to chant. "Show us now, or we will tell all who dwell in the pits of hell," they say.

Irritated that they are interrupting its joyful moment, the beast clutches its wrists to stifle their mouths. In protest, they nip through its sleeves. "I will only let you see if you show obedience to me, and if you choose to bite, you will never be free, remaining beneath my velvet no matter how much you plea," it says in a guttural whisper. They all immediately fall silent, giving in to its demands. Then, using its sharp, rigid nails, it climbs up the backside of the sign to get a better view.

Joel continues to reflect on the cause of the loud snap and tries to construct a logical explanation for what could have caused it. After much deliberation, his ideas regarding the disturbance drastically shift from a natural occurrence to one of intent.

His testosterone surges at the revelation as he becomes convinced that his wife is plotting to embarrass him. Knowing he must assert his authority, he stomps toward the sign to remind her she is not in charge. Clearing his throat, he shouts loud enough to be heard over the wind. "You know, I have been talking with God, Caroline. He told me that because of your childish behavior, I must take away your privilege of participating in making decisions," he says.

The beast silently perches at the top of the sign's thick ledge like a vulture watching its prey. Keeping its end of the bargain, it pushes back the fabric covering its companions to give them a clear view of the show.

Joel takes another step closer to the sign. "Honestly, I don't want this any more than you, but my hands are tied,

Caroline. If this is what God wants, we must abide by his will. It is the only way," he says.

Joel's body shivers uncontrollably, and he loses patience. Tired of the cold and feeling he is not receiving the respect he deserves, his demeanor becomes more assertive. "You need to get out here right this minute!" he says.

Enthralled by the show, the creature kicks its feet excitedly as it watches Joel's ego, leading him straight to them. Wanting to take part in the fun, it hatches a brilliant plan.

Starting with a whisper, it ensures its pitch perfectly emulates Caroline's voice and, once content with its rendition, it calls out. "Let's play a game."

Caroline's familiar tone grabs Joel's attention. Angered by her lack of compliance, his grasp crushingly tightens around his cell phone. Suddenly he remembers he still has essential photos on the device. Joel eases his grip and carefully places the device in his back pocket, knowing that once he gets his inheritance and returns to civilization, he can charge it and enjoy the photos again.

"You had better come out here this minute. Do not make me come over there, wife," he says. To conceal his rage, he chuckles sarcastically. "Believe me; this is me being nice."

The creature fights to control its laughter, snorting and spewing mucus into the air, which barely misses Joel. When the acidic snot hits the frosty ground, it sizzles.

Joel cannot stand being laughed at. "You think this is funny, Caroline?" he asks. Immersed in Joel's childish spectacle, the beast gazes down from above as the man scours his surroundings to locate his wife's hiding spot.

Joel's face flushes with rage as snowflakes cling to his glasses, obstructing his vision. "Damn it," he says as he yanks them off his face to dry them.

The creature leans in, eager to watch what he does next, and the sign makes a subtle creak. Joel stops what he is doing to listen. He smirks. "You must think you are quite clever, Caroline," he says.

The beast flashes a wicked grin and answers in Caroline's voice. "Mhmmm," it says.

Joel seethes over her condescending tone, and, unable to control himself any longer, he lets his anger get the best of him. Fixated on punishing her, he glances toward the top of the sign and shouts, thinking he sees something. "Gotcha!"

The beast remains silent.

Frustrated, Joel continues attempting to dry his glasses on his damp clothing while shouting at the blurred figure and stomping his feet. "I mean it, Caroline. If you do not get your ass down here this instant, I'll—I'll..." he says. Although he cannot distinguish the silhouette details, he knows it is Caroline, and seeing no movement makes him shake with fury.

The creature responds with a thunderous snarl. Startled, Joel fumbles to put on his glasses, but they are still too fogged to see. He frantically tries to dry them again, but his damp clothing only worsens the smears. With no alternative, he holds them out in front of his face and attempts to use them as a magnifying glass, squinting through the smudges to get a clearer view.

The beast shimmies itself closer to the sign's edge, giving Joel a better view of his antagonist. "Jingle, jingle, jingle," it says.

Joel slowly scans the beast's gruesome details, and even with compromised vision, he can identify enough to leave him terrified and trembling. "Who—who are you? What do you want?" he asks. His hands shake uncontrollably, causing his glasses to tumble from his grasp.

Jingles hops off the ledge, intentionally landing on the glasses and grinding them to smithereens using the ball of his foot. Joel jumps backward, catches his shoe on a fallen limb, and twists his ankle. Wanting to retain his manliness, he scowls and kicks the small branch that caused his snafu. "Stupid branch!" he says.

Jingles lifts its boot and, with its spindly fingers, scoops up the fragments of plastic and glass. Then, with a puff of its cheeks, it blows air into its hands and gleefully watches the contents flutter toward Joel's eyes like fairy dust.

The tiny fragments enter Joel's petrified stare, digging deep into the whites and turning them a shade of scarlet. He screams in pain while pawing at his face and shuffling backward, trying to escape.

The beast's companion's jeer. " The sinful man cannot be saved from the penance owed to those he betrayed." They say.

Joel cannot determine where the additional voices are coming from and mindlessly flings his hands to stop what he considers an unjust accusation. "I think you have the wrong guy. I am a churchgoing man. I live a life without sin," he says.

The elusive audience continues to heckle him. "Hypocrite, hypocrite, hypocrite," they say.

As their chants fade, Jingles takes in a deep whiff of air; its lips curl to the corners of its eyes. "Is that a bell I hear, harboring Christmas cheer?" it asks.

At once, Joel realizes he is referring to the bell he purchased at the airport. Having no attachment to it, he fumbles through his pocket to retrieve the small metal trinket. "Oh, you want the bell? Why didn't you say so in the first place? You are more than welcome to take it," he says. He extends his quaking hand and offers the object to the beast. "Is this what you want?"

Concerned about what may happen if the creature finds out it does not jingle, he quickly explains. "Before you take it, I must warn you it is defective and doesn't jingle. I think whoever made it forgot a piece."

The beast stares at the moon's glimmer reflecting off the metal. It moves closer, shortening the distance between them. "Fool! Only I can hear its delicate call until terror fills its metal walls. Through it, I track who is next to fall, hunting, killing, and watching them crawl. Stalking those who are sinful is the best part of all," it says.

Each of the melodic words makes Joel shiver. "Who... what are you trying to hunt?" he asks.

Thinking the question is naive, Jingles laughs. "It is written that a descendant from the Mittlerhaus tree will one day end my legacy. I am sure you see why I cannot set you free," it says.

Joel notices the figure briefly pausing and seizes the opportunity to take a step backward.

Jingles momentarily deliberates before reaching into its satchel and touching each bell containing its victim's fear-filled memories. Then, with a grimace, saliva foams from its mouth as it recounts the tale. "Somebody far down the Mittlerhaus tree decided it would be wise to try to trick me. It was a small boy whose name began with a 'T' and who, because of his dear sweet mother, attempted to flee. But, like everyone in this town, he was filled with sin, stealing one of my bells crafted for him, and that is where you come in. One of you is bound to be his kin," it says.

Joel retreats faster while waving the bell in the air to distract it. Knowing fully what the man is trying to do, Jingles increases its pace to follow him—the small faces cackle. "Let's eat his flesh and make a mess," they say.

Joel chucks the bell into the air with all his might, then turns to run. While frantically trying to escape, he trips over the pile of luggage, utterly unaware of the fact that his phone has fallen out of his back pocket.

The bell's carvings cause it to linger in the air like a wiffle ball until it finally lands in the creature's hand. Jingles, delighted with the turn of events, snickers while watching Joel scamper away.

Joel sprints past where the cab dropped them off and, picking up speed, continues to run downhill, following the road and hoping to find someone who can help. The unforgiving asphalt feels like needles stabbing his frozen feet as they break through the snow and impact its hard surface.

With the bell in hand, Jingles playfully spins the item through its fingers while tapping its foot. "Oh, this one is feisty—finally, some fun. Let us allow him a few more moments to run," it says.

As the snow flurries continue to fall, the terrain grows slicker, making it increasingly challenging for Joel to maintain his footing and gain traction. Abruptly, without warning, his feet slip out from under him, leaving him flat on his back and sliding uncontrollably down the hill. His panic escalates as he picks up speed and cannot slow down or stop himself. Even though he has poor eyesight without glasses, he can detect a faint glow on the road ahead.

As he approaches, he realizes that it's a pair of taillights. Shifting his weight, he skids toward the vehicle while frantically waving his hands to get the driver's attention. "Help! I need help!" he shouts. The brightness of the illumination increases as Joel approaches, providing him with the assurance that the driver heard him and stopped.

Joel grasps the back of the car to halt his slide, but not before his shins smash into the rear fender. The impact causes him to lie writhing in pain on the ground. Slowly, he regains his bearings and, grabbing onto the back bumper, pulls himself up onto his bruised shins.

A strong smell of burned rubber lingers in the dense air. Ignoring the smell, Joel continues to pull his way down the side of the car toward the back door. "There is not an ounce of decency left in the world. How can someone stop to help, then ignore the person struggling to get to the car?" he asks.

His feet skate out from under him, and as he places his hand on the ground to keep his balance, his fingertips brush against something. Immediately, he recognizes the object; it's a set of glasses. He is in disbelief and rushes to put them on. Even though the prescription only somewhat corrects his far-sightedness, he feels lucky that it at least allows him to see better up close. Now, nothing within his wingspan is blurry.

Joel hears heavy footsteps, reminiscent of a giant steer, moving down the hill toward him. Unfortunately, they are muffled by the falling snow, making it difficult to estimate their exact distance.

Desperate to escape, Joel shifts his focus to getting inside the vehicle. After fumbling with the door handle, he pulls it open and crawls into the backseat. He shouts at the driver. "Drive! Goddamnit, drive!"

The car does not move. Unnerved and desperate to get the driver to listen, Joel leans over the seat, confident that eye contact will help with the language barrier.

The illumination from the headlights hitting the snow outside reflects into the front of the vehicle, providing just enough glow to get a gist of the horrific, gore-splattered scene. The man who dropped them off a short time ago sits lifeless; one arm dangles from the smashed driver's side window. Something has eaten away his face, exposing teeth and bone. Deep claw marks filet his neck to the point of near decapitation. Even his eyes fell victim to the attack, torn apart by tiny bites. The front of his cranium is missing, and his scalp is now resting on the adjacent seat, still partially attached to the removed portion of his skull.

Joel sees his reflection in the rearview mirror and realizes he is wearing the driver's glasses, spattered with the man's blood.

The creature did not hunt the driver for his lineage but for his memories of the Smith family gathered during their car ride from the airport.

In a fight for his life, Joel scrambles over the front seat and, wasting no time to move the body, hoists himself onto the dead man's lap. He throws the car into reverse and hits the gas, but despite the pedal being pushed to the floor, the front tires remain trapped on the shoulder because of an earlier skid. The back wheels spin uselessly on the pavement. Smoke from the burning rubber fills the air as the rear tires cut through the snow and connect with the asphalt.

Joel's jaw clenches, his knuckles turning white as he grips the wheel and presses harder on the gas pedal. "Come on..." he says.

Even without Joel having the bell in his possession, the creature still tracks him down. By analyzing his movements earlier, Jingles discovered that Joel would opt for self-serving and the least clever options if given a choice. Unfortunately, that was enough information to determine that he would not deviate from the road.

Now only a few feet away from the car, the creature observes the vehicle's predicament. Chuckling, it knows it has time to spare and continues its prowl nearby, even adding a dance to its steps. "Jingle bells, jingle bells, jingle all the way," it sings.

Suddenly, the car jolts onto the pavement. Joel slams on the brakes to stop its backward roll and takes a deep breath. As he prepares to shift the vehicle into drive, something seems off. It's as though he has forgotten something. Feeling the corpse's lap underneath him, he realizes his phone is missing from his back pocket. He cannot stand the idea of not having it to call Barb after he escapes to a nearby town. "Shit," he says. Convinced it must have fallen out while climbing over the seat, he frantically pats the cushion on the passenger side, but it is not there. As he prepares to scale to the back to search further, he checks the side mirror to see how much time he has, and his eyes dilate.

Jingles silently waits next to the door, dangling the cell phone from its stick-like fingertips. "Ho, ho, ho," it says.

Seeing the matted human hair sewn into the end of its sleeve triggers Joel's gag reflex. He battles his nausea, but the ill-fitting prescription glasses have given him a migraine, making it impossible.

He struggles to concentrate, scrunching his face tightly to stay focused while battling the temptation to grab the device. "Look away, Joel. You don't need it," he says. He fumbles for the gearshift, but his hand lands on the wrong lever, causing the windshield wipers to turn on. Joel screams as the bloody gore smears across the glass, swishing back and forth.

With a playful shrug, the creature swallows the phone in a single gulp.

Joel catches the act from the corner of his fuzzy peripheral vision. Immediately, his stomach drops as he watches his memories move in a rectangular lump down the beast's throat. He finds it unbearable to watch; he is not ready to let the memories go. His heart races, and he struggles to catch his breath as anxiety takes over.

Jingles eagerly absorbs his fear. Then, seizing the whip from its belt, it snaps it against the ground to straighten it and sends the end through the shattered window with a flick of his wrist. The object tightly coils around Joel's neck, causing his eyes to bulge from their sockets. Grasping at his neck, he attempts to free himself as he struggles to breathe.

The beast's tongue writhes in its mouth, feeding off his suffering. "While I cannot offer clemency, I will reunite you with your treasured memory," it promises. Then, with a brutal heave, it drags his squirming body through the driver's-side window.

Joel's body slams against the cold, hard ground, sending his glasses flying. Then Jingles, with a firm grip on the whip, gives it another sharp yank, crushing the man's windpipe and triggering his limbs to convulse as he desperately struggles to stay alive.

With each desperate gasp, the carved faces of the creature contort in malicious glee. They take pleasure in Joel's suffering.

Jingles watches the color dissipate from his flesh and sneers. "You cannot flee, so follow me," it says. Then, spinning on its toes, it leisurely drags Joel's body up the hill, leaving a trail of cleared pavement in its wake.

Joel drifts in and out of consciousness. Lying on his back, he can see the blurred sky above. The road's surface is unforgiving, tearing away at his clothing and skin and leaving a trail of red-stained snow in their wake. With nothing fleshy left to grasp onto, the pavement latches on to muscle, then vertebrae.

Unable to take any more agony, Joel goes limp. Noticing his body's lack of fight, Jingles stops to check his condition. The creature tilts its head, studying him with the same intensity it had used when examining the crushed mouse. It gradually pulls back its sleeve to reveal a diminutive face with a full mouth, holding onto a bell.

At the snap of Jingles's fingers, the tiny jaws regurgitate the metal object back into its palm. Then, anticipating something in return for its help licks its lips. "Eye, eye, eye," it says.

Jingles moves its wrist toward Joel's cheek. The tiny mouth, not where it wishes to be, refuses to open and speaks through its clenched teeth. "I want the eye while he is still alive," it says.

Jingles grants it one nibble before jerking back its wrist to observe for any activity. Joel's eyelids twitch. The creature chortles and its abdomen emits a gurgling noise as if eager to participate.

Jingles is running out of time to harvest Joel's memories, and it gets to work without wasting another moment. With a wild grunt, it uses the pavement to bash open his skull. Then, after picking away his hair and bone fragments, it uses its nails to dissect the two desired sections from his semi-conscious brain. While it places the bits in their new metal home, it savors the aroma of fear emanating from the fresh tissue.

With a satisfying click, Jingles seals the lid of the bell and adds it to the growing collection in the satchel. Then, seizing one of Joel's legs, the creature drags the man's dying corpse deep into the woods for its companions to devour.

Without the intention of doing so, the patriarch has protected his family. Though his ending was not consensual, his sacrifice gives the remaining Smiths more time.

As they pretend to play a game of adventure, laughing and singing merry tunes, the close configuration of giant fir and pine trees behind them shields their ears from the brutality of Joel's dying screams.

Hannah looks ahead and notices the pattern of trees getting sparse. There is something in the distance; it appears to be civilization. The eldest daughter smiles and points. "Look! Mommy, it's Christmas lights!" she says.

Caroline stares in disbelief. Even though she knows she should shout to signal her husband of their discovery, something in her gut tells her to keep her composure. A grin forms on her lips as she gently squeezes her children's hands, realizing that this is their moment, not his. "You are right, sweety! Such a keen eye! It looks like we are almost there," she says. They all release a sigh of relief.

Overcome with happiness, Caroline's eyes fill with tears. "It's a miracle," she says.

Chapter Ten

ALWAYS WATCHING FROM ABOVE

Together, hand in hand, the remaining Smiths gallop through the last bit of forest toward the town like moths drawn to a flame. With the utmost ease, they dodge each obstacle, including tree stumps and debris.

As they arrive at the forest's edge, an overhang of branches decorated by lush green prickly pine needles shelters them from the gently falling snow.

Standing next to each other, they gaze in wonder at the picturesque village. Madelyn's eyes sparkle with excitement. "It's like the tiny town grandma used to display at Christmas," she says.

Her daughter's statement makes Caroline look closer at the intricate details of the quaint community. She is amazed. "Would you look at that," she says. The similarity stirs up feelings of nostalgia as she remembers her mother. "You are right, Madelyn. It looks identical. I know in my heart she is looking down upon us from Heaven right now," she says.

Madelyn immediately chimes in. "Amen," she says.

Caroline directs her attention towards the triumph of their discovery of Mittlerhaus to avoid becoming sentimental. As she takes a deep breath, the aroma of fir and juniper fills her senses and evokes memories of holiday gatherings.

Seeing her children's angelic faces brings Caroline an overwhelming sense of happiness as she watches them express their gratitude, silently bowing their heads to pray.

Even though Jacob stands beside them, looking at the same town, the small boy feels excluded and alone. The woman perished before he was born, so he never saw the miniature village or met the grandmother they spoke of. Like the others, he recognizes the buildings for a far different reason. His knees lock beneath him, paralyzed by fear as he recognizes the town that turned his dreams into nightmares, Green Hill.

Each string of lights and holiday decoration coincides with the vivid details of where he once called home. Seeing the resemblance sends him back to the worst night of his life, causing a chill down his spine and goosebumps on his arms. He desperately searches to find something dissimilar about the town but cannot. Even the bulbs on the flickering strands reflect an identical pattern to the flashes accompanying the creature's arrival in his dream world.

Jacob wants to warn everyone, but fear stifles his speech. Finally, opening his mouth, he stutters as tears stream from his eyes. "*Grün — Grün—Grüner Hügel,*" he says.

His attempt at German warms his mother's heart. "My little genius," she says. Thinking that her son has made a cute nickname for their ancestral home, she smiles to encourage him. "That's what we should call it from now on." Her eyes dart to her daughters. "Come on, girls, let's all say it together: *Grüner Hügel.*"

Madelyn and Hannah are quick to join in. "*Grüner Hügel! Grüner Hügel!*" they say. Even though his mother means well, the spectacle has the opposite effect on Jacob, worsening his brittle nerves. He refuses to participate as the others continue to chant and clap their hands. With each repetition of the name, the little boy's fists clench tighter at his sides. He tries to calm his panic by tuning them out but cannot escape it.

Finally, his gaze shifts toward them, and the stress causes him to crack. "Stop it. Please, stop," he says. Still singing the name, they cannot hear his meek voice over the happiness of their song.

He knows he must try again, so he frantically tugs on his mother's hand until he gets her attention. Recognizing he is upset, Caroline quiets the girls, then softens her voice to speak to him. "What's wrong, Jacob?" she asks.

The small boy thinks back to his father's encouragement to use their imagination and gathers his confidence to speak. His tiny body shakes as he pulls his mother closer. Then, keeping his voice down to a whisper, he says. "You are being too loud. It... it will hear you."

If his words are insufficient, she can tell by how her son's eyes dart around anxiously that something is wrong.

The two girls exchange glances and communicate amusement through silent smirks and eye-rolls.

His sisters regard Jacob as the weakest of the three, and they are proficient at hiding the severity of their bullying of him from their parents. As young women living under the roof of an obedient household, they would get whipped if caught preying on the youngest, especially the boy.

Jacob continues to sniffle loudly. Caroline wants to get to the root of his emotional reaction; to do that, she knows she must calm him down. So, playing along, she whispers, "Who, my sweet boy? Who will hear us?"

The mere thought of the creature's demonic face makes Jacob squirm. He is the only one aware of what is lurking and recognizes he must protect his mother. Fearful of summoning the beast, he tentatively surveys his surroundings before uttering its name. "Jingles. Its name is Jingles," he says.

Caroline leans toward him, wanting to know more. "Is it an imaginary friend?" she asks.

The idea of divulging more truths about the sinister being causes Jacob's voice to tremble. Overridden by the horrific memories of it infiltrating his dreams back in Utah, he shakes his head. "No, it's real. It's... it's the monster. The same one I told you about from my nightmares," he says.

Eavesdropping, his sisters catch the last part of the conversation and gasp sarcastically. Madelyn laughs. "That's silly. Monsters aren't real," she says.

Her accusation turns Jacob's face bright red. "They are too. I've seen one," he says.

As the two youngest children bicker, they are unaware that their argument is triggering Caroline's pregnancy-related nausea; she has yet to tell them another child is on the way. Her queasiness makes her impatient, and she gives them a stern glare. "Both of you, stop it," she says.

Thinking her mother is not looking, Madelyn continues her brattish behavior and sticks out her tongue. Caroline glimpses her from the corner of her eye and turns to scold her. "I mean it. Both of you!" she says. All three children freeze; they don't want to be in trouble.

As head of the household, Joel is solely responsible for implementing disciplinary actions for the children. Despite being inexperienced in holding authority, Caroline has quickly adjusted to the role. "Good. That is much better," she says.

Jacob is taken aback, not having seen this assertive side of his mother before. Caroline finds their obedience gratifying. Hiding her grin, she turns back to her son. "Jacob, do you think the monster could be somewhere around here?" she asks as she slowly scans each decorated building. He nods nervously. Not wanting to get in trouble again, Madelyn and Hannah look at one another, bulging their eyes while restraining their laughter.

Caroline continues to survey the festive village. She cannot imagine any horrible person living in a place where they love Christmas as much as her. Her view is that the amount of thought and care one puts into decorating reflects how they treat others.

Jacob's anxiety intensifies as she remains silent. To ease his nerves, Caroline smiles and gently squeezes his hand. "I understand your concerns and how scary seeing a monster must be. I know I would be just as frightened as you," she says.

Her words give him a sense of validation, prompting him to relax momentarily.

Caroline softens her tone and continues. "I fear that since our relatives have extended their hospitality and are expecting us, they may think we are rude if we don't show up. Don't you think we at least owe it to them to go give them a big Smith family hello?" she says. Jacob's body becomes rigid as if flash-frozen by fear.

The girls find his pronounced reaction amusing. Before he can answer, Caroline notices his apprehension and jumps in to redirect the situation. "I promise that if they try to do anything funny, upon your signal, we will all leave together, no questions asked," she says. Then, releasing her hand from his, she extends her pinky to solidify the promise.

A tree branch rustles behind them, startling Jacob. He quickly grasps her finger. Caroline smiles. "Good, then. It's settled," he says.

Regardless of his fear surrounding the town, it pales in comparison to seeing Tobias's mangled face at the airport, making his agreement more palatable. "What's the signal?" he asks.

Thrown off by his question, she swiftly thinks of something silly to lighten the mood. She spreads her fingers and places them on each side of her head. "In the spirit of Christmas, our signal will be reindeer antlers," she says.

Jacob's eyes widen over her fingers' moonlit rendition of horns. She appears as a radiant Devil to him, and he fervently nods to get her to stop. The girls remain quiet as they make faces at one another, snickering at their brother's anguish.

Caroline notices Jacob's serious demeanor and grins to lighten the mood. Then, clutching the children's hands, she confidently marches them forward to prevent additional fuss. The only thing on her mind is escaping the cold, and she picks up the pace.

The face of the town's clock, mounted in a spire atop the city hall, is barely visible as it strikes the hour. Its chime is a Christmas carol rather than the typical sound of bells. Madelyn's eyes light up; she is in awe.

They step out of the fir and pines at the forest's edge into a small meadow connecting to the cobblestone street. With the city hall in clear view, something odd about the clock catches Caroline's attention. As she glances at the time, the giant hands whirl wildly. "Either the clock needs repair, or they have some interesting customs here," she says. Laughing playfully, she does not give it a second thought.

The town is quiet, and she feels comfortable, despite the absence of people milling around. "Hannah, wait here and watch your siblings while I find whom to talk to about our accommodations," she says.

Hannah is annoyed at having to play babysitter and pouts. Caroline does not want to deal with her daughter throwing a tantrum and revises the plan. "As long as you stay together, you can explore. Just don't wander too far," she says.

Jacob nervously glances at the two girls, and they sneer back. The small boy lunges for his mother's hand. "Can't—can't I go with you?" he asks.

After thinking about it momentarily, she glances back at her daughters and shrugs. "Your brother is coming with me. You two stay out of trouble; we won't be long," she says. Her hand extends toward Jacob. "Come along now." Fearing being left behind, Jacob swiftly grabs onto her.

Jacob is happy not to be with them. He would much rather follow his mother than go exploring with the girls and be subjected to their bullying.

As they take their first step, Caroline turns back to give her daughters one last set of instructions, but they are gone. Jacob frantically scans the area to see where they went. "Shouldn't we find them?" he asks.

Caroline hears the girls' laughter, and even though she cannot see them, she can tell they are relatively close. "They will be just fine. We shouldn't be long," she says.

Jacob and Caroline walk together, hand in hand, down the main street until they arrive at the town hall. They hastily ascend the stairs to the building's front entrance.

Caroline's impatience gets the best of her, and she tries to pull open the large wooden double doors forcefully, but they do not budge. They are locked.

Frustrated, she turns around and leads Jacob down the main street lined with shops. As they walk along, they become distracted by the row of windows adorned with antiquated decorations. The heavy use of glistening tinsel in the displays perks up their spirits. "It is strange. Before you were born, your grandmother, my mother, had a small porcelain village that looked identical to this town that she would set up every year at Christmas," Caroline says.

As Caroline reminisces, Jacob investigates a storefronts plate-glass window. His attention is drawn to the reflection of his mother with a tear streaming down her cheek rather than the decorations on display. Afraid her son will see her upset, she shies away from her image. Jacob comforts her, tightening his grip around her hand. "Please don't cry, Mommy," he says.

His words surprise her. Typically, men in the congregation do not exhibit compassion towards women crying, so she knows he did not learn it from his father. She wipes the tear with her sleeve. "You know what my mother used to tell me when I would get upset?" she asks. Jacob nods for her to continue.

She had not thought about it in a while, and the memory of her made her smile.

With a subtle German inflection in her voice, she playfully shakes her finger. "Let no one tell you tears are for sadness; more often than not, tears are filled with joy. We are just blind to the positivity of the change accompanying them." She takes a scant breath, then continues. "Each drop is a blessing sent by the Angels in Heaven to remind us who we are and how far we have come."

Caroline has never opened up and shared that information with anyone else before, and releasing the memory feels like a weight has been lifted from her chest. "You know what's special about that?" she says. Giving his full attention, he listens closely. "Even though I never met her myself, she learned that from her mother, my grandmother, and now I am passing it down to you," she says. She gently kisses his forehead.

Her words spark his curiosity. "Mommy, why didn't you meet your grandma?" he asks.

Due to her limited knowledge of her grandmother, she found it challenging to provide a detailed answer. "My mother didn't enjoy discussing her past, so I never pried. It was not until I became an adult that I discovered her parents had passed away due to an illness when she was very young. That was how she ended up in our community—someone from our church adopted her while on their mission," she says.

Jacob's mind wanders to his sisters as his mother discusses their family history. Remembering that they are still off on their own, he scans the window's reflection for them. Caroline sees his look of concern, and it reminds her of something she wants to discuss with him. She knows her children are on their best behavior in front of her, but something she noticed in the earlier exchange between Jacob and the girls triggers her motherly instinct. "When I'm not watching, are your sisters mean to you?" she asks.

Jacob shrugs. "Sometimes, but they say it's okay because I'm the youngest," he says.

Caroline always knew Jacob differed from other children but kept it to herself. Her biggest fear was that he would be labeled, leading others to judge him unfairly. Since birth, she has been compensating for his delayed learning and social difficulties, even keeping them a secret from her husband, hoping they would improve. She could not tell if Joel did not notice or was in denial since anything less than perfect, especially where a son was concerned, would be considered a blight on his name.

The community considers differences unacceptable, and if they knew the secret, they would remove Jacob from home and enroll him in diversion treatment to make him 'normal.' It is the same program her parents protected her from. She knows not all kids have to fit into the same box, but those around her feel otherwise.

The prolonged silence worries Jacob that he has gotten his sisters in trouble. Caroline, reading his concern, kneels on the floor beside him. "Let me tell you a secret that helps me through difficult times: There are many bullies in this world. They come in all different shapes and sizes, and some are so sneaky you don't even notice they are being mean," she says. Reaching into her pocket, she pulls out the bell gifted to her by her husband. "Now, place yours next to mine."

After losing it once, the idea of not having his bell safely in his pocket makes Jacob nervous. "Why?" he asks.

She smiles, rolling hers back and forth in her palm. Unable to contain his anxiety any longer, Jacob blurts out, "We must keep them, or else the monster will get us." It's the rule."

Caroline's suspicion grows as she connects the dots. She believes the entity tormenting his imagination could directly result from his father's controlling personality and lack of empathy.

The past few days have opened her eyes to Joel's questionable character. This new insight prompts her to reflect on numerous interactions between Joel and Jacob that could be traumatic for a child. She understands Jacob better than her other children because of their similarities and knows that if she were in Jacob's position, Joel's parenting approach would be overwhelming. "You can trust me," she says.

Her calm demeanor and love envelop him in a reassuring warmth that makes him temporarily forget the bitter cold. Reaching into his pocket, he pulls out his bell. Fearful of what will happen when he releases it from his safekeeping, he closes his eyes and quickly places it beside hers.

Caroline thinks his concern over the bell is endearing. While Jacob nervously holds his breath, waiting for the world to collapse around him, he hears his mother giggle, and, realizing that he is still alive, he cracks a single eye to peek.

Caroline, spotting his distress, conceives an idea. "Come on, let's go. I have the plan—one that will get rid of the monster once and for all," she says. She takes him past the town square to the edge of the cobblestone street.

As they gaze at the meadow dusted with fallen snow, Jacob finds himself distracted; he worries about his sisters. Caroline notices his preoccupation and acts. She hurls her husband's gifted bells with all her might, fueled by her anger from years of oppression. As the wind takes away the two metal objects, she feels a sense of freedom.

The whistling noise of the bells traveling through the air causes Jacob to turn around swiftly. He notices her brushing off her hands; the bells are gone. Confused, he wants answers. "Where did they go?" he asks.

Noticing that he looks worried, Caroline conceals the truth. She pats the pocket of her dress. "They are in here, safe and cozy," she says. He breathes a sigh of relief and, feeling reassured, continues scanning the horizon for his sisters.

As snowflakes delicately fall from the sky, dusting the grass and pine needles, Caroline experiences a sense of rejuvenation. She grasps Jacob's hands, and they cheerfully whirl around in circles while heading toward the town square. The carefree moment shifts his attention to his mother; he has never seen this side of her before. Mid-spin, she glimpses the area where she had thrown the jingle bells, and the sight of them being concealed by the fresh snow delights her.

Jacob cannot stop beaming, swept up in her contagious joy. For the first time, she appears genuinely happy. As they dance across the path, it is as if each paver lights up beneath their feet, leading them back to where they started, in front of the city hall.

Caroline stops and looks up at the giant clock to check the time. "Well, would you look at that?" she says. "It looks like someone has gotten it working again."

The time is three thirty-three, and though the clock now runs with the ease of a Swiss watch, its face looks nothing like before. The hour and minute hands have been replaced, and the once-meticulously drawn black roman numerals are now crimson and smear as the unusual pointers tick around the dial.

Just as Jacob is about to focus on the timepiece's bizarre transformation, Caroline bends over to tickle him. She is oblivious, overlooking the clock's peculiar details and assuming the scarlet color is a festive holiday choice. "Who knows, maybe the color changed because of the magic of our dancing," she says with a chuckle.

Jacob giggles at the thought of having enchanted feet. Suddenly, Caroline's ankles throb and she realizes that all the walking and dancing has caused them to swell. It is an issue she has experienced with every pregnancy, and she knows she must sit and give them a rest. Her attention shifts to the concrete steps of the town hall behind them. They are inviting and—even more important to her—free of snow.

Above the steps is an overhang extending from the town hall's roof, shielding the shallow stairs from the weather. Draped along the perfect pleats of the awning's edge, a pine needle garland exudes the subtle warmth of holiday cheer. Within the prickles, strings of multicolored Christmas lights are tucked away next to glitter-adorned ribbons.

Caroline finds the beauty beguiling; she has only seen this kind of artistry in catalogs. Without wasting another moment, she guides her son to the steps, plunks herself down, and gently pats the ground beside her. "Trust me. We are safe here. Come, sit next to me and rest for a moment.," she says.

Jacob feels reassured by her words and obediently follows her direction. They exchange a smile, and then both giggles. Caroline removes her shoes and stretches the arches of her sore feet. The cold air brings relief to her swollen toes.

In her gut, she knows they could be there for a while. If her husband has handled their remaining travel plans like everything else, they will wait at least until the sun comes up.

Abruptly, Jacob stiffens, thinking he hears something in the distance. Noticing his rigid demeanor from the corner of her eye, Caroline turns to face him. "You can relax; there's nothing to worry about. Everything will be okay," she says. He fights his fearful urges by wiggling his body closer to hers.

A clamor blares from the clock above. The once-jolly Christmas carol, now flat and resonating an octave lower, resembles a funeral hymn rather than a cheerful melody. Suddenly, one by one, each bulb draped above them flickers in time with the unnerving melody's tempo. The chaos causes the small boy's heart to race.

A gentle wind travels down the main street, carrying young girls' laughter. Despite the voice's familiarity, rather than scanning for its origin, he eyes his mother to assess her reaction.

She is no longer at ease. Instead, she sits straight up; her hands shake as she fumbles to put her shoes back on her feet. Her gaze darts to check on her son. "This is sure a silly town," she says.

Jacob remains quiet and nervously nods. He has the confirmation he needs for the first time: like him, his mother sees and hears everything.

The wind's whistling grows louder, drowning out the girls' laughter.

Every surging buzz of electricity makes Caroline flinch as the pandemonium of the lights persists. She seizes Jacob's hand and pulls him to his feet. "All right, we should look around to see if we can find anyone. What do you say?" she asks. Jacob warily bobs his head.

While struggling to maintain concentration through the mayhem, they try each door down the main street, hoping to find at least one unlocked. Just as Caroline tugs on the last handle, the lights overhead stop their flickering, returning to normal, and the unnerving music from the clock ceases.

Something brushes against her skirt, causing a shiver to roll down her spine. She knows it is not her son; he is standing on her opposite side. Jacob stares at her for guidance as the tension pulsates through their clenched hands.

Out of nowhere, the pitter-patter of children's feet racing against the cobblestone resonates behind them.

Thinking it might be her daughters, Caroline spins around and sees three children running toward city hall. They are already halfway there, and her only view is of their backs, but she can confirm two identities from the clothing and stature—Hannah and Madelyn. The girls hold hands while playfully chasing the third child. The closer the pair comes to catching the adolescent, the more they laugh.

Something isn't right. Though the voices confirm Caroline's suspicions, their body movements seem uncharacteristic, almost mechanical. Jacob cannot take his eyes off the child in the lead as Caroline prepares to call the girls. He recognizes the coat as the one the little boy wore at the airport. "Tobias," he says.

Caroline stops dead in her tracks and her face drains of color. She looks at her son with confusion. "What—what did you say?" she asks.

Convinced he is in trouble, he frantically looks around. "Umm..." he says.

She returns her attention to observing the girls. "I didn't mean to startle you. It has been a while since I heard that name. On several occasions, my mother mentioned that she had an older brother named Tobias," she says.

The playful group darts to the right, skirting around the town hall, and continues to run further into the distance. Worried they are getting away, Caroline grabs Jacob's hand and sprints after them. "I told them not to go too far!" she shouts.

She drags her son behind her while yelling to get their attention. "Hannah! Madelyn! You two stop this instant!

I mean it!" she says. Jacob shudders; he knows precisely where they are going.

Ignoring her, they continue to run. The children's merriment grows louder as they move off the cobblestone into the snow-sprinkled meadow. Her daughters' unresponsiveness, paired with the frigid air, causes Caroline's face to turn red. "Girls, this is not a game!" she shouts between gasping breaths.

As Caroline drags Jacob's slight frame along, he trembles uncontrollably in response to the dropping temperature. Upon reaching the end of the cobblestone path, Caroline feels helpless as she watches the distance between her and her daughters grow. Her feet throb, and a sharp jab infiltrates her gut; she immediately doubles over to catch her breath.

Jacob watches in horror as his sisters get further away. Sensing his mother's despair, he attempts to help. "Hannah! Ma-Madelyn!" he calls.

Caroline gives her son's back a gentle pat to console him. "It's okay. This is what they call independence. I am sure they will come right back," she says. Then, in an attempt to break her worry, she tries to steer the conversation toward a more pleasant topic. "While we wait for them, why don't you tell me more about your friend Tobias?"

The mere mention of the name makes him flinch. Anxious, Jacob fidgets while he counts the cobblestones to distract himself while pondering the stories told to him in his dreams. "I don't know him. We never really met," he says.

Confused, she takes a moment before responding. "Oh? Then how do you know that is him?" she asks.

Her question provokes his memory from the airport, and he skips to the end of the story. "He died," he says.

His statement takes Caroline aback. "Oh my," she says. Then, reminding herself that they are talking about his imaginary world, she regains her composure so as not to overreact. "That is so tragic." Slowly, she softens her tone to dig deeper. "What happened to him?"

Jacob does not know the answer and swiftly disengages himself from the conversation by examining the nearby woods. "They told me he went in there to play and never came back," he says.

Caroline follows his gaze. "You mean those woods? The same one your sisters were running toward?" she asks. He nods.

Having raised her children in a community with no perceived crime, she has never worried about their safety. However, his vagueness causes her mind to race. Even though she knows the narrative stems from her son's imaginings, she does not understand how he could have crafted such a morbid story without context. She fights back her concern to ask further about the young boy. "Did they ever find out what happened to him?"

Jacob scans the horizon. "No," he says. Seeing his sister's silhouettes in the distance and realizing they have yet to enter the clusters of trees relieves him.

Jacob's uncertainty makes Caroline ponder. "Huh," she says.

Clutching tightly onto her hand, he shifts his eyes to lock on hers; his pupils widen. "Can I tell you a secret?" he asks. Even though she is uncertain where the conversation is headed, she nods. That is all the confirmation he needs, and desperate to get the information off his chest, he quickly whispers, "I know what happened. The monster got him."

The outlandish turn in her son's narrative reminds Caroline that she is listening to his fantasy, nothing more. "Your secret is safe with me," she says. Jacob feels a weight lifted off his shoulders. She looks back at the girls playing with the child and feels good that they have already made friends with what she assumes could be one of their cousins.

The town's lights flare before returning to normal. Caroline shifts her weight onto her aching feet and tightly grips her son's hand. "Rather than standing here, what do you say we go back to those steps to sit and wait for them to finish playing?" she says.

Before Jacob can answer, his mother is already dragging him toward the city hall. He looks over his shoulder and finds that his sisters have vanished. With urgency, he tugs Caroline's hand to make her stop. "Mommy, Hannah, and Madelyn are gone," he says.

Lack of sleep has left Caroline exhausted and with no patience. "What do you mean they are gone? I just saw them a minute ago," she says. She turns to look. Jacob is right. The three children have gone missing from the snowy meadow, leaving nothing but the shadows of the trees.

Jacob's breathing and heartbeat quicken. Caroline remains calm, convinced they have shifted play spots. She returns to the cobblestone's edge for a closer view. "I am sure the darkness is playing tricks on our eyes," she says.

But the small boy knows something far worse than the darkness is at play.

As she scans the trees, Caroline passes over where the children have been playing, and a sick feeling fills her gut. Frantically, her eyes scan the terrain. Each of her heartbeats wrenches at the veins that feed the pounding muscle in her chest wall.

What appears to be a child's jacket hangs from a single prickly branch of a giant pine tree, its arms flapping in the wind. Caroline gasps. Straining her eyes, she tries to analyze the style and color but cannot due to the darkness and distance. While clutching her son's hand, she keeps the discovery to herself, hiding her concern by lessening the emotion in her voice. "I am sure they will turn up," she says.

Jacob knows things are not okay, despite his mother's reassurance.

A piercing scream echoes through the cobblestone street, filling the frigid air with chaos and jarring the building's windows. It shudders Caroline's spine, prompting her to tighten her grip on Jacob's hand. Deep in her gut, she knows it is her daughter's cry, and the thought makes her nauseous. Suddenly, the temperature drops ten degrees, draining the pink from Jacob's cheeks.

Caroline cannot identify where the sound is coming from. Her heart pounds as she scans the area, searching for any sign of her daughters. As she glances toward the meadow, she sees the waving jacket again. A tall figure with distorted limbs is crouching, perched above it on the tree branch. On its head sits a hat reminiscent of Santa Claus.

Jacob catches sight of the shape before she can make sense of it; his eyes bulge in terror. "It's here," he says. Abruptly, the strands of Christmas lights renew their pulsation behind them.

Caroline trembles at the thought of the outlandish stories living in her son's imagination coming to life. Not wanting to believe it, she leans closer to get a better look. The shadowy figure copies her movement, leaning forward.

Jacob worries about his mother being too scared to move, so he tugs her arm to get her attention. "We have to go, or it will eat us," he says.

She emits a gurgle in reply, incapable of forming a single word.

Chapter Eleven

WHEN THE CLOCK TICKS

The vivid imagery of Jingles's victims plays through Jacob's mind. Consumed by paranoia, his unease builds like a ticking time bomb, ready to explode. Everything in him tells him to run and though he fears being next, he cannot leave his mother behind. His panic heightens, and he whimpers as he visualizes his ghastly fate of being devoured alive.

The sound of his desperation creates conflict in Caroline, sparking her mind and pulling her from her daze. Knowing she must protect her child, her maternal instincts kick in.

A rush of adrenaline sweeps through her body, giving her the strength to move. Jacob is reluctant to look away. Without warning, she grabs his hand and bursts into a dead sprint. Given that the forest is not a viable hiding spot, they rush toward the only alternative: the town square.

As the duo flees, the creature halts briefly before giving chase, allowing them a head start to prolong the hunt. Then with glee, it unhinges its elbow and swings its arm back and forth like a pendulum. "Tick, tock, tick, tock, said the clock. Each minute that passes, your fear I shall stalk," it says.

It surveys the hypnotic motion of its arm before releasing a grim sneer, its slithering tongue clicking against the roof of its mouth. "The luxury of time does not exist in a world overrun with material trysts," it says. Pondering, it continues, "Let's see what it will be; the choice is hers. Will she hide or flee? Will she yield to the terror I have in store? Or will she be like the others—a complete bore?"

The mother and son dash onto the village's main street.

The sound of teeth clacking and lips smacking echoes from the faces on the beast's body. "We hear their scurrying feet running through the cobblestone street. Let us sneak up, gouge out their eyes, and eat the delectable treats. Only if blind can they see the world as they wish it to be." They say.

Every word fuels the creature's hunger. "I am afraid it is time's up, my friends; this is the moment your lives shall end," it says as it dismounts from the tree. As its boots pound to the ground, the bag of bells callously tinkles, releasing a surge of static that pervades the air.

The energy of the underworld fills its limbs, inciting it to dance. "No one will ever take my throne. I am the king of this malignant home," it says.

The creatures' conjoined companions, large and small, sing along with the rattling chimes of the matter-filled bells. "Jingles, Jingles, Jingles. That is its name. Get ready to embark on its glorious game; soon, like us, you will scream the same," they say.

The wind strengthens as they chant, clearing the snow from the pavers. Static energy fills the frigid air, charging every electrical strand, resulting in bursts of bright, blinding light. With the sudden surge of power, the sockets blaze to life, and the filaments housed within the tinted glass coverings explode into sparks and jagged fragments. Caroline winces at each flash and crackle, knowing the aftermath will leave them in darkness.

She leaps into action with lightning speed, shielding her son's body from the dangerous splinters of glass that rain down like perilous glitter. Jacob feels a sharp poke near his eye, and he flinches. "Keep your head down," she says. The sternness of her voice coaxes him to listen. As the shattered bulbs rain like a hailstorm coating the cobblestones, the glowing face of the giant clock reflects off them.

Caroline holds a firm conviction that sunrise will provide the answer to her family's predicament. She peers downward to avoid tripping over scattered objects while heading toward the clock to check the remaining time. At that instant, she observes the clock's clear image mirrored on the glass shards.

The pieces fit together like a puzzle and read three thirty-three—the same time as when they first glanced at the clock from the forest's edge.

Caroline fights her panic. She knows she witnessed the hands move only moments before. The idea of time standing still takes away her last bit of security. Her mind becomes frantic as she feels her backup plan ripped from her grasp. She shakes her head to convince herself otherwise. "That's not possible. If we are moving, that means time *must* also be moving," she says. While they carefully navigate around the glass, her mind races with self-doubt and uncertainty.

Meanwhile, Jacob keeps a watchful eye as they pass the last brick structures while nervously peering through the shadows to check the surroundings for the creature.

Everything about the town's quaint appearance has shifted; the buildings' edges look sharper, and their darkened outlines make the doors and windows seem more cynical. Rather than inviting, the change in tone heckles them, screaming for them to leave. Nothing appears jolly anymore.

Glass crackles beneath their feet, and the grating noise causes Caroline to flinch with each step. They continue to run forward, keeping their heads down to avoid falling shards.

The sound of bulb fragments tumbling to the hard stone slowly dissipates around them, and Caroline decides it is safe to scan the area and orient herself to their location. She lowers her hand, which is shielding her eyes.

A sliver of glass hidden in her hair catches on the exposed skin of her wrist. "Ow!" she says. The pain causes her adrenaline to spike, and her pounding heart draws her attention from the sting. Blood slowly drips from the cut and runs under her sleeve. Despite her attempt to inspect it, the absence of light renders it futile. Besides, she cannot afford to waste any more time.

Navigating the remaining distance in pitch-black darkness, they rely on the faint glow of the clock and its reflection off the jagged debris to guide them safely back to the town hall. They pause briefly in front of the building to catch their breath and assess their surroundings.

Caroline winces as she lifts each foot to relieve the pain in her arches. The longer she remains stationary, the more her shoes exacerbate the pain in her swollen feet.

Their placement in the town square throws Jacob into a trauma-provoked stupor; it is the exact starting place of his horrific nightmare. His thoughts are in such conflict that he questions his wakefulness. "Maybe I am asleep, and this is a bad dream," he says. While his whisper lingers, he closes his eyes and digs his fingernails into his palm to test his reality. He experiences pain, but it is not enough to persuade him whether the experience is a reality or a dream.

Amid her son's mental turmoil, Caroline uses whatever reflective light is available to inspect their surroundings swiftly. She feels her determination slowing down as the agitation of her aching feet worsens, and her focus blurs. Knowing she must stay positive, she concentrates on the town hall to divert her attention from the pain.

The clock's illumination flickers above them. Caroline takes its glimmer as a sign and, answering its call, looks to the giant clock for a clue. It has stayed the same; it reads three thirty-three, the same time as before.

Her eyes anxiously twitch. Rather than comforting her, she feels mocked by the sight of the frozen time. Amid her frenzy, she notices a subtle detail she had previously overlooked: the red accents are much brighter than she remembered and contrast strikingly against the off-white background.

She takes a moment to listen. The eerie melody that chimed from the clock earlier has been replaced by muffled sounds reminiscent of human suffering.

At once, the disquieting change intensifies her worry, compelling her to take a closer look at the stark crimson decorations on the clock's face. It reminds her of when she cut her finger while cooking, and the memory sends a prickling down her spine. Her curiosity intensifies as she cautiously moves closer to see what else has changed. Jacob, still questioning whether he is dreaming or awake, submissively follows her.

The beast creeps through the night, timing each of its steps with theirs, concealing its approach. As a result, neither one hears the pair of heavy boots, which sound like the clop of hooves slowly prowling toward them.

The loud crackling of glass crushing underneath their shoes pulls Jacob back to reality as his mother leads him to the town hall steps. Hyper-focused on the environment's hostility, every slight noise makes him jump. Terrified, his eyes dart to each dark shadow, and he moves near his mother's skirt, burying his head in its fabric to hide.

Standing in clear view of the spire, Caroline grasps the horror hiding within the clock's face. The intense backlit glow meant to illuminate the silhouette of analog hands shines through the dripping patterns on the glass. Like a blood smear on the slide of a microscopic experiment, it highlights the scarlet gore, leaving no room for the imagination. She can no longer hide behind the naivety of thinking the substance is red paint used to decorate for the holidays. With the disappearance of her innocent perspective, a small part of her dies.

Caroline now sees the truth with unsheltered eyes—undoubtedly, it is blood. The thought makes her sick. Trying to manage her nausea, she pinpoints her attention on the clock's motionless second hand, but it offers no relief.

Something about its form has an air of familiarity.

Caroline strains to focus through the gore-stained glass surface. As she squints, her heart sinks as she realizes that a child's figure makes up the dial. Despite the desire to turn away, she forces herself to look closer.

The abnormal positioning of the body makes it nearly impossible to determine the child's identity.

Caroline is traumatized by the discovery, and the possibility of it being one of her girls terrifies her. As her mind spirals, she remembers the third child with them, making her selfishly optimistic.

While muttering a plea for the safety of her daughters, she fights to keep her emotions in check as she looks for any hint of the figure's identity. She instantly regrets her decision upon seeing birch sticks piercing the child through its torso, skewering it in place, and immobilizing everything below the waistline. It lies on its side, slightly bent at the hips, arms outstretched on either side of the bowed head, each limb pointing to different components of time–seconds and hours. The appendage representing the hour's hand rests on the three. The one allocating the seconds is closest to Caroline and in a position that makes it impossible to identify the child's face. Covering the child's lower half is a heavy pair of gray leggings and white sneakers tainted with blood. The feet are securely bound by thin strips of birch bark at the ankles and artfully positioned as a minute hand, securely fixed on thirty-three.

Everything around her moves in slow motion, allowing her to take in every detail of the child's slight frame and disheveled hair. "No. Please, God, do not let it be my child," she says.

Despite her attempts to remain optimistic, tears stream down her face. Caroline has reached her breaking point and is consumed by her terrifying reality. Her intestines violently churn in her belly. She whispers, trying to deny what she sees, praying the gruesome image will vanish. "Hannah?" She asks. Hearing her daughter's name exit her lips causes her knees to buckle.

Caroline notices a slight quiver on the clock's facing and is sure it stems from the child's movement. She calls out a little louder. "Hannah?" She asks. Convinced that she sees her daughter responding to her name, her body tenses up with anticipation. Her speech picks up pace as the emotional rollercoaster becomes too much to bear. "She—is she still alive? My baby is still alive!"

When Jacob hears his mother repeating his sister's name, he peeks out from his crinoline hiding place. His eyes light up with excitement at the thought of Hannah being okay. Confusion sets in as he scans the area but does not see her. "Where, Mommy? Where is she?" he asks.

Caroline is conflicted about whether to share her frightening discovery. Then, stumbling over her words, she points her trembling finger at the clock. "There—she's—she's in there," she says.

The little boy, eager for the reunion, stares up hopefully, and his happiness instantly transforms into horror.

Hannah's upper body shudders with another spasm. Her motion causes Caroline to become frenzied. "We—we must go get her," she says. After quickly surveying the town hall, she concludes that the entrance to the clock tower must be within the building.

Jacob cannot take his eyes off the little girl's mangled body. "Mommy, she's—she's..." he says. But, no matter how hard he tries, he does not have the heart to tell his mother that his sister is dead.

In a rush to save Hannah, Caroline pulls him toward the steps. "We cannot leave her like that. You watched her move. I saw it with my own eyes. She is still alive. I know she is. We will get her down, and she will be good as new. You will see," she says. As she nears the entrance, her hysterics become more vehement, leaving the collar of her dress drenched with tears. "Hannah, don't worry. Mommy's coming."

She yanks with all her might on the front door handle, desperately hoping it will open. But no matter how hard she pulls, it remains locked.

Jacob worries that the spectacle is drawing unwanted attention. Despite his distress, he tries to remain calm and not worsen the situation. Unlike his mother, he had seen no sign of life in his sister; to him, she is now another victim of the beast.

Caroline, unsuccessful in her attempts to gain entry, tries to devise an alternate plan. Pulling her son's hand, she returns to their original spot to check the clock and see if her daughter has moved.

As they enter the clock's illumination, Jacob's attention shifts to the cut on his mother's wrist. "Mommy, you are bleeding," he says. His eyes fill with tears at the thought of losing her from his life.

The concern in her son's voice causes Caroline to pause. Following his gaze, she sees the minor wound on her wrist and chuckles nervously. "I'm fine. Nothing to worry about; mommies are made of steel," she says. Then, using the cuff of her coat, she wipes away the streak of blood. "See? It's all better."

Caroline shows Jacob her wound, causing him to brush away his tears. A faint ticking interrupts him as he attempts to relax with slow, calming breaths. As the clock gradually gains life, the eerie clicks grow louder.

An unsettling tune fills the air as the cogs rotate, causing them to step back to view the scene. The clock's backlighting slowly transitions to a menacing red, emphasizing the scene's grisly nature. The details tell a story, not just of the child's fight, but of the intent of the thing she had been up against—it had no plans of letting her survive. Each of the deep wounds reflects a hateful vengeance.

The sinister illumination helps cement the truth. Despite the obviousness of her daughter's fate, the dramatic depiction finally forces her to confront the reality of her loss. No matter what she does, she cannot save her. Jacob's first conclusion was correct - Hannah was never alive in the clock tower. The gears shifting beneath the corpse caused the illusion of her earlier spasms.

As the clock's workings pick up speed, her right arm responds with a slight movement, taking on the role of the second hand. Jacob tugs on his mother to bring it to her attention, but the spectacle already entrances her.

Every tick unveils additional parts of the child's face. A cluster of long matted hair clings to a piece of her severed scalp. The strands that were once blond dangle from her forehead, partially covering her fixed and open gaze, composed of milky gray lenses.

Caroline does not recognize her little girl. The extensive disfigurement makes it nearly impossible to distinguish a single feature, and even though the figure wears her child's clothes, it feels like she is staring at a stranger. The disheartening sight causes her nausea to worsen. Fighting it, her body trembles, and closing her eyes, she whispers a final prayer. "Peace, I leave with you; my peace I give to you. Not as the world gives, do I give to you. Let not your hearts be troubled, neither let them be afraid," she says.

The ticking hand picks up speed. The child's arm moves under her chin, exposing the corners of her upturned mouth, forming a cynical smile etched deep into her skin. Jacob recognizes the expression; it is a bigger version of the same grin she had used when picking on him. Even though the horrid expression haunts him, he feels captivated and cannot look away. It triggers his guilt. Although he is not to blame, he worries that revealing his sister's cruelty to his mother has led to her death.

Holding one another's hand, they watch silently as the arm moves faster. It continues to pick up speed, unnaturally contorting past its point of flexibility. Then, releasing a muffled snap, it breaks away from the shoulder socket.

Horrified, Caroline clutches Jacob's hand tightly before enveloping him in a warm embrace. His emotions overwhelm him as he hugs her, causing a lump in his throat.

Glass grinding on the cobblestone beneath a heavy boot consumes the air. Still holding onto one another, they gasp in unison. Caroline, already facing the source of the sound, clenches her child to her chest as she strains her eyes to see through the darkness.

A sulfuric stench fills the square. As it wafts into Caroline's nostrils, it stings her sinuses. Jacob does not have to look to know what it is, and his body shakes uncontrollably. Squeezing onto his mother tighter, he whispers a warning. "It's here," he says. "It's... it's Jingles."

Upon hearing its name, the creature lets out a sinister chuckle and inhales deeply, relishing the scent of fear that permeates the air. It shakes its satchel and grimaces as each memory-filled tissue rattles, producing a malevolent jingle.

Caroline's body stiffens, and her eyes scan the area surrounding their feet. Worried that the slightest bit of noise will draw attention to them, she gently grabs her son's shoulders and stoops to look him in the eyes. Despite her lack of encounters with the beast, she knows staying silent is crucial for their survival. She places her finger to her lips to signal Jacob to remain quiet. Shivering, he clenches his jaw to silence his chattering teeth.

Caroline glances down the street, observing the broken glass on the ground. Each piece dimly reflects the clock's red illumination, causing a fragmented sheen. To her, the glints have no beauty - they look like little alarms. The monster will identify their whereabouts if they misstep, resulting in disastrous consequences. She must eliminate as much risk as possible and recognizes that one set of footsteps is better than two.

Even though she is exhausted, she does what she must to increase their chance of survival. Without hesitancy, she wedges her hands underneath the child's armpits and hoists him onto her hip. Then, steadying his weight, she lightly drags her toe over the cobblestone while listening intently. Upon confirming the absence of any glass scratching beneath her foot, she cautiously takes her first step.

A heavy footstep crushes glass in the distance; the beast is getting closer.

Jacob cowers his head into the nape of his mother's neck to hide. The building pressure of the situation causes sweat to drip from Caroline's hairline. She struggles to stabilize her breathing while fighting the terror running through her veins. Knowing they must keep moving to survive, she forces her shaking foot to brush the area before them. Again, she listens for any scratches against the cobblestone and, hearing none, takes another step.

As the creature inches closer, it craves a reaction. With intent, it pulverizes the glass under its boot toe. The smell of their fear makes it ravenous with hunger. "Come out, come out, wherever you are. You can try to escape, but you will not get far," it says. The beast's voice booms through the deserted street.

With a cackle, it claps its hands to the beat of the ticking clock. "There were five. All wished to thrive. Then, there were four; he was a bore. After that, there were three. I displayed her for all to see with a hammer's wrap and a *tap, tap, tap*." With its spindly hands, it clenches its fist, pretending to hammer the air.

Its accompanying faces mimic the creature. "Tap, tap, tap," they say.

Each horrific word reminds Caroline of the birch branches impaling her daughter's mangled body. As she fights back her tears, she notices something in its riddled words: the creature has only mentioned one male and one female, which must be Joel and Hannah. That means Madelyn must still be alive. With a rush of purpose, she places her foot down to take another step. Jacob's weight strains her arms.

A familiar giggle replaces the ticking sound as the clock's second hand completes its lap. It sounds like Hannah.

Caught off-guard and confused, Caroline stops to look.

The beast lifts a finger as if conducting an orchestra, and the little girl's expression behind the glass wall shifts. Then, reaching into its satchel, Jingles snatches the bell housing her harvested memories. With a grin, it places the sphere on the end of its serpent tongue, encircling it like a python before sliding the bell into its mouth. The child's last moments resonate from the object, permeating the air through its porous skin.

Caroline cannot tear her gaze away from the anguish on the young girl's face as she hears her desperate pleas for survival replayed. Frozen in place, she feels trapped in a personal hell as her child's distressed cries make her want to vomit.

The sound becomes too much for Jacob, and he clutches his ears, causing him to shift his weight. Caroline is too exhausted and distressed to reposition him on her hip, and her trembling arms cannot handle the sudden movement. He begins to slip.

Hannah's cries grow louder. "No. Please leave me alone. Please, I want my Mommy. Don't hurt me," she says. The noise plays through the creature's pores and seems to project from the clock.

Every shriek adds to Caroline's torment. Knowing that her daughter had cried for her suffocates her with guilt; it is worse than trying to save her and failing. She struggles for breath as she battles her sorrow, and her trembling arms give way, letting the young boy fall.

Disorientation grips Jacob as he lands on the cobblestone. His ears are still covered, and his eyes are tightly shut. His feet scramble beneath him, crushing glass with each frantic step.

Hannah's screams cease.

Instantly, Caroline's eyes widen with fear, and cramps form deep in her side. Her entire body trembles as she looks at her son. But unfortunately, it is already too late.

Jacob does not know what to do. The sight of the creature's outline in the distance leaves him paralyzed.

As the creature spits the bell back into its hand, its smile bends unnaturally; it knows where they are. "Peekaboo. I am ready to eat you," it says. It carefully places the bell back into its satchel and intently listens.

The beast's comrades hiss with laughter. "Eat, eat, eat," they say.

Caroline tightly grips her child's hand as she witnesses the beast's emergence from behind the clock before it slips back into the shadows. It is far worse than she had imagined.

Now convinced that her son's stories are true and that he has already been to this place, she is certain he is their best chance for survival. Caroline has no choice but to trust his memories to lead them through the darkness to safety.

"I want you to show Mommy where you hid from the monster in your dreams," she says. Jacob hesitates momentarily but then quickly nods to show his agreement.

Caroline releases his hand and points into the distance. "Now go. I will be right behind you," she says, each of her words quicker than the last. He remains still, causing her anxiety to intensify. With shallow breaths, she fights back the unrelenting pain to whisper in her son's ear. "Run," she says. Obediently, the little boy takes off at a dead sprint down the main street, his chosen route echoing the sound of cleared cobblestones. He does not look back.

Caroline holds her side as the pain migrates to her lower abdomen. She realizes that a distraction is necessary for her to escape. Gritting her teeth, she stoops down and takes off her shoes, hurling them in the opposite direction of Jacob's escape.

The creature's head snaps around to follow the clip-clop of the kitten heels as they bounce across the stone street, stopping near the meadow's edge. Its fingers tap together playfully, feeding off the building anticipation. "Let's see, my friends... which will it be? Have they been naughty or nice? Will they flee or plea? Hmm, which will it be? " It says. It crouches down gradually to all fours, and its mouth seethes with froth, leaving traces of foaming saliva that create a bubbling red puddle on the ground.

Jingles' associates emit an assortment of growls. "Naughty, naughty, naughty," they say. The chanting creates a tingling sensation throughout the creature's body, culminating in a twitching sneer as it prepares to hunt. The beast's pinpoint pupils lock onto where the heels have landed. It shakes its satchel back and forth, causing the metal balls to clank in the pouch like the bells of a sleigh ride.

Overwhelmed with crazed excitement, it sings, its melody mimicking the tone of a raven's cry. "Dashing through the snow, in a one-horse open sleigh, O'er the fields we go, laughing all the way." Then, at the height of the bells' chaos, it grips the cold stones on all fours, propelling its way forward like a bear toward the shoe's location. "Ho, ho, ho, look at me go!" It says. Shards of glass crunch under its palms' leathery skin while the ball of human hair bounces at the tip of its hat. The faces cackle.

Caroline's trembling body triggers her muscles to tense, worsening the pain in her stomach, and she digs her fingers into the ache to make it stop.

She tries to identify where the creature is in the dark, relying only on the sound of its movement to confirm its location and ensure her disruption is successful.

As the beast barrels across the glass and cobblestone toward the meadow, it snorts and pants like a wild animal. The monstrous sounds provide Caroline the confirmation she needs, and not aspiring to be its next victim, she stares in the direction of her son's escape and runs.

Chapter Twelve

I HEAR THE BELLS

Caroline attempts to ignore the unsettling noises of the being behind her while chasing the sound of Jacob's footsteps in the darkness. As she nears the end of the storefronts, she slows down her pace.

A childlike figure darts across Caroline's path, startling her and stopping her dead in her tracks. It is so quick and unexpected that she does not have time to get a clear view. "Jacob?" she asks.

The youngster continues running, disregarding her. When it reaches the edge of the street, the clock's glow momentarily illuminates it, but not enough for her to be sure of the identity.

It playfully darts back toward her, tauntingly zigzagging across her path multiple times before running away in the opposite direction.

She recognizes the child. It is the small boy who had been with her daughters earlier. But, unfortunately, by the time she makes the connection, it is too late. He has already disappeared behind the edge of the last storefront.

Caroline's mind races as she wonders whether he may know of Madelyn's whereabouts. Her confusion causes her to waver, and she is torn between following him and holding back. Suddenly she lets her impulsivity lead, and, fixated on what she will ask him; she becomes complacent about her surroundings and steps on a large sliver of glass. The wind had carried it further than the other fragments scattered across the street.

As the jagged edge lodges in her foot, the sudden pain causes her to gasp. She pinches the skin of her arm to stop herself from crying out.

A burst of wind flutters across her cheek, temporarily distracting her. It carries a child's laughter, and she pinpoints the sounds' direction to the edge of the last building. Caroline attempts to move toward it but is stopped by the agony encountered on her first step. She knows what she must do. Taking a deep breath, she pinches the glass between her finger and thumb and hesitantly pulls it from her foot. After tossing the bloody fragment aside, she returns to listening for any sign of Jacob's movement.

Instead of her son's footsteps, a child's giggle fills the air in front of her. It grabs her attention, and feeling drawn to it; she limps closer.

The little boy's puffy blue jacket peeks out from the corner of the brick building, then disappears. Caroline's mind fills with guilt as the fleeting glance at the material evokes memories of Madelyn. Wanting answers, she swiftly weighs her options while staring toward the town hall.

The creature has discovered the empty shoes; now, in a frenzy, it combs the area surrounding the building, looking for them. "Come out, come out, naughty ones," it says. With each step, it takes in whiffs of its surroundings. "I swear I will not bite. I am just having some fun. I am not angry that you deceived me once or twice, but you will rue the day if it happens thrice."

The sound of the jingling bells raises Caroline's anxiety. Not knowing if she can live with the guilt of losing another child, she discards thoughts of her well-being and, pressing through her pain, limps toward the area where the small boy is hiding.

The wind funnels inward from the surrounding trees, clearing the street of debris as it sweeps its way through town. The gales become stronger, pushing heavily against Caroline's chest, weighing down each step as if she is swimming upstream.

As the beast's emotions intensify, the weather storms, causing sleet to pour from the sky. Caroline's clothes become saturated as she reaches the building's edge.

Abruptly, the temperature plummets, triggering the sleet to transition to snow and her clothes to freeze to her skin. Her entire body shakes, and her lack of shoes causes the warmth to flee through her feet.

Once again, Caroline hears the giggling of a child, and this time it is louder. As she approaches the building's edge, she ignores the sight of her discolored toes while turning the corner to look for the child.

Moonlight breaks through the clouds, creating an orange hue that reflects off the puffy surface of a child's coat. The small boy sits on the ground, his upper body hunched over his knees as he hides in a nook, shielding himself from the weather.

The wind's howl fades to a whistle.

Preparing herself for whatever may come, Caroline inhales deeply as she limps toward the boy. She notices the

shallow movements of his ribcage and his muted whimpers; he is crying. Even though she wishes to paint him a
villain, her love for children far outweighs her common
sense.

Based on his stature, Caroline can tell that he must be
around her son's age. No matter how much she wants to
stay angry, she can only picture Jacob being in his position,
alone and afraid.

Then, remembering her son mentioning his name earlier, she whispers. "Tobias? That is your name, right?" The
boy does not answer and continues to cry. Concerned that
he has no one to comfort him, she inquires further. "Are
you okay?" she asks. Her eyes scan the area as she fights her
weakness. "Is your mother somewhere nearby?"

The child remains silent, avoiding eye contact and
shrugging his shoulders. Without warning, the air becomes sharply colder, and the unexpected shift causes Caroline to feel unsteady. As the world spins around her, she
places her hand on the brick for stability. She carefully
eases herself to the ground, firmly shutting her eyes to
regain her composure.

The wind wails as it floods between the buildings,
drowning out the child's cries. Caroline's eyes spring open,
and as she glances beside her for the child, she finds he
has vanished. The odd encounter startles her. Quickly, she
looks from left to right, feeling like she has seen a ghost.
"Tobias?" she asks.

No one answers; she is alone.

As she scans where he had been seated, a shiny object
catches her eye—a metal bell peeking out from the snow.
She looks at it with confusion, her teeth chattering from

the bitter cold. Convinced that someone is trying to torment her, she grits her molars to stop their clacking and leans closer to get a better look.

Something about its silver luster is magnetic to her. As the moon reflects off the object, creating a shine, it reveals an idiosyncrasy. Unlike the others, it is crammed full, and she cannot resist the urge to touch the strange material protruding from its crevices. Caroline stretches her hand toward the item, and the nearer her fingertip gets, the more she is compelled to unite with it.

In a wave, a gust of wind howls from above; each screech beckoning for the snow-driven flurry to return. As flakes of ice pelt Caroline's pink cheeks, she finds an odd comfort in the bell; the cold metal pressed against her fingertip makes her giddy. But the euphoric bliss is short-lived, and the longer she touches it, the more her reality blurs, and with a single whistling chime, the object transports her into a state of hell.

Though she is stuck inside an unfamiliar room with no open windows, her skin still feels the harsh elements of the winter climate outside. Unable to speak, she sits at a rustic wooden table, only able to observe the scene as a woman with red hair cut into a perfect bob paces the room, panting heavily. She is clearly distressed. With each sharp turn, her Christmas apron twirls in unison with the circular skirt of her green dress, revealing layers of crinoline and frilly accents of eyelet lace. Her fingers frantically wipe underneath her puffy eyes, smearing the makeup that runs down her cheeks.

Caroline does not recognize the setting, but there is something familiar—she has seen the woman before. She combs her mind, wondering where she knows her from, but cannot place her face.

Her feet fidget, and oddly, no matter how much she stretches, she cannot feel the floor beneath them. As she gazes down to inspect the problem, she discovers that her fully grown legs have been substituted with considerably smaller ones. Caroline's mouth opens to call for help, but nothing emerges, leaving her distressed and helpless.

Seated at the table is a man who appears agitated. When he hears a babble, he looks toward Caroline but does not acknowledge her presence, instead; he seems to stare directly through her. Despite her inability to feel it, she is conscious of the child's gurgling, which has captivated his focus as they share the same seat. Suddenly, terror overwhelms her as she realizes she has been transported to the past and is now witnessing a moment from her mother's childhood.

The man nervously twists the wedding band on his finger and attempts to straighten his discombobulated suit, which matches the woman's outfit. He flinches with each thud of her pacing footsteps. "Ada, sit down. You are going to upset the baby," he says.

Their lack of sleep is apparent; it wears heavily on their faces. It is clear from the woman's wild eyes and frenzied expression that she is not paying attention to anything around her. "The beast is going to take her. That thing will take my child away from me, just like the last one. It told me so. Last night, it told me," she says.

The man clenches his fists, and his entire body tenses up in anger. "For the last time you heard the church: Tobias ran away," he says. His fists pound against the table. "And that's that!"

She leans closer to her husband, determined to make him listen. Her suffering is evident. "Do you believe that?" she asks. Tears stream from her eyes. "You didn't hear his screams. *I* did."

Not wanting to hear anymore, he abruptly jumps up from the table. "When the community's children turn one, they stay overnight with the others. Those are the rules. She must go," he says. "Without them, we wouldn't have gotten through our time of grief."

The woman clenches her jaw. "That was torture for me. Do you want to know what I saw each time I looked into those children's eyes? I saw our son staring back at me. It was a constant reminder of what I did not have and what I had neglected to keep safe," she says.

The little girl's babbling interrupts the conversation. Her cooing causes Ada to snap as she looks into the girl's doe-brown eyes. "It's either we watch her die like the others, or we take her elsewhere, somewhere safe," she says.

He laughs without a second thought. "Where are we going to go, Ada? This is our home. Our families have been here for generations," he says.

The quarrel causes the child to become upset, and she cries. Ada rushes over and lifts the little girl from the highchair. "If you don't do something, I will," she says.

Frustrated that he cannot get through to her, he storms out in a rage, slamming the door behind him.

Caroline watches the mother as she cradles the child. Their situation reminds her of the dysfunctionality of her marriage.

The woman wraps her arms around the baby and rocks her back and forth. Tears roll down her cheeks as she kisses the infant on her forehead. "You will always find safety here." She says.

Her gaze slowly shifts toward the kitchen window, and as she looks out to the forest, she whispers in her ear, "Let no one tell you tears are for sadness; more often than not, tears are filled with joy. We are just blind to the positivity of the change accompanying them. Each drop is a blessing sent by the Angels in Heaven to remind us who we are and how far we have come." She says.

Violent knocking at the front door shatters the woman's moment of reflection. The room's temperature plummets and her breath becomes visible in the air as she stares at the door with a look of horror. She clutches the baby tightly to her chest. Her eyes dart around the room as she desperately searches for a place to hide the child. Then, she catches sight of the oven...

A shaking sensation spreads across her shoulders as Caroline hears a voice calling out to her. "Don't, Mommy. You can't touch that," he says. She smiles upon recognizing it is Jacob.

Slowly, his voice brings her back to reality, and as she regains her bearings, she notices she is still seated on the cold, hard ground behind the store. Jacob tugs on her arms to get her to move.

Despite her state of confusion, the sparkle of the bell still draws her attention, and she extends her hand toward it. Jacob's mind flashes back to the crazed look in Mrs. Rigby's eyes when he sees her fingers nearing the object. Fearful his mother will end up like her, he swats her hand away, his voice quivering with fear, "Stop! The monster will get you." Then, with a swift kick, he sends the object flying out of her grasp. "If you touch the ones that jingle, bad things happen." He says.

The bell softly chimes as it skips through the snow.

Caroline redirects her attention toward Jacob as he pulls her to her feet. He quickly scans left and right to ensure that no one is nearby. "Hurry, Mommy," he says. He quiets his voice, thinking he may have heard something. "We have to hurry before it comes."

Her eyes dart around, trying to find a familiar landmark to orient herself.

The longer she stands, the more excruciating the pain in her feet and stomach becomes. Feeling the prickling on her toes prompts her to look down, and she notices the skin blistering. A small whimper escapes her throat as she tries to hold back her tears.

The wind sweeps against the bricks and mortar, mimicking the sound of nails scratching their surface. Jacob motions for her to be silent as he listens.

Footsteps with a clopping resonance methodically make their way down the street. "I know you are hiding somewhere. Now, where can you be?" it says. As it spits out its words, its tongue catches snowflakes in the air. "Come all ye faithful. *Vexilla regis prodeunt inferni.*"

Panic sets in for the small boy when he feels his jacket pocket and discovers it is empty. "You have our bells, don't you, Mommy?" he asks.

Even though she knows they are long gone, Caroline nods; she does not want to worry him. "Of course, sweety. They are in my pocket, safe and sound," she says.

Relieved, he grabs onto her hand. "Okay, they will protect us. But we have to stick together," he says.

Every time the creature steps, the bag of bells attached to its belt jingles. As the footsteps approach, the wind's howls escalate. Jacob quickly uses his hand to shield his ear from its battering.

Having already explored the town in his dreams, the little boy knows that only one door will be unlocked, the Rigby residence. Jacob cautiously glances at the darkness between the rows of houses, aware they must avoid being seen. He tugs on his mother's arm, urging her to follow him.

As it gets closer, the beast plays a game. Tapping its toes and heels against the slick cobblestones, it shifts its voice to mimic the sound of each of the Smith family members. The imitation sequence starts with Joel, continues to Hannah, and concludes with Madelyn.

The sound of her youngest girl's voice hits a nerve in Caroline. Her mind deceives her as she loses touch with reality, leading her to believe that her daughter is following behind them. The child's voice gives her a reprieve from her pain, and, wanting to hold her, she turns to follow the voice's direction. With her first step, the snow penetrates the blisters on her feet, worsening her injuries.

Jacob tugs harder on her and sternly whispers to get her to listen. "It's not her," he says. He sniffs to hold back his tears. "Mommy, we have to go."

The distress in Jacob's voice is impossible for Caroline to ignore. Looking at him, she makes her choice, but not before stealing one last glimpse toward the main street to mourn the thought of her daughter.

As the freezing temperature exacerbates her pain, she clutches her side. She realizes she must find somewhere warm to recover. She follows along as Jacob leads them into the dark abyss, weaving their way through the rows of brick structures. Underneath the dim moonlight, it is difficult to tell the buildings apart, as each one looks like the next.

The creature's skin acts as a filter, sifting through the air's scent while it pays attention to the wind's direction. Every adjoined face mimics the beast's unique sniffing pattern. As a gust blows up each sleeve, they catch a whiff of the nearby bell's odor; the metal's scent makes them froth from their mouths. "Jingle, jingle, jingle," they say. With a grin, Jingles peers into the neck hole of its garment to better hear the chant.

Suddenly, the wind shifts directions, sparking the creature to raise its head. A forceful gust strikes it head-on. The scent of tin enters its system as the icy breeze jostles the fur beneath its chin. The face on its belly gurgles, tickling the creature's organs, causing the crusty patches of hair above its eyes to twist.

As it listens to its stomach's stirring, it reaches down to the satchel on its belt to count its collection and chuckles. "Sly, sly, sly," it says. It knows exactly which one has vanished. "Someone has stolen Ada in the blink of an eye." The creature cackles. As it recollects the taste of her flesh, it licks its lips and whistles a merry tune.

Hidden beneath the snow, the bell waits for the creature's summons. It lightly pulsates with a dim glow, bubbling the white powdery blanket covering it.

Jingles's elongated digits playfully form a funnel around its eye to mimic a telescope; it searches the ground. "Come out, my child. We must make haste. Our journey awaits us through hell's fiery gates," it says.

The frozen cover bursts open, revealing the shiny surface of the bell. Spotting the volcanic snow, Jingles frolics to pluck the treasure from its hiding spot. Its shoulders shake with excitement as its spindly fingers place it back in the pouch with the others. "Safe and sound, returned to me, back in your home, where you should be," it says.

As the creature eagerly waits for its friends to acknowledge the bell's return, it shakes its arms and legs, hoping to incite a reaction. Still met with silence, it angrily flicks each of its sleeping companions, then hisses. "Do you hear them? Do you hear them like me? Do you hear my precious bells jingling with glee?"

Each of them sneers. "Yes. Yes, we hear the bells. Their charm begins the misery that you will inflict on the final three," they say.

The beast puffs out its chest. "Indeed," it says. The tips of its lips curl, revealing its blackened gums and jagged teeth. "They are not as clever as they think." With a deep cackle, it picks up a tracking scent; the elements have yet to discard the misery-laden fumes the Smiths left behind. "I will find them by their fear-filled stink...." It opens its mouth, and its pores widen to absorb the aroma. "Come out, little ones, now do not be shy. You cannot escape your fate to die."

The concealed beings try to inhale the fragrance, but all they do is fill their gaping mouths with the cloth of the sleeves. They are oblivious that Jingles has already depleted the scent from the air. The agitated crew chews on the fabric as they cough to dispel the velvet. "Where, where, where?" they ask.

The creature relies on the sound of the bells to hunt, so it hushes the minions to be quiet and refocuses on filtering through the surrounding noises to find its prey.

But beyond the chatter of his companions, everything seems to cause a distraction.

As the snow flurries migrate, clustering in the sky, they create a thunderous cyclone. The static in the air pushes the dense clouds down, forming thick layers of fog against the ground.

Even though Jingles can barely hear the faint chirp of Jacob's and Caroline's bells over the tumultuous storm, it enjoys the challenge. Denying its limitations, it looks to the road, then scans the dark abyss.

As it investigates the shadows, it translates the details of the lingering taste left on its palate with a lip-smacking sound. "Their fear tells me the bell has acted as a mirror, illuminating secrets that laid buried for years," it says.

Tobias's laughter carries through the forest with the wind, enraging the beast. "That little boy thought he was clever, but I know much better as they scurry like rats, more terrified than ever," it says.

As the creature ponders, it knows precisely how Ada's bell has escaped its pouch. "Mischievous child!" It says as it looks back to the road. "That conniver stole his mother's bell to guide the Smiths on where to hide. There is only one place her thoughts will lead. It is her home sweet home where she carried out her most horrific deed, leaving every child in this village to cry and bleed. So, to Ada's house, I shall go stalking them quietly through the snow."

The members of the creature's entourage interject their opinion in unison. "They must die, die, die," they say.

Their words of encouragement tickle Jingles's bones, making its cheeks pucker with a twitch. "Let us journey one last time down memory lane and delight in the warmth of the kitchen's flame. The story culminates with Ada succumbing to her family's demands and a couple of my nefarious commands. Now it is time, my little friends, to satisfy our curiosity about this poetic journey's end," it says.

Unaware of Jingles's lament, the pair have found themselves in front of their destination, the Rigby house. Jacob leads his mother up the steps and places his hand on the doorknob. He cannot help but notice a few patched areas of splintered wood he had overlooked when making his rounds earlier, and the sight causes his knees to shake.

The haphazard repairs signal that something is different; he feels blindsided. Even though the scary scenarios of his dreams shift each night, one constant remains: anything damaged resets with each subsequent visit to Green Hill.

Immediately, as the horrific memories of meeting Mrs. Rigby flood his mind, he questions his perception of his current state. Is he dreaming or awake?

Despite many things aligning with his dreams, he questions his state of being because of subtle differences.

Caroline watches her son freeze in terror. She anxiously scans the darkness behind them as she tries to remain patient. Simultaneously, with a break in the breeze, the creature's rusty jingle bells echo between the stone and brick in the distance. Her eyes bulge. The familiar noise sends shivers down her spine. "Oh, God," she says. Swiftly, her hand jolts over her son's shoulder and clutches the knob, inadvertently squashing his finger as she hastily unlatches the door. As they let go of the handle, the weighty wooden door opens with a groan.

Jacob stands at the threshold, paralyzed by fear, with his heart pounding like a drum as he peers inside. The room's darkness taunts him, fueling his imagination with every conceivable horror lurking in the pitch-black space.

Caroline shallows her breath to help minimize her pain. With their lives at risk, she no longer has time for hesitation; she gives him a stern nudge and follows his stumbling body through the doorway.

The little boy, overwhelmed by shock, gazes into the distance with dilated eyes while his mother frantically tries to close the door. As she secures the locks, she spots the outline of the beast's body through the peephole. Its grotesque appearance makes her want to scream.

Jacob can tell something is wrong. "Do you see it? Is the monster coming?" he says.

Caroline winces at his words. She tries to steady herself, smiling as she shifts her gaze to him and changes the subject. "Come on, Jacob, let's show Mommy your hiding spot," she says.

Chapter Thirteen

THE OVEN

J acob slowly looks toward the closed kitchen door; his body shudders. The image of his friends' dismembered bodies floods his memory. As the child contemplates the damaged front door, he cannot help but wonder if the corpses are still inside the kitchen, waiting for him. The thought of seeing the gruesome scene again makes him conflicted about entering the space.

He fumbles for his words as he looks to the floor while thinking of a different hiding spot to tell her. "Um... um..." he says. Feeling his world closing in, he panics and shifts his attention back to his mother for comfort.

His silence is painful to Caroline. The small stained glass crescent window behind her is darker than before; something lurks behind it.

Jacob squints to get a better look. A pair of bony hands cast a shadow through the ornamental pane, giving him an ominous puppet show. He focuses more intently, and despite his inability to see what is happening outside, he recognizes the silhouette of the protruding knuckles and jagged nails. "No...no..." he says. His body trembles and his fists tensely grip into tight balls.

Ignorant about what he is fussing over, Caroline stares at him, her back toward the door. Her aching smile causes her cheeks to quiver as she tries to make him feel more comfortable.

Jacob's pupils dilate to twice their usual size in fear. He wants to warn her, but his terror prohibits him from forming a complete sentence. "Mom-Mommy," he says.

The chaotic dancing of the spindly fingers turns violent, simulating a child's attack by a monster. While the hands twist and bend, the faces on the creature's wrists are exposed, revealing their ferocious teeth. Their tongues hiss as they cackle at the show, the sound resonating through the splintered wood.

Jacob, unable to speak, silently lifts his trembling finger to point at the door. The horror in her son's eyes makes her terrified of what is behind her. Overcome with a sense of powerlessness; her body shakes uncontrollably. Liquid trickles down her legs, and she expresses no embarrassment; her numb thighs protect her dignity.

Still staring at the small window, Jacob sees the emergence of a tiny, dark pupil swimming in a sea of white peering back at him. The sight of the small boy makes the beast neigh like a stallion. "Ho, ho, ho," it says.

Startled, Jacob stumbles backward until he hits the darkened corner of the room, bringing him to a sudden stop. Her son's sudden movement causes Caroline's adrenaline to spike, and she reluctantly pivots to see what they must face.

The door shakes violently as a thunderous thud creates a splintered break in the wood. Caroline's face turns ghostly white as she stares directly into the soulless face of the beast through the breech.

While cackling like a rabid hyena at Caroline's misery, it knocks on the door in a recognizable Christmas carol tune. The wintry cold is freezing my skin. Now open the door and let me come in!" It says.

Not getting a response, it strikes the door again. This time, the rattling of the frame causes one of the board-ed-up patches to fall off, letting in the sulfuric smell of death.

Its hand bursts through the gap created by the missing chunk of wood, aggressively feeling for the bolts on the other side, but they are just out of reach. "Shutting your friend out in the icy air, I am afraid, is quite naughty if you are cozy in there," it says. Jingles raises a finger and gives a scolding shake, jostling its sleeve and revealing one of its tiny companions. Its confusion over the sudden exposure mimics the reaction of a naked mole rat exposed to light.

Caroline glimpses the miniature face and it's gnashing teeth. Terrified and with no intention of waiting to see what happens next, she sprints to her son, hoping to take shelter in the corner's darkness.

Jacob tries not to cry as he burrows his head into his mother's chest. She brushes her fingers through his hair. As she tries to tune out the pounding on the door, she rocks him and whispers in his ear. "Mommy is here. It will be ok. Mommy is here," she says.

Her voice calms him, keeping his tears at bay. But, instead of feeling relieved, the absence of her child's hysterics adds an eerie hush to the room, enabling her to detect even the slightest sound. Caroline's muscles tense up as she distinguishes faint echoes from the charred fireplace, resembling a rat foraging. She covers Jacob's ears to protect him from becoming more scared.

She believes that something is watching them from inside the room. As she listens more closely, she hears soft breaths and a muffled sneeze that sounds nothing like the monster.

After concluding that the noise is harmless, she peers through the darkness toward the fireplace. A splash of moonlight seeps through the small window and cracks in the door, casting a reflection off a tiny set of blinking eyes peering out from the brickwork cave. She can identify by the delicate features that it is a child. Then, with a spark of optimism, she whispers, "Madelyn? Is that you?".

Swiftly, the figure responds. "Mommy!" it says. Then, with a burst of energy, a little girl erupts from the ashes, springing to her feet.

Caroline resists the urge to reply as the child appears in the faint light. Instead, she takes a moment to scan each of the little girl's facial features to confirm it is her daughter, and then, ignoring her severely disheveled state, she grins. Her warm expression fills the small girl with excitement, triggering her to squeal and hop up and down.

Suddenly the walls shake with the force of the door being battered. Its chaos reminds Caroline of the more significant threat at hand. Even though she wishes to reciprocate her child's happiness, she worries they are drawing unwanted attention. Lifting her unsteady hand away from her son, she silently motions for Madelyn to approach them.

The influx of hammering blows causes Caroline to flinch with each impact. Panicked, she whispers to her daughter, desperate to silence her, "Shhhh...You must be quiet; it will hear you," she says. Madelyn glances at the door and then rushes toward them, fighting back a smirk.

As Jacob watches his sister approach, his attention focuses on her clothing.

Every inch is drenched in blood.

Even though the dim lighting softens the appearance of the stains covering her, Jacob still finds her appearance terrifying. Their mother continues to scoot Madelyn closer. Jacob becomes anxious; he does not want to be near her. Little by little, he snuggles into his mother's side to get away.

As the little girl settles under Caroline's opposite arm, her gaze fixates on Jacob's fidgeting body. The sight of gore stippling her cheeks makes his eyes widen with fear.

Caroline wraps her arm tightly around Madelyn. She is thankful that her daughter has miraculously returned. Though she has endless questions regarding her disappearance, the sheer relief of her return makes them seem unimportant for the moment.

The thunderous knocks abruptly stop, creating an eerie stillness in the room.

Jacob leans his head against his mother's ribcage. He feels her stomach muscles clench and her heart rate spike; he can tell she is in pain. The small boy refrains from questioning her and instead opts for a different approach to help, lightly tugging her arm to gain her attention. "I'll show you where the hiding spot is," he says, then motions to the kitchen door. "It's in there."

Caroline quietly nods, fighting her fatigue; she is ready to get somewhere she can rest. Madelyn's feet are stationary while her ears perk up, and she intently listens to Jacob's words. Caroline gently pulls on her hand. "We have to follow your brother," she says.

Having made it this far alone, the girl despises being told what to do; she feels she does not need anyone. Despite trying to conceal her annoyance, Madelyn's scowl at the little boy's back gives her away.

Caroline carefully guides her children in front of her while vigilantly keeping a watchful eye on the front door.

Now side by side with her brother, Madelyn seizes the opportunity given by their mother's preoccupied state. She grabs her brother's hand and yanks him closer, capturing his attention. As they continue to move forward, she whispers in his ear. "I wish it were you," she says.

Her words startle him, and he flinches. Jacob attempts to wiggle his fingers away from her, but her hold grows tighter. His eyes nervously flutter as he tries to comprehend what she is saying. "What do you wish?" he asks.

She quickens her words without pause, cruelly filling his tiny ears with toxic notions. "Hannah would not be dead if you came with us to play. The monster would have gotten you, not her, so it's all your fault she is gone," she says.

Not knowing how to respond, his nerves create a stutter as his heart races. "That-that-that's not true," he says.

Madelyn peeks behind them to check if their mother is listening, and seeing that she remains distracted, she quietly continues. "Yes, it is. You should be dead," she says.

Her cruel words overwhelm Jacob; his eyes fill with tears. "But... I don't want to die," he says.

Madelyn knows that if she hopes to survive, she must be the strongest. Seeing him cry elicits a smirk from the little girl, as she sees it as a sign of his weakness.

The pressure of her grip increases. "No need to be sad, baby brother," she says. Then, pausing, she shrugs callously. "We will all die someday. It's not a big deal."

Jacob looks at his sister with terror as they stop at the closed kitchen door. Noticing their mother turning her attention back to them, Madelyn wants to make sure that her brother does not snitch on her, and releasing her grip, she gives him a threatening glare. He timidly looks away.

As Caroline reaches over their heads to open the door, she notices her son's pale complexion. "Don't worry. Everything will be okay, I promise," she says.

The little boy peers up at his mother. He desperately wants to tell her what has just happened, but as he begins to speak, he catches his sister's merciless glare from the corner of his eye. Afraid of the consequences, he holds his tongue and responds with a silent nod.

Caroline is confident that her words were helpful and shifts her focus to her daughter. Madelyn smirks as she reflects on her brother's torment and is caught off-guard by her mother's sudden attention. She quickly wipes the smugness from her face, shifting her expression to mimic her brother's look of fear. Caroline glares at her with disapproval. "We will face this together," she says. "You hear me?" The little girl nods in agreement.

Caroline opens the door to the kitchen. The two children immediately funnel inside, and she rushes in behind them.

The kitchen's odor triggers Jacob's memories to return. Timidly circling the island, he scans the floor for the mounds of his friend's body parts, but they are not there. Despite the kitchen layout resembling his nightmares, he finds minor differences that soothe his distress, permitting him to focus on the room's idiosyncrasies.

As she follows her son's every step, Caroline surveys the area around the kitchen's center island, still trying to figure out what he is looking for. The moonlight reflects through the sizable kitchen window, highlighting the chopping block in the center of the room. A deep burgundy-red color has saturated the wood.

Startled by the sight, she feels woozy and reaches for a counter to keep her balance. As the room spins around her, the snowstorm worsens outside. Ice and snow pelt the home's exterior walls, chipping away at the brick like a sharpened ice pick. They look to one another for stability, but a worrisome noise shortens their connecting moment.

Something is stirring on the roof.

Booming footsteps overhead echo through the room, making them stare up at the ceiling in unison. Amid the chaos, the air resonates with the unmistakable sound of jingles whistling a holiday tune. Its heavy boots batter the shingles, kicking them off with each punishing step.

The commotion overwhelms Caroline, causing her to panic and triggering her heart to beat erratically. She lowers her head to catch her breath, but instead of providing a moment of respite, it worsens her anxiety. The sight of red stains smeared across the floor's tile plunges her into a deeper state of shock.

She tilts her view to follow where the bloody trail leads, and what she discovers causes even more distress. Children's bloody handprints cover the walls surrounding the door. Each smudge tells a story of torture and desperation. She knows that whoever the victims were, they had been trying to escape a horrific fate. She shakes uncontrollably while her eyes fixate on the children's grisly warnings.

Jacob notices his mother's debilitated state as Jingles continues a destructive tap dance across the roof. He knows he must protect her. Fighting his anxiety, he shifts his gaze to the oven's door.

Madelyn still pretends to look at the ceiling while watching Jacob from the corner of her eye to monitor his actions.

Without a second thought, Jacob races to the oven, and, trying to ignore his apprehension of what might be there, he turns his head aside as he throws open the door. Taking a deep breath, he reluctantly forces himself to look inside. A dim light flickers from the back of the large metal box, barely illuminating the space between the metal racks. Again, like the rest of the kitchen, he finds the area clear of limbs and body parts; the only things left behind are remnants of bloody encrustations and stains.

Having become accustomed to the darkness, the flickering light grabs Caroline's attention. Slowly, she slides her hands along the counter's edge to stabilize herself and approaches the oven. The closer she gets, the louder and more vigorous the footsteps on the rooftop become.

Watching her brother getting all the attention irritates Madelyn. Unable to maintain her charade, she sprints toward them, almost slipping on the tile's crimson coating.

Jacob, oblivious to her approach, continues looking inside the metal appliance that had previously saved him. "That—that's where I hid. The monster could not find me there. I-I—that's how I..." he says.

Before the small boy can complete his sentence, the creature's movements on the roof cause a shower of plaster to fall from the ceiling, covering him and the floor in a fine layer of debris and dust. Jacob looks around in confusion before quickly brushing himself off.

Everything goes silent, and the plaster's peppering stops. Jingles stands next to the chimney and, leaning over the top, peers inside. Purposefully projecting its voice into the hole, it cackles. " Come out, come out, from wherever you are. I know you are in there. You will not get far." It says. Then it continues with a roaring howl. " As your friend, I promise your fate will differ from the driver of the car, and I will only leave you with a teeny-tiny scar. Come out, come out, from wherever you are,"

Loud thuds echoing from the chimney follow its words. Item after item clatters down the bricks and into the firebox, accompanied by the creature's heckling laughter.

Caroline reluctantly turns her attention from the oven and, steadying her wobbly legs, inches herself toward the wooden butcher block. She hides behind it and looks through the open kitchen door to better view the falling things. Jacob follows her, latching tightly onto her skirt, scared of being left behind.

The creature joyfully sings as it yanks shingles off the roof and hurls them down the chimney. "Hail the Heaven-born Prince of Peace! Hail the Son of Righteousness! Light and life to all," it sings. Not remembering the rest of the words, it loudly belts a jumbled chorus, then continues, skipping to the ending. "The herald angels sing, 'Glory to the newborn king!" With one last grunt, it emphasizes the grand finale. Then, after flinging the last item down the hole, it stops to listen.

Caroline winces at the sound of the object tumbling into the basin of the fireplace. Unlike the clamor of the shingles, the sound upon impact is a hollow thud. The gravity of the fall causes the object to roll through the fireplace entrance. Its pace diminishes as it moves across the floor and stops within the kitchen doorway. The dim flicker of the oven reflects off the white ceiling, illuminating the object. Caroline and Jacob both lean closer to identify what it is.

Curious, Madelyn creeps up behind them to see what they are looking at. The trio's gawps are met with gaping eyes staring back at them. Though death has clouded the irises, the familiarity is undeniable, leaving no doubt that it is Joel's severed head. Madelyn is unfazed by the sight of her father's mangled skull. Instead, she views it as the perfect distraction. With a mischievous grin, she tiptoes back to the oven to climb inside.

Caroline stands paralyzed. Even though she has already learned of Joel's death from the monster's earlier clues, she is unprepared for the gruesomeness of the outcome. Unable to look away, she motions for the children to cover their eyes.

As she leans in for a closer look, she spots something shiny wedged in her husband's front teeth. Her eyes widen as she realizes it is his cell phone.

Caroline's heart races as she turns her attention from the eerie silence of the roof to the device poking out from his mouth. She finds no comfort in the sudden stillness of the air, as it means she has lost track of the creature. Knowing she has no time to consider her options or to determine whether the device has any charge remaining, she extends her arm to take it. As she plucks it from between the molars, she cringes; a slimy coating from the beast's stomach covers it. She wipes the device clean with a few swipes of her skirt and tucks the phone away in her pocket before returning to her hiding spot behind the center island.

A thunderous boom reverberates from the kitchen window. Startled, Caroline spins around to look and her hip collides with the side of the butcher block.

More ravenous than before, the beast snarls, its crooked lips curling back, exposing its jagged teeth. Jingles savors the moment, delighting in their escalating fear as they anticipate his grand entrance. Each pound of its fist further cracks the square panes of glass.

Overwhelmed, Jacob closes his eyes and covers his ears. Madelyn smugly watches the commotion from her curled-up position in the oven. Then, without care, she slams the door closed, locking herself safely inside.

The abrupt noise and the disappearance of the oven light trigger panic in Caroline. Frantically, she scans the kitchen for her children. "We must hide. Now!" she says.

Frosted shards from the broken window stick into the beast's fist like a pincushion. Its snarling tongue laps them up, crunching them like potato chips as it sings. "Jingle, jingle, jingle," it says.

Each of the beast's companions joins in, singing and snapping their teeth in unison. "Where, oh where, have the naughty ones gone? Oh where, oh where can they be?" they ask.

The creature's smile stretches in response to the chanting. Its finger taps the window, creating a squeaking sound against the foggy glass. "Look inside, my friends. Oh, what fun! Watch them panic! See them run!" it says.

Caroline spots Jacob and hurries toward him to help him hide. As they approach the oven, they grasp why the flickering light disappeared.

Jacob's pulse quickens. He lowers his hands from his ears and pulls on the handle, but the door will not budge. Immediately, he spots his sister peering through the glass. He is horrified; she has stolen his hiding spot.

Caroline looks desperately at the window before pivoting her attention back to Jacob. Seeing her preoccupied, Madelyn sticks out her tongue at the little boy. The contemptuous look on her face causes him to replay their earlier conversation, and, in a panic, he pulls the door harder.

The creature's fists have created webs of cracks in the last surviving panes of glass, which, like the others, are about to shatter. Caroline knows they will not hold much longer.

While laughing at her brother's anguish, Madelyn looks at her mother and wiggles her fingers to wave goodbye.

Caroline flinches at the alarming sound of her nefarious giggle and briefly shuts her eyes to contemplate what to do next. "Think, Caroline, think," she says. Then, turning her attention to her son, she pulls his hands from the oven handle. "Jacob, we have to go. Now. We don't have time for that."

He whimpers as he struggles against her grip, reaching out to the oven door to attempt it again. "But... but where are we going to hide? I don't want the monster to get us," he says, tears streaming down his cheeks. The air in the room has become so frigid that it freezes the droplets on his skin.

Caroline yanks his arm, dragging him away from the oven. Then, fixing her eyes upon him, she speaks sternly to ensure he listens. "Look at me, Jacob. Be thankful that your sister is safe. I will protect you, but we must find somewhere else to hide," she says.

Jacob opens his mouth, but before he can utter a word, she makes a swift decision and guides him to find a place to take refuge. Caroline's mind flashes back to her child-hood home, and she remembers how her mother's pantry was just a few steps away from the refrigerator. With a deep breath, she extends her arm toward the shadowy wall enclosing the icebox, her fingers searching for the store-room's cold metal knob.

The bay window shatters with a loud crash, sending shards of glass flying in all directions. Caroline jumps at the sudden noise. She drops to the floor, hoping to remain unseen, and Jacob follows. Despite her fear, her trembling hands persist in feeling their way along the wall. Then, just as she is about to give up, she encounters a small metal lever. Hoping for the best, she grips the handle and pulls with all her might.

Instead of a pantry, it opens to a dark abyss that reeks of decay. Having no alternative, Caroline takes a deep breath and assists her son to climb inside. Then, lightly kissing him on the forehead, she hushes him to be quiet, and he disappears into the darkness. She pauses, uncertain of their fate, and tenderly looks back at her daughter, secure in the oven.

A blast of cold air rushes into the kitchen as the last remaining glass panes shatter. Barely visible through the flurry, the creature teeters in the window frame, half in and half out.

Caroline moves cautiously, terrified that sudden movement will draw the beast's unwanted attention. After reciting a quick prayer, she hoists herself through the wall's small square opening and shuts the door behind her. She fights back a scream as her body's weight drops beneath her, pulling her down a dark tunnel to a pitch-black pit filled with the smell of rotting garbage.

Jacob scurries to find her, having been listening for her to land. His hands wave around in the dark, searching for his mother, and when he brushes her shoulder, she quickly pulls him into a tight hug. Caroline opens her mouth to offer words of assurance but promptly stops herself. She hears something—a muted version of the kitchen's activity.

While they cower in the dark, embracing each other in fear, Madelyn smugly waits in her secure hiding spot above. The racks feel cozy beneath her body as she huddles in a tight ball. She peers out the oven's tiny window for her mother and brother and, not seeing anyone, assumes the beast must have taken them. The thought of outsmarting it twice makes her grin in victory. Amid her triumph, she closes her eyes and luxuriates in her secluded haven.

Stepping onto the piles of shattered glass, the beast slowly stands up to its feet. As it stretches out its contorted spine, the sight of Joel's decapitated skull makes its mouth water. Unable to control itself, it tiptoes across the kitchen to retrieve the body part.

The sight of the snack delights the creature, and, wanting to share; it lifts its shirt to reveal the surprise to its stomach companion. Hearing no reaction, it looks down and notices it has drifted off. "Wake up, my friend. It is time to eat. Take it now, or it will be my treat," it says. Then, irritated by its lack of readiness, it angrily slaps its gut.

Jingle's stomach growls as its muscles clench, and the scabbed skin surrounding the eyes and mouth slowly cracks. Then, smelling the fetid offering, the face releases a yawn. "Hungry, hungry, hungry," it says; it is ready to eat.

Holding onto the skull by a dangling patch of hair, the creature waves it back and forth in front of its stomach to tease it. Impatient, it spits gastric acid, burning holes into the cheeks of Joel's severed head. "Feed me now!" it says. Its mouth stretched wide in a state of anticipation.

Jingles chucks the bloody object into the opening. The bones crack between its molars, and its tastebuds savor the tang as the fragments swirl on its gyrating tongue. While it chews, the creature scans the floor for more morsels. Then, hopping around the room like a rabbit, it gathers the few miscellaneous body parts tossed down the chimney earlier and eats them.

Madelyn's eyes remain closed as she basks in the serenity of her soundproof refuge. She uses her imagination to paint a beautiful image of what her future family will look like. The thought of it all makes her smirk; she has always wanted a Labrador Retriever.

Jingles finishes its snack and licks its lips. With its hunger momentarily satisfied, the creature can now focus on finding the Smiths. As it takes a deep breath, its pores enlarge and sift through the room's air while listening for clues. "Where are you hiding? Oh, where can you be?" it asks. With a smirk, it turns to scan the room. "You are free to flee, but your bell will betray your location to me."

Madelyn feels something wiggling in her pocket. Thinking it's a bug, she continues planning the details of her new life and mindlessly swats at the annoyance, trying to get it to stop.

Unbeknownst to her, it is her bell, and with every shake, the metal rings a silent song that only Jingles can hear. The sound of it causes the creature to salivate.

As the monster strides through the space, it purses its lips and whistles a festive tune while sniffing the air. Upon hearing a slight clatter, it follows the noise to the back of the kitchen.

As its steps get closer, its parasitic entourage chatters. "It is the wicked one. The wicked one who tripped her sister so she could run. My, oh, my, this should be fun," they say.

While perusing the kitchen, Jingles glimpses Madelyn through the stove's window and snickers; it is not ready to reveal its discovery. The creature paces back and forth near the room's entrance; its excitement causes its drool to heat to a bubbling boil. "Those who are bad meet with endings that are sad. I admit a dash of evil can be fun, but you, my dear, have homicidal tendencies, and the penalty for those you will not outrun," it says. Continuing to ponder, the creature moves closer to peer at her.

Surrounded by the muffled silence of the oven, Madelyn finds her day's exhaustion creeping up on her, and she soon dozes off, snoring lightly. Jingles looks at her sleeping face and cannot help but smirk, seeing it as an excellent opportunity to surprise the little girl. Tiptoeing across the kitchen, its spindly fingers stretch to turn the oven's dial to the "on" position, and with a gentle clicking sound, it ignites the gas. "Maybe some heat will turn her sourness sweet and make her tasty enough to eat," it says.

As the temperature escalates, the adjoined faces hiss. "Cook, cook, cook," they say.

Jingle's cohorts quiver with crazed delight as it spins the dial to the highest setting. Its expression twists as it fights back a chortle. The anticipation of hearing her scream is almost too great for the creature to bear.

As the temperature rises, the child gradually wakes up. Spotting a slight twitch of her arm through the window, Jingles lowers its body to the floor to watch her squirm.

Madelyn, sweating and confused, scans her environment, and the sight of the orange glow from the metal bars below plunges her into a state of panic. She kicks and screams, her fists pounding on the door, desperate to be released.

Despite the creature's glee at watching her suffer, it understands the importance of keeping her brain intact to harvest her memories. Reluctantly, it springs to its feet and turns the dial to stop the child's roasting. The smell of cooking flesh fills the air as it opens the oven door.

With a jig in its step, it grabs the birch lasso from its belt loop and, allowing itself one lick of her flesh, sneers, then hogties her limbs together. Despite its temptation to take a bite, it resists the urge, saving her for later. Jingles whistles joyfully as it chains her dangling body to its hip. Her petite frame swings like a pendulum with the creature's steps, each sway causing her to scream as the metal links cut deeper into her toasted flesh.

Hidden below the house, Caroline covers Jacob's mouth to keep him quiet. Her eyes fill with tears as Madelyn's tortured wails carry through the floorboards; she can do nothing to save her. If she tries to help, she will risk the lives of Jacob, her unborn child, and herself.

Without warning, a powerful gust of wind sweeps through the shattered kitchen window. Something catches the creature's attention as the iced air sifts through its porous skin: the eerie melody of the two missing bells. "I find it quite curious and perplexing," it says, scratching its head in contemplation. "Their triumphant escape. I was not expecting." Then, with a shrug, it hops out the window to follow the sound.

Each tiny face chants. "Jingles, Jingles, Jingles, king of fun. If they do not wish to become a meal, they had better run," they say.

As it strolls down the main street, the creature waltzes to Madelyn's screams, shaking its hips occasionally to incite her to cry louder.

Caroline and Jacob stare at each other in shock without uttering a word.

Chapter Fourteen

IS IT OVER?

Caroline Cradles her son tightly to her chest, closes her eyes, and focuses on the surrounding sounds.

They are shrouded in darkness. The only thing visible is the slight glow of the whites of Jacob's wide-opened eyes.

Caroline oddly finds solace in the decades of garbage that cushioned her fall, each mound evoking memories of her lumpy mattress back home.

She takes a deep breath, inhaling the pungent aroma of decay and mildew. Instead of being disgusted by the putrid smell, she sees it as a sign of their freedom.

By choosing to enter the mysterious door, she surrendered herself to an uncertain destiny. She had already come to terms with the possibility of an unfavorable outcome due to her injuries, so deciding required little thought.

Caroline lies on her back, shuts her eyes, and soaks in the peaceful calm surrounding her. After a few minutes of deep contemplation, she concludes that, no matter what, she still has faith.

Jacob silently cuddles up to her, his arms wrapping securely around her waist. Caroline's eyes remain closed as she manages the ache from his increased pressure on her body. The fight to remain conscious becomes more challenging as she combats pain and exhaustion. Sweat pours down her forehead, and her limbs shake uncontrollably.

As the small boy settles beside her, he feels the dampness of her sweat-soaked clothes. Immediately, he can tell that something is wrong. "Mommy, are you sick?" he asks.

Her sprawled position worsens the ache in her side. Despite her discomfort, she draws him closer. "Jacob, there is no need to worry about me. I am fine," she says. Even though he cannot see her face in the dark, she sends him a warm smile.

Caroline's shaking intensifies as she battles to keep the pain at bay. Then, without warning, her cramping suddenly disappears, and with it, the movement of her unborn child.

She desperately slides her hand over her stomach, her eyes brimming with tears, yet the stillness remains. Jacob hears her muffled crying, and even though she says everything is fine, he knows it is not.

Jacob gently places his hand on Caroline to comfort her and quietly whispers, remembering what she had told him earlier. "Let no one tell you tears are for sadness; more often than not, tears are filled with joy. We are just blind to the positivity of the change accompanying them. Each drop is a blessing sent by the Angels in Heaven to remind us who we are and how far we have come." He says. Caroline can feel her mother's presence radiating through the little boy's words, making her certain she is with them.

Jacob rubs his mother's hand. "Are those tears of joy?" he asks.

She sniffles. "Each drop is a blessing sent by the Angels in Heaven," she says.

A scurry echoes among the trash. Jacob's hand tightens around his mother's as his eyes nervously scan the room. The darkness makes it impossible to make out anything as the sound draws nearer.

Abruptly, the air around them plummets in temperature, irritating Caroline's lungs and prompting her to cough uncontrollably. Jacob nervously glances down to check on her. She has entered a hypothermic delirium, leaving her without the strength to open her eyes; her mind is lethargic.

As his mother's hand turns clammy and cold, he hears the eerie sound of raspy breaths next to his ear; it sends shivers down his spine. Fearful of what is beside him, he attempts to distract himself by focusing on his mother's breathing.

The subtle whisper of a woman's voice fills the air of the murky space. "You are home. Welcome home, home, home," she says. Each word traipses into the next, replicating the skip of a scratched record. He trembles in response. There is something eerily familiar about the voice. It has a similar resonance to his mother's.

Methodically, it moves through the towering mounds of scattered debris around him. Each crumpling noise makes Jacob flinch.

The entity slinks up and perches beside him, its presence looming over his mother with a piercing glare. Then, without breaking its gaze, it strikes a match and lights each discolored fingernail on its right hand like a candelabrum. As light floods the dismal space, the face of an old, withered woman is revealed, her lips curling into an evil grin.

"I knew everything would be all right. It told me not, but I knew you were bright," she says.

Jacob senses the woman's unyielding stare and slowly lifts his head, dreading what he will see. It is far worse than he imagined.

Her hair that remains is colorless, brittle, and has wiry ends that twist in all directions. After Prolonged exposure to darkness, her anxiety has caused her to tear out nearly every strand, leaving abraded bald patches crusted in blood.

The dark has warped her figure with disease and has taken the warmth from her skin, turning her complexion a sickly, deathlike shade. Wrinkles of a dull blue-gray blanket her face, drooping like a melted candle's wax, leaving her humanity almost unrecognizable. The flickering light fills her eye sockets, left empty from a frenzied act of self-mutilation.

As he analyzes her manic behavior, it is clear that her focus lies on Caroline.

Trembling with fear at the woman's bizarre actions, Jacob slowly retreats into the darkness to hide.

The woman emits a piercing screech like an owl searching for prey as she shifts her posture, delicately holding Caroline's head in her lap. Her hand waves the flames back and forth over her skin to illuminate her tears.

The flicker of light reveals the irregularity in Jacob's mother's breathing as he watches her chest rise and fall. Despite his longing to be near her, a foreboding feeling consumes him that something sinister is at work, leaving him paralyzed with fear.

The woman leans forward, focusing solely on Caroline's face as she delicately collects each tear with her long, sharp nails. "You were well aware your son had to die for the female lineage to thrive, and if you gave into your desire to keep him alive, there was a risk that the chosen one would not survive," she says.

As she sucks the underside of her nails dry, she assimilates every agonizing memory of Caroline's past. "You had an older brother who came before you, but, knowing my place, I did what I had to do. Without a moment of dwelling in the gloom, I ensured that the boy never left my womb. Your grandmother did the same, murdering her dear Tobias in the wooded terrain. Just like you, she tried to hide him as well, and her lot was determined by the monster's bell.

She suffered considerable damage to her emotional state, sacrificing others' children, hoping to alter her fate. Unfortunately, she did not realize her effort was in vain until it was too late.

Despite her attempts to keep Tobias stowed away, he still found a way outside in the snow to play. As he journeyed home that fateful day, the monster, using the boy's sight, discovered where our lineage stayed.

Fortunately, the beast's ego controlled its will, savoring its stalking of them for weeks leading up to the kill. Ada understood that to keep the girl alive, she had to eliminate the monsters' ability to spy long enough to hide the one who needed to survive. After Ada killed Tobias, she had little time to carry me through the snow and pine to a safe place where I was found by a couple who took me to a small Utah town.

Without the beast's watchful eyes on me, I could continue to grow our family tree, safely hidden away in the isolated community.

It should be obvious to see that without the sacrifices of your grandmother and me, you would not have a chance of being free."

Her horrific words trigger Jacob's anxiety. As he nervously shifts his weight, his leg accidentally nudges a piece of trash. Its movement creates a faint, rustling sound reverberating through the confined space.

The woman's head snaps in his direction. She wields her flaring nails in the air, the flames crackling as she uses them to incite fear in the child. The wrinkles on her face cluster together, blocking her nose as she squinches to smell. She lifts the skin away from her nostrils with a single nail to get a better whiff, but the rising temperature in the chamber feeds the putrid stench, hiding the boy's identity.

Her fingers cast a sinister glow, exhibiting enough facial peculiarities to be identified. Jacob fights back a gasp as his suspicion is confirmed. "Grandma," he whispers.

With a grunt, she turns her attention back to her daughter to continue scolding. "We made a pact with Hel long ago to bear the child fated to remove the beast when it began rampaging its way from the woods through the snow, disregarding all rules to gratify its ego. Naughty children were to be taken by it once a year, but its bloodlust grew, leaving villagers running in fear as it crept from house to house, slaughtering all who lived here.

When you had that boy, it became your turn, but you selfishly kept him alive, earning you a punishment that is stern. You risked more than our fate because now the creature knows what lies beyond the village gate. That is how it finds us, through our little boy's dreams, spending night after night spawning its wicked schemes. Now the devilish creature appears every season, desperate to kill for the primary reason of ensuring the chosen one does not survive, allowing the worst evil to thrive. So, we must continue with our sacrifices until the one chosen to destroy it arrives," she says.

Jacob's eyes widen.

In shock, the small boy keeps quiet, continuing to listen.

Her mouth froths with resentment for all she has sacrificed. "Upon my deathbed, you lied! You kept your family a secret, ruining our lives," she says.

Then, pointing with her flaming fingers, she spits her words. "As I laid there, taking my dying breath, that thing visited me, clinging to my chest, harvesting my memories, no matter how much I begged. As a punishment, it has kept me waiting in this purgatory with my bell until this day, claiming that for your deception, I must pay."

Jacob observes her personality shift, noting a growing venomous quality of her words. "I will kill the small boy, taking matters into my own hands. It is what I would have done a while ago if I had lived to have the chance," she says. Her spitting words cause saliva to drip onto the lids of Caroline's closed eyes.

The woman's morbid intent is clear to Jacob. Panicked, the small boy frantically scans the darkness for a way out but pauses, a tear rolling down his cheek. His mother's unconditional love and protection make him feel guilty for considering her abandonment. He cannot face the harsh reality that she might die and feels pulled to look at his mother's lifeless face one last time.

As another drop of spittle lands on her skin, her hand twitches. Her movement, though small, causes the child to freeze, making him wonder if she has been conscious enough to hear the woman's horrific words.

Caroline's mother's tone softens to compassion as she slowly runs her fingers through her daughter's hair. "Sleep, my dear. Do not worry. The child will barely feel a thing as I handle the rest. I promise it will help remove the fear that weighs heavy on your chest. In the end, you will see it is a small price to pay as we await the chosen one's return to take the monster away," she says. As she leans forward to kiss her daughter's forehead, she puffs out her cheeks, preparing to blow out the flames on her fingers.

Jacob watches with horror as the woman's scraggly hair wiggles between his mother's lips. Trying not to make sudden movements, Caroline allows each strand to fall into her mouth as she patiently waits for the woman to get closer. Her mind drifts to reflect on the woman's wicked soliloquy. She finds it strange that her mother claims to have warned her of the monstrous beast; she remembers it much differently.

The only time her mother had alluded to a family curse was on her deathbed. When Caroline made her last visit, she joyously announced her pregnancy with her son; however, instead of a warm response, a rambling tirade erupted. She attributed the strange occurrence to the onset of end-of-life hallucinations and preferred remembering her mother differently, so she blocked it from her memory.

Jacob watches as the woman blows out two flames, then touches her lips to his mother's skin. Still lost in her thoughts, Caroline cannot elude her downward spiral.

Reflecting on her early years, she recalls how her mother skillfully deflected questions about their family's ancestry. Caroline vividly remembers an incident in second grade where she flunked an assignment that required her to create a family tree.

At her mother's advice, Caroline included Kennedy, Washington, and Lincoln as ancestors in her drawing. Not only were they not related to her, but they also had no family ties to each other. As a result, her teacher, Mrs. Miller, accused her of lying, and the assignment received an F.

Caroline defended her mother's information staunchly, believing she was unjustly singled out. However, when she entered sixth grade and studied US History, it became clear that her teacher's assessment was correct; the information was false.

The woman had been a walking contradiction. She never acted with her children's best interests in mind, only her own, and any alignment that may have occurred was entirely by chance.

Even concealing Caroline's eye color and uniqueness was not a matter of safeguarding her daughter but her own reputation in the community. The woman failed to realize that hiding the girl's qualities would shatter her confidence and deplete her self-esteem.

Each second that passes with her mother's clammy lips pressed against her skin, Caroline's resentment grows.

Jacob cannot hold still any longer and nervously squirms. The rustling of his coat breaks the eerie silence, causing the vile woman to turn her attention away from Caroline. As she does, her lips disconnect from her forehead, leaving a string of drool behind.

The mere thought of her child being harmed causes Caroline's body to fill with distress, leading to a surge of adrenaline and causing her to bite down on the strands of hair in her mouth.

Unsure of what is happening, the bewildered woman lets out a high-pitched shriek while frantically wriggling and pulling away to free herself. She feels for the end of her hair and rams her fingers into her daughter's mouth to pry it loose. "Let go of my curl, you senseless girl," she says.

In a fit of anger, Caroline opens her eyes and locks her gaze on the woman's withered face. Her acidic drool burns her daughter's skin everywhere it drips. Fighting through the searing pain, she reaches over her head, grabs the woman's neck, and begins strangling her. "Jacob, run!" she shouts. Not hearing any movement, she yells louder. "Now!"

Jacob looks at his mother struggling, then scans the room. No matter how obedient he is, he cannot leave her behind. Quickly, tripping over trash in the way, he races toward her to help.

During the clash, his grandmother's hands flail, illuminating every corner of the space with her flaming fingertips. A wave of horror washes over Jacob as he looks around with newfound clarity.

The cold cellar is far from what they had imagined, with evidence of a troubling shift in its intended purpose. Blended with the decades-old trash bags are mounds of mutilated human remains, limbs, heads, and torsos deemed too spoiled for the monster to eat. What his mother had thought to be a comfortable pile to rest her head on was a man's torso, partially preserved by the room's chill.

Not a single body is left intact, making it impossible to determine the total number of victims occupying the space. One thing is clear; the body count is significant and far surpasses the creature's appetite.

As Caroline's strength diminishes in the battle, her laboring gasps grow louder. Terrified that she will not last much longer, Jacob holds his breath and searches the putrid debris for a makeshift weapon to defend her.

The woman can smell him behind her and, fighting her daughter's strangling hands, frantically swings her arms out to reach for the little boy. Then, just as her fiery hand is nearly within reach of grabbing the child, it gets entangled in a pile of garbage.

Jacob watches with terror as the heap lights up in flames.

With renewed vigor, Caroline tightens her grip on the woman's neck, causing her venomous tongue to protrude from her mouth and her limbs to fall limp. Caroline senses a tingle in her fingers from the force of her grip as she releases her clutch. She can feel the weight of the lifeless body crumpling beside her.

Smoke infiltrates her lungs and burns her eyes as the chamber fills with charcoal-plagued air. With each passing moment, her panic rises as she scans through the dense smoke, her eyes straining to find her son.

Her body tries to clear her lungs with deep guttural coughs, all while feeling around the trash with her hands.

"Jacob, Jacob!" she cries. Then, her fingers brush against his thick winter coat.

He is unresponsive.

Worried that he has succumbed to smoke inhalation, she seizes the collar of his jacket and pulls his body behind her while searching for an exit.

Burning debris falls onto the piles of trash as the flames engulf more of the home's structure. As the kitchen floorboards plunge into the roiling abyss below, bits of natural light escaping through the crevices in the ceiling above go unnoticed amid the searing flames.

Glancing back at her son, Caroline notices the color has drained from his cheeks and, panicking, drags his body faster.

Unexpectedly, the illumination of the flames reveals a precarious set of stairs leading to a wooden-planked cellar entrance. She hastens her strides, towing her son toward the symbol of hope. While carefully dodging the falling debris, she experiences a rush of adrenaline and, at the bottom step, uses it to hoist the weight of his limp body over her shoulder.

Behind them, the room is a raging inferno, devouring the chronicles of the home's sinister secrets. The intense heat chars the skin of Caroline's lower extremities, and with the combination of the frostbite, her toes throb with pain as if walking shoeless through hell.

Fighting with all her might, she reaches the top of the staircase and, with a last surge of energy, forces open the wooden doors. A loud, thunderous crash reverberates through the street as each access panel slams against the cobblestones.

The sight of daylight confuses her, and she shakes her head to regain her focus, knowing she must get her son to safety. Caroline quickly leaves the building and gently lays him on the ground. Charcoal has smudged Jacob's clothes and cheeks, and he remains motionless.

She drops to the ground in a panic, the cold stone against her knees, and lays her head on his chest to listen for his heartbeat. "It's okay, Jacob! Mommy is here," she says.

Caroline unbuttons his jacket collar and leans in, trying to detect any signs of life, but there is nothing. All she can sense is the stillness of death.

The woolen fabric falls further from his skin, revealing a bruise shaped like a bell. Its impression, which includes the initials AR, intertwines with handprints that circle his tiny neck.

Her mind is consumed with confusion, leaving her paralyzed with trembling hands and wide eyes filled with terror. "That—that is impossible. I know I had a tight hold on her. She didn't leave my grasp. I would never have let her hurt him," she says.

Caroline struggles to overcome her shock. Her rapid inhalations of the cold air sear her lungs while her heart races as she refuses to accept reality and continues to scan his body for a sign of life. She desperately clings onto his jacket and shakes him, only releasing her grip when she notices something shocking, a peculiar mark on her hand. "Dear God, this can't be," she says.

Caroline warily turns over her hands to view the whole of her palms, each imprinted with half an image. She fears confirming the answer, forcing herself to push her wrists together to join the two pieces to solve the puzzle. Staring down at the mark, her insides twist upon seeing the intricate patterns from her son's neck mirror the designs before her.

Overwhelmed by sadness, she places her trembling fingers on her son's neck again in search of a pulse, already knowing the answer but unable to accept it. The oppressive silence engulfs her, intensifying her anguish and causing tears of exhaustion and sadness to flow uncontrollably down her face.

As the Rigby house goes up in flames, it warms her chilled body, and along with the cremation of its nefarious past, the fire decimates the truth behind what started it: the gas oven.

Caroline is left lost and alone, with no family members remaining and no plan. She cradles Jacob tightly in her arms, swaying back and forth gently while watching the house turn to ashes. Tears flow from her eyes, running down her cheeks and dripping onto his as she weeps. The air is heavy with defeat, and she can feel herself on the brink of surrender.

Through her fatigue-driven delirium, she hears a voice coming from the direction of the cellar door—it is her mother. But, unlike before, this time, her tone is calming. "Let no one tell you tears are for sadness; more often than not, tears are filled with joy. We are just blind to the positivity of the change accompanying them. Each drop is a blessing sent by the Angels in Heaven to remind us who we are and how far we have come." She says.

Caroline looks up at the sun and, closing her eyes, whispers part of the phrase to calm herself. "We are just blind to the positivity of the change accompanying them," she says. Then, slowly, she opens her eyes and looks at her son. " We are just blind to the positivity of the change accompanying them," she says again.

Twigs snap in the distance, reminding her that the beast is still lurking. She takes a deep breath and kisses Jacob's forehead, knowing she must keep moving to stay alive. "Despite anything said, you are not responsible for any of this. I regret encouraging everyone to go on this journey, as it exposed you to evil. Regardless of destiny, I cannot forgive myself for bringing you here. The what-ifs plague me, making me question every decision and action I took that led us to our current fate; I swear to God, I will be the one to end this nightmare.

My life is unimaginable without your presence, Jacob. I love you so much.

I pray that you have found a peaceful sanctuary where kindness and love surround you," she whispers.

The fire roars. Caroline feels the warmth on her cheeks and slowly leans toward it. It brings her a sense of solace. With a heavy heart, she looks at Jacob's lifeless body and cannot bear to walk away and leave him to the monster. She gently picks him up and carries him over to the fire, where she lays him down softly amid the compassion of the flames.

Caroline walks toward the forest's edge, the crackling blaze echoing behind her. Tears stream down her cheeks as she turns and takes one last look at the town. The flames from the Rigby home have spread, jumping from rooftop to rooftop, setting the entire village ablaze.

Dropping her head in reverence, she touches her womb and senses the delicate flutter of a baby's kick against her hand. Her eyes turn to the heavens, a slight smile crossing her lips as a glimmer of hope is rekindled within her.

The breeze rustles the branches of the trees as she makes her way through the woods. Her hands lay flat on her abdomen, and each gentle movement drives away her fear and provides her the will to live. "Hello, there, my little one. I promise I will always protect you," she says.

With nothing but her intuition to lead the way, she returns to the same spot where her journey first began. Seeing all her family's suitcases beside one another causes her grief to resurface.

She takes a deep breath. "Let no one tell you tears are for sadness; more often than not, tears are filled with joy. We are just blind to the positivity of the change accompanying them. Each drop is a blessing sent by the Angels in Heaven to remind us who we are and how far we have come." She says.

As Caroline reaches to unzip her bag to retrieve a change of clothes and shoes, her attention is drawn to a children's picture book resting atop her belongings. She feels compelled to pick it up, and upon doing so, she notices the cover. "*Green Hill*," she says. The name makes her shudder.

Regardless of her apprehension, she opens it to the first page. She grins at the dedication. "To Helena..." she says. Upon hearing the name, the baby reacts with a flurry of kicks. The movement elicits a sense of joy in Caroline.

She sets the book down and changes into a fresh set of clothes. While slipping on her shoes, her eyes glimpse her holiday dress and winter jacket lying on the ground, triggering nothing but painful memories.

She momentarily considers the phone tucked in the skirt's pocket. Caroline knows she cannot change her past but can control her future. Realizing that a fresh start is necessary for her and her child to have a fighting chance, she knows they must leave it all behind.

As she closes her bag, Caroline suddenly catches sight of the book, prompting her to pause. She picks it up again, and as she rereads the dedication page, a sense of warmth overwhelms her. Placing her hand on her baby bump, she smiles. "That will be your name: Helena," she says.

The pine needles rustle as a gentle breeze passes through the trees. As the wind flips through the pages, they rest on several whimsical drawings of the familiar Christmas town with a sign that reads, *Welcome to Grüner Hügel.*

A peaceful stillness envelopes her as she delicately closes the book and embraces it. She senses Jacob by her side. "You know what Helena? I think I will keep this to read to you when you are older. That way, you will never question where you are from," she says.

A soft breeze swirls around her, carrying the distant tinkling of a bell. She swiftly pulls a few more items from her suitcase, layers them over her outfit, and zips her luggage shut. The metallic zipper's noise conveys a sense of finality as it resounds within her ears, sending chills down her spine.

With the book securely tucked under her arm, she bravely heads down the hill without looking back.

As she advances, the snow gradually vanishes, and the ringing of the jingle bell grows faint. Despite her lack of knowledge about where their journey will lead, she has faith that it will all work out as it should.

GLOSSARY

ACH?

OH?

AUSSTEIGEN

EXIT.

DIE ADRESSE?

THE ADDRESS?

DIE DUMMEN AMERIKANER

THE STUPID AMERICANS.

EINHUNDERT

ONE HUNDRED.

GRÜNER HÜGEL

GREEN HILL.

GUT, RAUS HIER

GOOD, GET OUT OF HERE.

JA, ADRESSE

YES, ADRESS.

ICH WERDE DICH DORTHIN BRINGEN

I WILL TAKE YOU THERE.

IN NOMINE PATRIS, ET FILII, ET SPIRITUS SANCTI

IN THE NAME OF THE FATHER, AND OF THE SON,
AND OF THE HOLY SPIRIT.

IN ORDNUNG

IN ORDER.

MITTLERHAUS

MIDDLE HOUSE.

O MI IESU, DIMITTE NOBIS DEBITA NOSTRA,

**SALVA NOS AB IGNE INFERNI, PERDUC IN
CAELUM OMNES ANIMAS, PRAESERTIM EAS,
QUAE MISERICORDIAE TUAE MAXIME INDIGENT**
OH MY JESUS, FORGIVE US OUR SINS, SAVE US FROM
THE FIRES OF HELL; LEAD ALL SOULS TO HEAVEN
ESPECIALLY THOSE WHO ARE MOST IN NEED OF
YOUR MERCY.

**SIE KÖNNEN IHRE TASCHE IN DEN
KOFFERRAUM LEGEN**
YOU CAN PUT YOUR BAG IN THE TRUNK.

SO WEIT KANN ICH GEHEN
AS FAR AS I CAN GO.

WARUM WILLST DU DA HIN?
WHY DO YOU WANT TO GO THERE?

WILLKOMMEN IN
WELCOME TO.

WOHIN MUSST DU GEHEN?
WHERE DO YOU HAVE TO GO?

GITTE TAMAR

Brigitte, "Gitte," Tamar was born in a small rural Oregon town. Growing up, she was enthralled by scary tales featuring poetic tones and consistently gravitated towards writing darkened narratives. In the different storylines, Brigitte explores the harsh realities of social issues faced by today's generations. This includes the dark outcomes brought on by peer pressure, addiction, homelessness, mental illness, childhood trauma, and abuse. She feels it is essential to share narratives that refrain from sugarcoating the topics society tends to shy away from.